I0680841

Novels
Brimstone and Lily
Jasper's Foul Tongue
Jasper's Magick Corset
Paragon of the Eccentric

Drama
The Three Musketeers
Coolness and Courage
Blood and Beauty
Gentle Rain

Nonfiction
HeartSnark

Anthologies (contributor)
Customs, Castles, and Kings, v. 2
Broken Links, Mended Lives
False Faces
You Belong
Found

Awards
Colorado Gold Literary Award
Paragon of the Eccentric (winner)
Brimstone and Lily (finalist)

Independent Publishers Book Award
Brimstone and Lily (Bronze Medal)

Next Generation Indie Book Award
HeartSnark (finalist)

Colorado Short Story Contest
"The Day the Earth Couldn't Stand Still"
(winner)

Rapiers & Rogues

A Captain Treville adventure

Terry Kroenung

Rare Moon Press

ISBN: 978-1-7378947-2-8 (paperback)

Printed in the United States of America

Cover design by Safeer Ahmed

"In all times and all countries, especially in those countries which are divided within by religious faith, there are always fanatics who will be well contented to be regarded as martyrs."
— Alexandre Dumas

Rapiers & Rogues

CONTENTS

Rapiers & Rogues

1

MARCH 1605: OSTEND, SPANISH NETHERLANDS

A SNEAKY, DISHONORABLE FIGHT IT IS, THEN. LIKE USUAL.

Treville had to admit that the Protestants took their murdering seriously.

No threats, no boasting, no warning. The tall one in gray wool had stopped him in the dim street, pretending to ask directions, while his squat comrade in black leather had slipped in behind with a business-like dagger. If it had not been for his elk-hide buff coat he would have bid good-bye to a kidney. As it was the wicked point punctured the expensive jerkin just below his red officer's sash and plunged into his side, just above the hip.

Luckily Treville had caught the triumphant anticipation in the first fellow's eye as his friend came in for the kill. A quick twist not only preserved his life but trapped the blade in a fold of the thick leather. Before its owner could retrieve it Treville seized the set-up man's collar and jerked him close as if to kiss him. Snapping his own head to the left, he smashed his new friends' faces together over his right shoulder. With a vicious elbow to the rear and a front boot to the bollocks, he managed to free himself from their attentions and plunge into the crowded market.

He ducked into a hatter's stall, browsing the merchandise while keeping a sharp eye out for pursuit. Had they penetrated his disguise or were they merely reacting to his speaking Spanish to that fruit seller? Treville had been reared in the Pyrenees foothills and spoke the tongue like a native. Hard to say if they merely wanted to dispatch an officer of the occupying forces or if they knew that he was spying for the French. Either one was a splendid reason for killing, in their eyes. After all, one only had to give Ostend a cursory glance to see what the Catholic army of Spain had done in its three-year siege. Close to a hundred thousand dead. It was said that Queen Isabella had wept when she had seen the destruction wrought by her own troops. Six months later the town had hardly recovered. Only the rebuilt fort looked serviceable. Buildings were burnt-out shells. Disease savaged conqueror and subjects alike. A stench of unburied dead competed with the gagging reek of sewage flowing in rivers. Only a handful of civilians had returned.

Just my luck that two of them came out hunting Spanish troops today.

He winced as he leaned out to scan the narrow street. The wound throbbed like a hoof-kick from Lucifer. Clearly it had been a nastier thrust than he had first thought. If it grew any worse, he would have to find a doctor. That could be a problem. It would not do to lie in a Spanish military hospital, growing delirious with fever and blurting out God only knew what secrets. Then this little pinprick would be the least of his concerns. Their interrogators were notorious for mixing devilish creativity with their enthusiasm for torture. And if he managed to see a local surgeon the man might just poison him out of spite, not knowing that he only impersonated a hated invader.

Both assassins came into view, peering into every stall for him. The tall one walked with a limp and the stabber's nose bled. As gratifying as that was, they still seemed perfectly able to pursue him. Judging from their grim faces, they were intent on doing so until the Last Judgment. Now that he got a good look, they seemed suspiciously well-fed and free of sickness. Their garments were simple and had seen hard use, but these men did not have the bearing of siege survivors.

How did they even get back in? It's not like the Spaniards have thrown open the gates and welcomed Dutch men of fighting age to repopulate the place.

Questions would have to wait on answers. A well-placed silver *real* bought his whereabouts from a ragged urchin, who was more than happy to earn it by pointing directly at him. With the ill will that the Spanish had earned with their bloody siege, the killers could probably have gained the information gratis. He would find few friends here if it came to a stand-up fight. Gripping his rapier hilt to narrow its profile along his leg, Treville snaked through the crowd and headed for any place that offered escape or at least a more defensible position. Now the wound was stiffening as well as hurting. Warm blood trickled inside his breeches and pooled in his tall riding boot. *No doubt about it. Going to need a doctor.*

Or an undertaker.

Masking his limp as well as he could, Treville adopted the haughty manner seemingly installed as a permanent feature on all the Spanish lieutenants he had seen since arriving two days before. His moustache curled into a hard black sneer and he glowered like a rabid dog to make civilians get out of his way. He stomped into the nearest grimy alley as if he were the Habsburg Emperor. Once there he surveyed his new kingdom and found it populated by a bony cat picking through garbage and a snoring drunk. Beyond them lay the next street and the safety of his rented room. Freed from observation, he relaxed his assumed character and screwed up his face in pain while dragging his half-paralyzed hip and leg behind him. In a few more steps he would be behind his own door and could take stock of the damage.

Naturally, God punished him for such hubris. The light from the far end of the alley grew dark as someone entered it. At the same time heavy footsteps crept in behind him.

Well, this is going to look bad on my report.

He toyed with the idea of trying to over-awe them with the majesty of the Spanish Empire, threatening them with all manner of dire consequences for assaulting the King's officer. Such bluster had worked before. But one look at the dark faces before and behind told him that would be wasted air. They had cast their dice already and would accept whatever the roll brought them. Treville sighed and drew his rapier, pulling the matching main gauche as well. Though he settled into his best guard, back flat against the wall so that he could keep both in sight, he had few illusions. One against two was nearly always a losing proposition. No sense letting them know that, however.

"Señors," he said, trying to sound cheery though the wound felt decidedly wider than a church door now, "I'm so dangerous that it requires the pair of you? I'm flattered."

Still the Protestants said nothing. But the tall one to his left, narrowed eyes proclaiming that the offense to his abused bollocks would not be overlooked, yanked out his own rapier and pointed it at Treville like an accusation. The bloody-nosed short man, knife already in hand, looked even less forgiving. Treville debated which one might be the easier mark. He needed to take the fight to them, one at a time. Waiting for their simultaneous rush would be suicide. Deciding that the shorter weapon and swollen face made the dagger man less dangerous, he advanced on him while humming a happy tune. That cued the one with the rapier to come after him from behind, his boots squishing in the mud. But he had waited too long and Treville had stolen a march on him.

The French spy feinted a thrust at the smaller man's tender face, causing him to pull up short and attempt to parry it. But Treville had anticipated that and dropped the point for a lunging thrust at the fellow's plump thigh. His opponent proved to be nimbler than he looked and pulled the leg back just in time. He had also kept an ace in reserve. Like a striking snake his free hand whipped up from behind his back and brought down a stout oak cudgel directly onto the crown of Treville's head.

The alley rang with a metallic clang as the club smacked against the crown of the wide-brimmed leather hat. Giving thanks that he had chosen to insert the steel skullcap that morning, despite its irksome weight, Treville smiled, winked, and dug the point of his own dagger into the soft underside of the man's wrist, straight into an odd V tattoo. With a surprised yelp the victim dropped the cudgel and hopped back out of range.

There was no time to savor the triumph, however. The other man had arrived to join the dance.

Treville heard him coming and slid to his right to remove the easy target while also spinning and sweeping his sword in a wide arc to make the assailant halt his advance. The tall man slid to a stop in the muck, leaning his upper body back to avoid the hissing tip. But he did not turn and flee, nor did he flail his sword about in response to Treville's move. Instead, he nodded, gave a little salute, and assumed a guard position that told of much training and experience against serious enemies.

Ah…a veteran soldier, this one. No surprise there. The whole damned Flemish population's been at war for longer than either of us has been on this earth.

His first impulse was to return the salute and flee, but both ends of the alley were still blocked. The burly fellow was using his headscarf to tie up his wounded wrist, but he still barred Treville's exit there, dagger in teeth. And the man with the steady rapier would certainly object to the bleeding Frenchman exiting past him. Treville gazed longingly at the man on the ground, praying that he would leap to his feet and intervene on his behalf. But all he did was continue his snoring while hugging a leather wine bottle like a lover.

With his wound growing ever more agonizing, the pain creeping down the leg and up his ribs like a serpent of flame, Treville was left with bad options. He thought of rushing the injured one like a bull, thinking that his recent stabbing would make him wary of engaging again. That would leave the rapier man on his arse like a river leech, though. No matter how quickly Treville might overwhelm the shorter one, if at all, it would slow him down enough that he would feel that sword's point between his shoulder blades.

Right. A sneaky, dishonorable fight it is, then. Like usual.

He advanced with care on the tall foe, alert for any surprises while preparing one of his own. His point flirted with the other's eyes, drawing attention away from Treville's dagger, which had edged down so that his gloved little finger could tug at a button on his sash. Once he felt it give way, he launched a furious assault on his enemy, easing his rear foot up against the front one to give his lunge an extra few inches.

But it fell short, nonetheless. His canny opponent had spotted the preparation and retreated just enough to remain safe from the point. He snapped a stop thrust at Treville's forearm that nearly landed. At the last instant Treville cocked the wrist. The point grazed his gauntlet. Before it could be withdrawn, he caught it on his blade's forte and enveloped it, snaking his point in a corkscrew motion toward the other's arm. When he tried to ram it home by pushing off his front leg, however, Treville found that it had lost nearly all strength. It proved to be child's play for his foe to pull back the arm and escape out of range.

Cursing his luck, Treville struggled to his feet again and took stock. Behind him, the tattooed fellow seemed content to block the alley and let his friend do the hard work. That was fortunate. If they had both pressed him Treville knew he would be doomed. As it was things looked bleak enough. His wound now felt like imps from Hell were jabbing salty pitchforks into it. He had next to no feeling in his hip and the leg was practically unresponsive. Chasing down the man facing him was impossible. The Dutchman would evade him with ease and take advantage of his obvious weakness. All he could do was lay a trap…if the calm veteran could be lured into it.

Treville took a step, exaggerated the spasms in his wounded side, and inwardly winced at how little playacting that required. He would only get one opportunity with his scheme. If it failed, he would collapse and be at their mercy. Lurching forward, he gasped and dropped his dagger as if at death's door, clutching his belly to sell the possibility that he might be bleeding inside. When the other fellow saw that and moved toward him, Treville lifted his sword in desperation, mumbling at him as a further distraction. Those eyes needed to stay locked on his while his left hand fished into the hidden pocket of the sash to dump its contents on the ground. Thankfully, the soupy mud and manure hid the items.

He groaned and sank to one knee, the tip of his sword dropping as he sold his despair. The actors at the Hôtel de Bourgogne in Paris could have done no better. Chuckling in victory, the Protestant swordsman spanked the blade aside and strode forward, no doubt preparing to gloat a little before ramming home his point into Treville's vitals. Instead of a crow of success, however, the alley echoed with a completely different sound: a screech of surprised pain. For his boot sank down upon Treville's hidden toys. In reflex the man's eyes dropped to see what he had trod upon.

Caltrops.

Smaller than those used against cavalry horses, the wicked twisted spikes nevertheless had no difficulty puncturing the boot's sole and the tender foot inside it. He automatically lifted his foot, unbalancing him and taking his concentration completely from the fight for a moment. That instant was all Treville needed to raise his rapier and plunge it one inch beneath the breastbone. It slid through with no more resistance than might have been offered by a bale of hay. Considering how little force Treville was able to muster, that was fortunate indeed. His hapless enemy dropped his sword and his foot together. After a single cough that sprayed an aerosol of scarlet from his bearded mouth, the swordsman stumbled back, his body yanking Treville's blade from its owner's nerveless fingers. With a sigh he slumped against the wall, then slid down until he half-sat, sightless eyes open, the rapier that slew him swaying.

Treville also slumped to the foul ground, giving up a silent prayer of thanks for survival, and also asking St. Joshua, patron saint of spies, to make his inevitable imminent death less painful than it looked likely to be. He had lost all strength, all will to move. The dagger wound was a Vesuvius of misery now. Blood pounded in his ears with a rush and his breath already rattled. Even if a surgeon took him in right that moment it would take a miracle to preserve him.

Something stirred a few paces beyond him. He rolled his head enough that one eye could take it in. The sleeping drunk had finally realized that something was amiss in his cozy corner of the world. At this extreme angle the man -- a boy, really, not yet twenty -- seemed to be hanging onto the edge of a wall. His bottle rolled down that wall, revealing the surprise beneath. To Treville's amazement and horror he raised an ornate wheel-lock pistol. Its inlaid ivory grip proclaimed it to be so valuable that one could only marvel at it being in the possession of such a lost specimen as this. Why had he not sold it for a warm bed and warmer woman? This question fled his feverish mind, to be replaced by a more urgent one: *why is he aiming that thing at me?*

Alarm lent Treville a lost burst of vigor. He slapped his palms into the muck and shoved just as the pistol's dog snapped forward. The pyrite sparked against the wheel. Heat and sound roared past his ear as he rolled to his right, landing on his back, grimacing and gasping, unable to move again.

So this is how it ends. Lying in filth in a ruined Spanish town, done in by a rummy.

Something gurgled at his feet, like a half-obstructed storm drain. Forcing his eyes open, Treville saw through the lashes that the stout man he had twice wounded had pursued him, after all. In fact, by the time he had run his partner through this one was only three paces from Treville's back. The short blade was still in his hand, ready to cut the Frenchman's throat. All that had prevented that had been the drunken stranger's pistol ball. It had punched through the man's throat. He lay there, choking on his own blood.

The shot had been intended for him, not me. What the devil ---?

A tall slender shadow appeared above him. It resolved itself into the face and form of the drunk, now completely sober and smiling down at him. The clean-shaven youth was as handsome as Adonis, with a sharp eye and a cheeky grin. Golden ringlets hung down from beneath his ragged headscarf. He crossed his arms and said, in Gascon-seasoned French, "Well, you hardly look worth the trouble to bury, eh? But as I don't get paid unless I bring you back alive..."

Before Treville knew what was happening the boy had hauled him up and slung him over his shoulder like a bag of grain. Though the pain was spectacular, the wounded man managed to mutter, "Who are you?"

"I'm your master's insurance policy. Been following you ever since you left Paris. Never spotted me, did you? He told me to make sure if your useless arse failed its mission, I was supposed to bring it back so he could kick it." He began walking toward the far end of the alley as if Treville weighed nothing, even though he also packed the wounded man's weapons. "Let's hope you have an arse of iron. Oh, and the name's d'Artagnan."

2

OSTEND

"IT IS CERTAINLY POISON, ATTACKING THE BLOOD.
HE WILL BE DEAD IN AN HOUR."

"You're fevered already," said d'Artagnan, mopping Treville's dripping brow. Sweat poured down the victim's face, soaking his dark moustache and pointed chin beard. "Could bake a baguette on your head." He frowned. "That's odd. The bastard must've used his knife for something nasty. Scraping manure off his boots maybe."

"Or poisoned it," Treville suggested, voice so faint as to be barely audible.

"Wouldn't put it past those heretical scum."

They had just returned to Treville's room above the only inn in Ostend that had more-or-less survived the years of artillery bombardment. The roof had collapsed at one corner from a cannonball strike, but the building remained serviceable. It was reserved for Spanish officers and his forged papers had secured him a place. It offered a fine view of the harbor. A formidable Spanish flotilla rode at anchor there now, replacing the Dutch and English ships that had supplied the town during the siege and kept it viable. Though the Spanish had spent a staggering amount of blood and treasure taking it, bankrupting their kingdom in the process, the Dutch had taken Sluis and already made Ostend redundant as a naval base. But privateers had begun operating out of it, nevertheless, doing their best to harass Dutch warships and rich merchantmen. And the town and the countryside around it were aswarm with troops, preparing for a march north against Maurice of Nassau. After three dozen years the war still dragged on, devouring men like some mythical monster.

None of that much concerned Treville at that moment. His pulse raced like a drum beating the fast roll at a hanging. Sickly colors flared across his vision, while ominous blackness crept into its edges. Venomous demons gnawed at his right side. Twice already he had puked his guts into the chamber pot. Since it smelled even worse than what would normally be deposited there, he knew that something very wrong was roiling inside of him.

"We'll need a doctor," d'Artagnan said, not for the first time. "This is well beyond my talents." He had carried the groaning Treville two blocks to the inn and up three flights of narrow stairs. The whole way he had explained to all they met that his friend had boldly challenged the cavalry to a drinking contest. Lost? Why no, he had been the victor. "You should see what the losers are going through. Not even Dante's imagination could describe it, señors."

"A doctor will just bleed me and alert the town governor that I might be contagious," Treville protested. "I'll either be quarantined or shipped off somewhere."

"If we don't get help they'll be shipping you off to the churchyard."

"The fate of many a spy. We die unknown and unmourned."

"Speak for yourself. I plan to live to a ripe old age. Father many fat Gascon babes."

"Then you'd best leave me and get back to France before someone finds those two dead rascals and trails us back here."

"Again…I don't get paid for burying you."

"Why are you getting paid? Why the devil are you here at all?"

The young man half-rolled Treville so he could inspect the festering wound. His reaction resembled that of a man peering into the maw of a rabid wolf. "I was told to follow you and stay out of sight. You weren't to notice me. And I wasn't to reveal myself unless you got into serious trouble. If that happened I was to get you back to Paris."

"Why wasn't I told of this?"

D'Artagnan shrugged. "It's a sort of an audition."

"Audition? For what? The Forty-Five? Impossible! We don't take inexperienced boys off the street."

The Forty-Five were the personal bodyguards of King Henri IV, a monarch unfortunately prone to attracting all manner of eager assassins. As he had managed to make enemies of French Catholics and Protestant both, as well as nearly all of France's neighbors, during his unlikely rise to the throne, protecting him was more than a full-time occupation. Ironically, the Forty-Five had been assassins themselves, openly killing the Duke of Guise at the previous king's orders. Now they were more circumspect in that role, but it was understood that they were expected to undertake any task, however unpleasant, to preserve the life of their king. Becoming one of their number, like Treville, was by invitation only and generally they were soldiers of the minor nobility who had proven their worth with hard-won experience in battle, cunning, and above all, loyalty.

What court connections does he have that would get him through the door of the Louvre, let alone considered for such a position? He's clearly more than he seems.

The lad loaded his pistol, then wound its mechanism with the key. He threw Treville's officer's sash over his faded and frayed blue doublet, taking the other's hat and rapier, as well. "Who said I was inexperienced? Don't let this pretty face fool you." A brief haunted shadow in his eyes hinted at what the cost of that experience might have been. "I'm off to fetch a man I know who might be able to help you. It's long odds but a forlorn hope is better than none. Don't open the door for anyone."

Treville coughed, breath rattling deep in his chest. "Do I look like I could get up to do that?"

"To be honest, you look like the arse end of a plague-riddled dog."

"Ah…not as bad as I feel then."

With that d'Artagnan let himself out. No sooner had the sound of his footsteps trailed away than the door opened and he entered again. Another man followed close behind him. So delirious was Treville that all sense of time passing had been lost. He would have sworn that only seconds had gone by. But in those fleeting moments horrific dreams had churned his brain, making him feel that death had already claimed him. Looking up at the stained ceiling, cobwebs hanging in the corners like hell's lacework, only reinforced the thought. Just as disturbing was the sight of the stranger's face viewed upside-down as he bent over to examine his patient. Dark-complected, with unusual angles of eye and cheek, he had a hairless chin and splendid white teeth.

"Your description was accurate," he said in halting Spanish. His accent was odd, like nothing Treville had ever heard. "A particularly ugly dog's arse, at that."

"This is your physician?" asked Treville, every word a twisting knife in his belly now. "I've had more respectful torturers."

The newcomer smiled and moved toward Treville's feet. Now he could be seen at the proper angle. His skin glowed with a copper sheen, and his hair rivaled a raven's sleek black as it flowed from beneath the high-crowned buckled hat. An eagle feather sprouted from the hat's band, which had bear claws ornamenting it. Though he wore an expensive suit of the newest fashion, dark plum colored with a large white ruff at his throat, he seemed ill at ease in the clothes.

"Funny you should mention torture," d'Artagnan said, grasping Treville's arms and pinning him to the bed with all his weight.

A searing agony flared in Treville's back as the other man probed the festering wound. Only a dagger sheath thrust between his teeth by d'Artagnan prevented Treville from cracking the plaster walls with his screams. The misery seemed to slow time to a crawl as the brown fingers poked and kneaded. Treville's back arched and every muscle clenched. Just as he was about to beg to have his throat cut to mercifully make it stop, the stranger backed away. Treville sagged, panting, tears in his eyes.

"May I speak French?" he asked d'Artagnan. "I am more familiar with it."

"If you must,' the youth replied. "But keep your voice low. No sense in giving any eavesdroppers an excuse to come prying for a payday."

The doctor nodded and did as suggested. His French was excellent, though the accent remained. "The wound is not deep. No vital organs have been struck. Yet, as you see, he is in great distress.

"Can you do nothing then?"

"Perhaps. As you mentioned that this might be the case, I brought what medicines I had at hand that could possibly aid him." He took off his coat and began to roll up the sleeves of his linen shirt. "Boil water, quickly."

Through the sickly haze that masked his vision Treville watched the healer prepare his treatment. It interested him to note that none of the expected bleeding or enemas seemed to be planned. Instead, pungent herbs and powders were turned into a yellowish paste. This mass became a hot compress slathered all over his wound. The first application made him grit his teeth and hiss, but soon the pain began to ebb. At the same time, he was made to drink so much acrid tea that he feared he might explode like a rotting corpse.

Again time ceased to have any meaning, though changes in the weak light coming through the filthy window told him that many hours passed. His fever grew worse for a time and his caregivers grew alarmed. But eventually it broke. Perspiration and ugly fluids soiled the sheets. Clean pain replaced the rotting anguish in his side. Treville even managed to keep some soup and bread down.

At dawn the next day d'Artagnan shook his head. "You are a magician," he informed the doctor. "They may burn you at the stake for it."

The dark one laughed. "Magic it may be, but not the illicit kind. Merely the bounty of Mother Earth, along with Father Sky's blessing." His fingers tapped the pouches he had brought with him. "Bloodroot. Chickweed. Echinacea. Common charcoal. Myrrh. A few others."

"Take care. One man's medicine is another's sorcery," Treville croaked, so sore that he felt that his horse had rolled onto him. He held out his hand to his savior. "My thanks, sir."

Taking it with a firm grip, the physician said, "I am happy to keep you out of the Wi-htikow's embrace for a while longer." When Treville frowned at the odd word, the other man translated it for him. "You would call it an evil spirit."

D'Artagnan lay a hand on his shoulder. "Chipay is a marvel, eh? Learned our language from explorers sent to Canada by King Henri. Taught them how to survive in that wilderness. They brought him back with them, but the

Spanish dogs took his ship. Made him a prisoner, then a pet. When sickness seized the crew, their pet saved most of them. Not being complete fools, they gave him an informal post here as an army doctor. Naturally, being the Habsburg idiots that they are, their own surgeons took offense and drove him out. He's been stranded in the Low Countries for two years, often trapped between the lines."

"I'm glad of it," Treville said, "for purely selfish reasons."

"His Cree name is Chipay, but the men who first befriended him called him Fantôme, because he could move through the forest like a ghost."

"One learns that as a child," Chipay explained as he packed up his kit. "There are many enemies in the trees. Bears, wolves, snakes…men." Anxious sadness crept into his face. "Wolves are easier to survive than the men."

"Speaking of enemies," mused Treville to d'Artagnan, "I don't suppose you went back to that alley to see what you could learn about our own wolves?"

"I did. They both had that tattoo. A large V with a smaller interlinked O and C in the center. Don't know what it means. Secret Protestant society, perhaps? I made a drawing. Maybe they know about it in Paris. And that was no ordinary dagger he used on you. It was more of a spike, with a triangular cross-section. Specially made to punch through your buff coat. Would probably get through joints in armor, too. If I were a betting man, and the good Lord knows that I am, to my shame, I'd say he'd cut down a sword that had been designed for that -- an estoc, most likely." He pulled a document from his jerkin. "The only other item worth noticing was this. Hidden inside a pocket in the tall one's boot."

Treville's new partner held up the scrap of parchment close to him, as he was yet too weak to lift his own head. Oblong holes had been cut into it at seemingly random intervals with a very sharp blade, possibly a surgeon's scalpel. On the top right corner was inked **ZE1**.

"Code overlay," he ventured. "He puts it on top of an innocent-looking letter and the words visible are the real message. We use them sometimes."

"And these letters?"

"Hard to say. Could be the version of the codebook they use. You change them if the enemy breaks one. We do that on a regular basis just to be careful. Or maybe the name of the office issuing it."

D'Artagnan stuffed it back into his jerkin. "More work for the brains back home. I'm only good at stabbing and shooting people."

"I'm glad for that. Otherwise there wouldn't have been much for Fantôme to work with."

For six more days Treville kept to his room, with d'Artagnan using his own forged documents and Spanish soldier's disguise to go out for food. Chipay returned daily to look in on his patient and inspect the wound. It made rapid and remarkable progress. The festering mess gave way to a tight clean puncture and Treville's fever gave way to returned strength and appetite. Soon he could sit up and even walk about the room a bit.

He would talk with his physician, who was polite but not greatly forthcoming about his life in New France. But he did say that his healing talents had made him enough important friends among the Dutch that he generally did not suffer the sort of indignities and harassment that he had endured when first arriving in Europe.

"But this," he sighed, gesturing at his exotic brown face, "still makes some people think that they have a right to insult me, to spit at me, to call me demon."

"You aren't alone," Treville told him, touching his wound. "The man who did this would probably have said the same about me."

"But he took offense at your belief about the Great Father, not merely because of how you looked. He hated a choice you made, yes? Or at least a choice he believed you to have made. I receive abuse solely for appearing different than those in this world. No man selects his ancestors."

"True enough. If we could, I wonder what sort of world this would be."

The door opened and d'Artagnan burst through, out of breath. "Just as hellish as it is now. Men always look for a reason to butcher one another. If it isn't looks or religion, it'll be how many fingers and toes he has." He began packing up everything he could lay his gloved hands on. "Get dressed. You have to go, no matter your condition."

Treville sat up with a grunt. "What's happening?"

"The garrison's provost has found those two vermin that we danced with. I should've taken more time and hidden them better. God knows why they care about two dead Protestants, but they're acting like we killed the princes of the realm. They're asking questions. And the locals in the market are more than happy to trade their knowledge for gold." He gave Treville a hard look. "Apparently there is an embarrassing number of witnesses."

Wincing, every muscle stiff and sore, Treville levered himself upright and reached for his doublet. "My apologies. The next time somebody decides to stab me in the back I'll be sure to have him book an appointment for a more deserted spot. And I wasn't the one discharging a bloody pistol, was I?"

D'Artagnan stuffed some last items into his saddlebags and tossed them over his shoulder, addressing Chipay as he did so. "They want you, too, Fantôme. Maybe they've seen you here too often and are suspicious or maybe it's just an excuse for your enemies to persecute you. Either way, I heard some nasty talk in the street. They're laying a trap. You dare not go home."

Chipay responded with surprising composure for a man being told that his world was upended. "I wish I could say that I am surprised. But the sour hearts of these people are as difficult to change as is the course of a river." He threw his bag over his neck. "All that I possess of any worth is in here already."

"You'll come with us?" asked Treville as he finished buttoning his doublet and seized a boot. "Our people will be more welcoming to a man like you than the Spanish."

"And you'll be able to speak a proper language there," added d'Artagnan with a laugh.

Fantôme shrugged. "Well, if I must speak a barbaric tongue, I do prefer yours."

"We'll need a plan to get out of this wretched town in one piece. And getting through the Spanish army won't be a picnic, either. Do you have a horse?"

"Alas, no."

"Ours are in the army stable. I doubt we'll be able to get them now." D'Artagnan sighed and turned to Treville, palms up. "So tell me, clever one, have you any ideas for getting us home in one piece?"

The wounded man started to laugh, then thought better of it as pain bit into his side. "I do, but I doubt you'll like it."

"I haven't liked anything about this assignment since it was forced upon me. How bad can your little scheme be?"

3

OUTSKIRTS OF OSTEND

"WHEN YOU KILL A MAN YOU DO NOT ONLY DISPATCH HIM.
YOU SLAY ALL WHO LOVE HIM."

"Congratulations," grumbled d'Artagnan, voice muffled by the stained grave shroud cocooning him, "I truly hate your stratagem."

"Hush, dolt," his partner whispered, "dead men are supposed to be silent."

They bounced in decided discomfort at the foul bottom of one of the Spanish army's corpse wagons. It was an open affair, taken from a luckless Dutch farmer, with ladder-like racks for sides, normally good for hauling hay. In this instance it also proved an excellent choice for transporting the fortunate dead of Ostend, as the disgusting smells and fluids did not remain. Pulling it was a transcendently ugly yellow pony with a hairless tail and a drunken gait. They expected the brute to collapse and die at any moment, but somehow it had kept going for nearly two leagues. Treville marveled at the ability of the oppressed of the region to survive despite all the outrages visited upon them by decades of cruel war.

Fantôme drove the wagon, as that was what the Spanish would expect. As there was an understandable shortage of volunteers for the duty of hauling corpses to the burial pit, and forcing a soldier to do it would not only take him from his martial assignment but expose him to contagion, the town's governor had hit upon the brilliant idea of having the detested pagan doctor do it. If he caught the plague or some other dread malady from one of the bodies, no one would mourn him for long. His mournful expression, mirrored by the overcast late winter day, required little acting ability on his part.

They had experienced little difficulty obtaining the cart, as it was hardly

15

the sort of military equipment anyone desired to be close to. Chipay simply told the sergeant in charge that there had been an unpleasant episode during the night and he was tasked with lugging the results out to the mass grave south of Ostend. He had been given the sad pony and rickety wagon without argument. It had been simple enough to detour into a still-wrecked part of town and have Treville and d'Artagnan hop aboard, swaddled in old shrouds that suggested that the shapes inside had passed away from something best not touched, or even inspected. Then all that had been required had been for the supposed bodies to remain still despite the constant jarring as the wheels struck gullies and projecting stones. Behind them, bands of soldiers searched the town for the murderers of two supposed upstanding citizens.

Their luck had held until they had passed through the rear line. Then a captain had raised a hand to stop them. All three men in the wagon had laid gloved hands on their hidden weapons in case a desperate fight might be required. But all the officer had wanted was to toss four more bodies into the wagon, as the camp fever was raging in his sector. It had taken great self-control for Treville and d'Artagnan to remain quiet and unmoving when the slack burdens had been thrown atop them. Though decidedly unpleasant, the incident did them a service, for now they were hidden at the bottom of a heap that no one wished to approach.

"Ready your wits, gentlemen," muttered Fantôme. "We have arrived."

He slowed the wagon as it approached three men. Two were local citizens pressed into service, with the sour expressions one would expect. Their clothing looked to be the worst that they owned, so as not to ruin anything worth keeping as they handled the leaking dead. A glum Spanish sergeant sat on a stump several feet apart from them, whittling a branch into a pile of pointless strands out of boredom. As his job was to check in each load, and to ensure that the unwilling workers did their jobs, he wore a proper uniform, though his officer would doubtless not approve of precisely how he did it. His big-brimmed hat lay on the ground, beside his sword and pistol, and a garish red scarf covered his large round head. The doublet should have been buttoned all the way to his unshaven throat. Enormous graying mustachios hung below his beak of a nose like a great bird had just landed there. Farther off, beneath a large tree, three horses were tied beside a medium-sized army tent with a table and bench in front.

A prodigious stone's throw beyond the men lay a great steaming pit. Some fifty feet across and fifteen deep, it was half-filled with the mortal remains of the diseased, the murdered, and all else who had recently left brutal Ostend for a hopefully better world. Barrels of quicklime stood beside the enormous heap of earth that had been made when an idle infantry regiment had dug the huge grave. The white powder was intended to reduce the sickening odor. If so, perhaps more was needed. Sadly, several other pits had already been stuffed full of their awful cargo and covered over. Partially-overgrown mounds littered the area. Such was the tragedy of the Spanish Netherlands and its unending war.

"What you got, savage?" the sergeant demanded, managing to look up at Chipay and down on him at the same time. They were in luck. The order to seize Chipay had not yet come this far out. He spit at the feet of the pathetic pony.

The physician mastered any anger he might have felt at the soldier's sneering attitude, having had long practice at it. Saluting the sergeant as if the man were a great commander, he jerked a thumb back at his load. "More dead of the swamp fever, my master. Santiago's company."

"How many?"

"Six."

"A damned awful lot. I swear, his men have the constitutions of old women. They don't stay upright long enough for the enemy to shoot them."

"We all must go when God calls us."

"What would you know about that, heathen?" The Spaniard turned to hurl curses at his civilian workers. "Hop to it, dogs! You know what to do. Follow them to the pit and heave the guts in." He snatched up his belongings and headed toward the tent, where a bottle waited for him on the table.

With looks of loathing for their boss, backs carefully turned so that only Chipay could see, the pitiful Dutchmen nodded and trudged toward the open grave. Fantôme shook the reins and got the pony back in motion again. He guided the wagon to the edge, turning it about so the wagon's open back faced the pit. After setting the brake, he climbed down and stood beside the rear wheel, whip in hand, pretending to inspect it so that he could whisper to the two Frenchmen.

"We are at the precipice, monsieurs. Two impressed civilian workers to remove the bodies and one soldier in charge. He has remained far off. I believe he has a flagon of wine."

"So much the better if he's impaired himself," said Treville. "So our plan holds?"

"It does. Ready yourselves. These men appear simple, quite amenable to suggestion."

The pair of Dutch conscripts arrived to perform their detested task. One climbed atop the pile of shrouded dead to ease each burden off so that the other could pull it loose and drop it upon the ground. When all were free of the cart they would each seize one end of a body and swing it out into the pit, pouring quicklime atop it before repeating the process. Later they would shovel soil atop the day's arrivals.

While the truly dead were being maneuvered, Fantôme slyly unwrapped the feet of his friends. For their ploy to work they would have to be able to move. The rest would be accomplished by their thespian talents and the native fears of the workmen. If it went as they hoped they would soon be riding Spanish horses across the French frontier. And if not, well…there was no alternative plan except d'Artagnan's preferred shooting and stabbing.

Naturally, there was no trouble with the first four corpses. Each was duly dumped into the mud at the pit's edge. Chipay had an anxious moment when Treville's turn came. With his wound still not completely healed, a hard landing might make him cry out. To make sure that this did not happen, the doctor assisted the workers with the burden, claiming that they looked fatigued and touching the dead did not distress him. He did the same with the inert d'Artagnan, taking care to grasp the youth's middle so that his pistol was not accidentally discovered.

"I commend you, gentlemen," he said in Flemish, removing his hat and mopping his brow. "Many might let their imaginations run away with them in such a macabre setting as this."

"Macabre?" frowned one. "That mean spooky?"

"It does. You do not fear ghosts and the like here?"

The man scoffed. "Tales for children! Dead is dead."

His partner scrunched up his face in doubt. "Don't know about that. Seen a strange thing or two in my time that I couldn't explain."

Naturally, that required him to tell his story, giving them all a break from their labor. He took his time, spinning an impressive yarn about a churchyard in Liege where he swore upon his mother's immortal soul that a newly-buried child had crawled out of her grave and chased him up a tree. His friends had insisted that it had only been a feral cat that had fallen into the hole and had dug itself out, but he was not so sure, describing its unearthly shrieks in terrifying detail. By the time he had finished the mood had grown decidedly gloomy at the rim of the death pit.

Which was precisely the moment that two of the corpses moaned and stood up.

Chipay played his part well, howling in feigned terror even though he had signaled his friends to resurrect themselves by a well-placed nudge to Treville's booted foot. As the supposed ghosts made horrifying gurgles and waved their shrouded arms, the workers turned white and cried for their mothers while wetting themselves in terror. They turned and fled toward the soldier's tent. Fantôme noticed that the fellow who had declared ghosts to be imaginary was far in front.

Still pretending mortal fear, the doctor stumbled backward after them. But he was leading Treville and d'Artagnan toward the horses that were the object of their ruse, as the shrouds did not permit them to see well. In a few moments they arrived at the tent, where the tricky part of the plan lay. The frightened workers were hiding behind the sergeant, babbling that the dead walked again and that it was his duty, as a sworn officer of the great empire of Spain, to protect them.

His face flushed with wine, he rose from his seat to squint at the oncoming specters. Apparently satisfied that the absurd sheeted figures, which made wooing noises like shades in a children's play, were a threat, he scooped up his pistol from the table and took aim. With a triumphant laugh he pulled the trigger. A cloud of white smoke spewed forth from its muzzle like the breath of a tiny but dangerous dragon. The ball had no chance of missing one of the disguised men. They were too close to the sergeant and to one another.

But miss it did. For Fantôme's whip had struck his wrist like an adder, slashing it to ribbons and tugging the whole arm down. Mud exploded as the heavy ball plowed harmlessly into the ground. Numb fingers opened and the matchlock tumbled from his grasp.

The sergeant, veteran of many hard-fought campaigns despite his foolish demeanor, knew how to change tactics. Not easily cowed, he snatched up his sword with the other hand and charged, eager to send the pagan to whatever hell his kind believed in. Those fools in the shrouds could wait their turn. Then he would make them completely dead and ensure they remained so.

Chipay dropped his whip and backpedaled away from the blade, for it was always good policy to presume that a man trying to run you through had skill in that arena. After all, this man had survived the apocalyptic battles that had slain eighty thousand of his comrades. He must have ability, even if the wine degraded it somewhat. As he retreated he led the sergeant away from the tent and his friends, toward the vast trench full of dead. Making certain to stay just out of range of the thrust, but still near enough to entice his foe to keep up the pursuit, he concentrated on not tripping on some hole or hidden root. Keeping his feet was the way to stay alive.

Back at the tent, Treville and d'Artagnan sensed that the drama had run its course. They threw off their borrowed robes and revealed themselves to the poor workmen, cackling in glee. Treville restrained his partner, whose first thought was to shoot the sergeant who threatened Fantôme. Satisfied that the doctor had the matter well in hand, the Gascon casually pointed the weapon toward the Dutchmen, who gulped and fled toward Ostend as fast as their quivering legs could take them. Still laughing, the pair helped themselves to the Spaniard's wine, which was of better quality than he deserved, and to his pistol, which Treville loaded while they observed the engagement near the pit.

Though he had failed to pierce his enemy's hated hide, the sergeant still had great expectations of doing so. Panting with the exertion, he maintained the chase until he caught his prey near the rear wheel of the wagon. Now Chipay had nowhere left to run. He seemed to realize this, for he grew calm and assumed the attitude of a condemned man facing a firing squad. Bumping up against the barrel of quicklime, he sighed and nodded as the gloating soldier approached.

"Just like a cowardly savage," he sneered, sword point aimed at Chipay's bosom. "Can't manage a stand-up fight. Only good for raids and sneaking ambushes. When a real soldier takes you on, all you can do is run." With that he cocked his arm back and sent a vicious thrust straight at the doctor.

But he struck only air. Without seeming to move Fantôme let the sword slip just past his waistcoat. In the space of a breath he glided along the steel and set himself behind his would-be killer. Before he knew what had happened the Spaniard found himself facing the edge of the pit with no one in range of his blade. Realizing what had happened, he turned his head to spot his target and loose another strike. Too late. A shove from Chipay launched him over the lip and down into the mass of reeking dead. Then the fellow began to screech as if feasted upon by demons from the underworld.

"You could've simply killed him," observed d'Artagnan when Chipay walked the pony and wagon back to the tent. "He's only a black-hearted Spaniard, after all."

Chipay removed their belongings from under the wagon's seat and freed the pony from the traces to wander free. "Only is a hard word, monsieur," he said. "I have killed too many men to count, back in my country. In my youth I thought as you do, that a certain kind of man is only an enemy, only an animal to be hunted, only a piece to be removed from the board. No thought to his father, mother, children, friends. When you kill a man you do not only dispatch him. You slay all who love him. Their souls grow black, they grow thick, become callused. As did mine."

He pointed toward Ostend. "A man's lifetime. That is how long the Spanish and Dutch have been butchering one another here. That speck of land was worth a hundred thousand lives? For what? Gold? Power? Can you eat those? Can you bounce them on your knee and teach them stories? Will they keep you warm at night?"

The physician set d'Artagnan's saddlebags atop one of the tethered horses. "No. I will defend myself when necessary. And others, too. But I have scars upon my heart that are not yet worn away. So I will do as the bravest of my people do. Touch the enemy without taking his life. And I have sworn to heal ten times as many as I have killed. To my soul's disgrace, that will take a considerable number of years." He pulled a double-stranded cord from around his neck. One strand bore black beads all the way to its end. The other had white beads only a third as long. "This is the tally. My life-debt. Every ten lives I preserve removes a black scar and a white honor replaces it. When all is white again, then I may go home. Come, we must go."

Neither Treville nor d'Artagnan had any retort to Chipay's speech. The youth seemed to think it was all a great joke. Treville was struck at how much wisdom could come from the mouth of an unsaved heathen from the dark forests across the sea. He vowed to observe this man, to learn from him. Clearly he had thought long and hard about the world and his place in it.

Getting back to Paris proved to be easier than they had dared hope. They had to avoid the heavily-guarded coast, so they meandered inland, squeezing between the garrisons at Nieuport and Furnes to cross the frontier into France at night. Twice they had to turn aside and hide themselves in copses or behind barns as patrols thundered past. Though it was unlikely that orders had gone this far and wide to find them, discretion urged them to be cautious. Friendly French-speaking local peasants along the fluid border proved more than eager to aid them against the hated Spanish. If Treville's wound had permitted him to go longer and faster the trip would have been child's play. But in two days they reached the safety of France. And in only three more they stood in the headquarters of the Forty-Five.

Under arrest.

4

PARIS: THE LOUVRE

IT'S PROBABLY A CAPITAL CRIME TO SOIL THE ROYAL FURNITURE

After ten minutes of his master's sarcasm, Treville longed to be thrown into the Bastille.

The balding, long-bearded Marquis du Rosny, Maximilien de Béthune, hardly raised his voice above the polite tone one might use with one's mother at breakfast. While Treville struggled to stand at attention with his aching back, the king's first minister carefully ticked off the regrettably-long list of his failures on the aborted mission. Every phrase felt like a new blade being twisted in the half-healed wound. Though his commander looked like a splendidly-dressed banker (which, as the king's Minister of Finance, he essentially was) in a burgundy-colored doublet, black velvet gown, and magnificent white lace ruff, his every word stung, dipped in the acid of fatherly disappointment that hurt so much more than mere rage would have. Risking a quick sideways glance, Treville saw that d'Artagnan suffered identical agonies at the great man's censure.

They had plenty of reasons to fear Rosny, not the least being that he was the governor of the Bastille and nominal captain-general of the queen's Gens D'arms, to say nothing of being the king's close friend and most trusted advisor, and the most powerful Protestant in the realm. At a single word he could make them both vanish as if vaporized by witchcraft. That was why they had felt such terror at being informed that they were under arrest for having failed the king. But he had no need to rely on such authority. His position as commander of the Forty-Five Guards, whom he regarded as if the very sons of his own loins, was more than enough. Falling short of his expectations made Treville and his comrades want to hide beneath a rock and die of humiliation. The irony was that his own son, also named Maximilien, was an eighteen-year-old drunken wastrel and gambler who had proven utterly immune to his father's scorn.

"So," he said, "to recapitulate: your false identity was immediately compromised, you let yourself be ambushed, my apprentice here had to pull your fat from the fire, and you bring me no actionable intelligence. Oh, and you lost a government horse." He sighed like a man who had been saddled with a half-witted nephew in the family business. "Have I forgotten anything?"

Treville knew better than to attempt to justify himself. Perhaps later he could return when Béthune's anger had subsided into mere irritation. Then they would coolly re-examine the operation, learn from its defects, and plan the next one. Right now speaking up would only earn him more scorn.

However, young d'Artagnan did not have the benefit of his experience in these matters. "M'lord," he ventured, "we were not entirely unsuccessful."

An imperious eyebrow went up as Rosny's gaze shifted to his smooth pretty face. "Yes? Pray enlighten me as to your spectacular achievements. Because all I see that you managed to do was to bring me back damaged royal property." He nodded at the pale Treville, who was silently screaming at his partner to shut his pie-hole. "Small comfort."

"The vermin who assailed us were no ordinary street trash. They weren't interested in robbery and they didn't seem to care who witnessed their crime. It was the bold murder of a French agent who to the locals appeared to be a Spanish officer. Someone had trained them well in their craft. Their plan was to distract, stab, and walk away whistling. And from what I could tell, most of the people in that market were either in on the game or had been paid to look the other way. No one screamed, no one called for help, no one interfered. That alley was as empty as a pauper's purse, despite it usually being full of traffic. Not a soul came through it while we were fighting there, not even when I discharged my pistol. They knew Treville was coming, where he would be, what identity he had assumed, and how best to kill him. Does that not suggest something to you, m'lord?"

Rosny tone and expression proclaimed that he was impressed with his cadet. "You think we have a spy here in the Louvre?"

Treville winced, more in pique than in pain. He could have told his master all of that. Yet he had held his tongue while the upstart basked in his respect. The day was getting worse by the minute.

"God forbid, but it would explain how this happened."

The great man turned without a word, walked to the enormous window overlooking the Palais des Tuileries. To his left the construction of the Grand Galerie, which would connect the Louvre to the other château, was a hive of controlled chaos, much like Henri's reign. It was Rosny's duty to help moderate that, particularly when the king was in one of his periods of besottment with a particular mistress. At the moment, the royal disposition was especially goatish, which only made the queen consort more irritable than usual. As Marie de Medici's Italian temper was naturally volatile, affairs were quite touchy these days.

"Treville, sit down before you fall down. D'Artagnan would rather not have to carry you again and I'd prefer that you not leak on my expensive carpet. Be at your ease, both of you."

With a grateful gasp Treville sank into the chair that his fellow agent immediately pushed up against the back of his quivering legs. Though much improved since the day of the attack, his wound still troubled him when he was forced to stand for long stretches. Doubtless the hard riding had done little to speed its healing. If Fantôme had not proven to be such a wizard of a physician, he would be at his own funeral rather than sinking into soft cushions. He pulled at the small uncomfortable ruff he only wore when forced to don his best for special occasions, like a dressing-down in the Louvre. D'Artagnan suffered alike in a green doublet borrowed from his new friend. *At least we had the wit to bathe and change clothes before reporting here. It's probably a capital crime to soil the royal furniture.*

Rosny also sat, assuming a more relaxed position behind his three-acre desk than either soldier expected. Even more amazing was the impish smile that peeped through his lush graying beard. Though only in his mid-forties, he already showed some of the wear of suffering through the innumerable Wars of Religion and campaigns for the throne at Henri's side. And keeping his friend's kingdom intact was proving no less stressful. But right at that instant, at least, he was smiling.

"Poisoned blades, Indian savages, and corpse pits. Ha! I must say, Treville, you always bring me a good story, even when you fail to deliver in other ways. Where is that red fellow, anyway?"

Unsure of the reception his new friend might find at the palace, Treville had thought it wise to leave Chipay at his lodgings. He told his master as much.

"Well, bring him when next you report. The king would no doubt be fascinated by a citizen of the New World, and one we owe a debt to, as well." Rosny lifted his chin to d'Artagnan. "And you! Quite the find. You'll either sit in this chair some day or get run through by a jealous husband. Or hang. Difficult to tell which at this juncture. Perhaps all three."

The abrupt change in tone drained much of the discomfort from Treville's abused body. Though hardly forgotten, the painful upbraiding of a few moments before faded somewhat. Another look at d'Artagnan confirmed that he felt the same way, possibly more so. As a new recruit his fellow Gascon had not had the experience of several tongue-lashings to callus his self-respect.

"My lord," Treville offered, "I fear that d'Artagnan may be right. I may fall short of perfection on occasion, but it beggars belief that I could give myself away so completely after barely arriving in Ostend. There is betrayal here."

That drew a cackle from Rosny. "Of course there's betrayal here! It's the bloody Louvre. Look about you. Catholics dine with Protestants, Italians sleep with the French, old enemies kiss cheeks while looking for the best place to thrust a knife. If all were sweetness and light, I'd begin to think that the Last Judgment were upon us. Heresy, treason, and corruption at every turn. We have more spies in this place than we have rats. Welcome to government service."

He knew of this first-hand, being a Protestant veteran of the Massacre of St. Bartholomew in 1572. That bloody day the eleven-year-old Béthune had survived, when untold thousands of his co-religionists had been butchered, by snatching up a Catholic prayer book and toting it like a divine talisman. His king had learned the same lesson, adopting whatever religious guise necessary to keep his head upon his shoulders. They had both seen that Europe's religious strife could not continue without shattering nations and the tenuous balance of power.

Thus Henri, influenced in no small measure by his chief minister, had issued his controversial Edict of Nantes seven years before. Though not popular with the majority of his people, it did enforce a kind of religious tolerance and civil rights for the Huguenots. But in the halls of the Louvre it created innumerable factions, for and against the policy and all else that the king was attempting to accomplish. Much of Rosny's work day was occupied with anticipating and countering the inevitable plots of people who were quite accomplished at lying through their aristocratic teeth.

"I tolerate a certain amount of it," he continued, "because it is the simplest way to get the troublesome ones to reveal themselves. If I keep the lid on too tightly, everything remains so covert that we discover the truly dangerous plots too late to take effective action. Much of it is simple self-serving corruption. That we can ignore unless the thievery reaches absurd proportions. Truth be told, I include it in my budget as a legitimate royal expense. However, there are also schemes that could bring down the monarchy and even make France the vassal of another power. Those we must be sure to quash."

He took a roll of documents from a drawer. "I sent you to Ostend because we captured a spy who told us...eventually...about a plan to join certain Catholic forces with unscrupulous Protestant ones in a truly unholy alliance. It will not surprise you to learn that money can take the place of God in the hearts of all too many." After thumbing through the stack of papers he pulled one out and held up a printed design identical to the tattoos of Treville's attackers. "This is the device of the Vereenigde Oost-Indische Compagnie, the United East India Company. The Dutch government created it three years ago to exploit their holdings, and those of all others there that they can gain control of, in the Spice Islands. Nowhere else in the world can nutmeg, cloves, and mace be found. The cursed English created their own company two years before that. There is a spirited war beginning on the other side of the world between them, with particularly vicious local pirates also involved. The trouble is, the Dutch have given their company too long a leash, I think. Almost carte blanche to do as they wish. You may have stumbled onto an uncontrolled faction.

"Naturally, this enriches the Dutch government beyond the dreams of avarice. 1700% profit! It's like they discovered how to transmute lead into gold. If they establish an outright monopoly, as looks likely, they will be able to buy enough ships and mercenaries and banks to make themselves masters of us all. Spain is already weakening. They've bankrupted themselves with the Netherlands adventure and by spreading themselves too thin. English sea wolves prey on their New World shipping. And plague has devastated their population, making it harder for them to maintain their troop levels."

D'Artagnan frowned. "Is not a weakened Spain to our benefit, m'lord?"

"It's true that we are hardly in mourning for their predicament. After all, we were at war with them until only a few years ago. But last year they made peace with England, as well, freeing them to retrench and build up their resources. They have improved their naval tactics and are losing fewer treasure ships lately. If they free themselves of Dutch entanglement, and my sources tell me that could be imminent, they may recover their power and influence in all too short a time."

Béthune sighed. "But I think a great war is coming, possibly the most dreadful ever fought in Europe. The Protestant states hate us, want to be free of us. They are motivated, ambitious, clever. If they become wealthy, too, then they will make common cause against us and try to assert their dominance. If the Holy Roman Empire collapses – and Rudolph is a weak and feckless ruler – then the fiends of hell will ride across this continent. Alone we cannot stem that tide. We will need a Spain with strength, with good infantry and better ships. However, they must be prevented from merely aiding their Habsburg brethren, rather than all of us. Though they are fellow Catholics, they may be more interested in territorial aggrandizement than defending the faith. Religion does not often trump blood ties."

"Pardon, m'lord," said Treville, "but is not our queen consort a Habsburg, at least partly?"

"She is. And now you know why I get so little sleep most nights. This requires cunning and diplomacy on our part, not to mention good spies."

D'Artagnan tried to bring the conversation back to his own part in the affair. "You spoke of a scheme between Spain and this Dutch company?"

"Ah! Yes. Best not to confuse you with grand politics, eh? Particularly since they change with the moon." Rosny held up another document. "Getting back to that unfortunate Dutchman. He had the same tattoo that you found in Ostend. According to him the Dutch government has granted sweeping authority to this new trading company, as they will be on the other side of the world and much too far away for effective central control. Essentially they will be their own state. They can found colonies, coin money, make treaties with other nations, hold and execute prisoners, even wage actual war. And he claims that they plan to do all of that.

"But a few in their ranks have already gone further. There is a secret agreement to meddle in European state matters that are hardly connected to the Spice Islands. Apparently some renegades in Spain's Council of the Indies are involved. We don't have exact details of the plan, but it involves bringing down governments, princes, religious affiliations. The fear is that it may reach as far as kings and the Pope. Much of the rationale is pure greed, but some appears to be sincere desire to save populations from perceived heresies.

"The odd thing is the partnering of Catholics and Protestants. I gather that an unusual bargain has been struck wherein each faith is willing to abandon some of its co-religionists in certain countries to gain the cooperation of the other side in helping with their own opposing aims. Very odd, yes, but with the combined wealth and might of these two colonial powers, many dark things are possible.

"The specific matter at hand requires you to go back to the Netherlands. Our man's confession states that his friends in the Dutch company are aiding a band of English Catholic rebels in some sort of wild scheme across the Channel. It's called Saltpeter, whatever that might mean. He wasn't privy to the particulars but he did give us a few names, likely aliases, of contacts there. With more persuading he also provided passwords and codes." Rosny handed Treville several papers. "There they are. Make good use of them, and don't get caught this time."

D'Artagnan raised his hand. "Sir, if there is a spy here, won't he just give us the same treatment as before?"

"I wish him luck. This time I have kept the relevant facts entirely in my hands. The only others who know anything are the poor bastard we questioned, who is in the deepest hole in the Bastille, and his two interrogators, who have been packed off on a mission to Sicily that they sincerely believe to be real. I doubt that you will meet with an ambush this time. If you do, I will have to blame sorcery."

Treville stood, doing his best not to grimace. "Are we no longer under arrest then?"

Rosny snorted a laugh. "I suppose not. Take care that I don't have to re-arrest you after this mission."

"When do we leave, sir?"

"Ten days from now. That should give you time to heal and make necessary preparations. You'll need solid disguises, and money, and the usual tools of the trade. See your quartermaster."

Both agents bowed and turned to leave. But when they reached the ornate gilded door they found themselves bowing much lower, as King Henri burst into the room without so much as one attendant.

"Ah! Maxi!" he said in a hoarse whisper, brushing past the two young men as if they were invisible. He left a strong smell of garlic in his wake. "You've got to save me. My very soul is in your hands."

This alarming declaration hardly caused Rosny's expression to so much as twitch, though Treville automatically braced himself to stop a horde of assassins and d'Artagnan's hand went to his sword. But when no assailants presented themselves, they shrugged and turned to see what the king was so worried about.

Henri IV, anointed King of France by the grace of God, was unprepossessing, to say the least. He had the worn face of a particularly ill-used hunting hound. It was dominated by the spectacular sort of prominent yet drooping nose that only the French produced, preceding him into the room by half a league. Mournful eyes bulged below brows that were the same dark gray as his receding hair and wooly moustache. His full beard, however, which hid a nasty scar where a Jesuit assassin had stabbed him in the mouth, was nearly white. Currently the corners of his mouth sagged with his mood, though that feature generally was animated by good humor and impish charm. Completing the effect was his plain brown doublet with simple linen collar and baggy trunk hose. All in all, he looked more like a moderately-successful shopkeeper than the monarch of the French. A stranger, unfamiliar with Henri's undoubted warmth of personality, would have marveled at the man's stupendous success with the fairer sex.

That success was both the cause of his distress and somewhat in doubt. "They've made common cause against me," he complained as he glanced back at the door in apprehension, his familiar Gascon accent taking on a plaintive tone.

Ah, the accent. That may be how D'Artagnan got his interview.

"Who has, Your Majesty?" inquired Rosny, knowing full well what the problem was. The king had acquired a fetching new mistress, more of a week's dalliance than anything serious, and both his wife and his principal lover had taken more than the usual offense at being kept on the shelf.

"The harpy and the gorgon, of course," was the whispered reply. For a warrior who had achieved the throne with sword and lance, Henry was remarkably fearful of two overdressed women.

"Who is which this time?"

Henri glowered at him, an expression for which his beetling brows were well-suited. "Marie is a punishing fiend who snatches away my happiness. Clearly she is the harpy."

"As you say."

"And Henriette can only be a gorgon. That cold accusing stare positively turn me to stone."

"Indubitably, my liege. But did you not force her into retirement at Venteuil for that plot last year?"

The king's face twisted into a mixture of self-recrimination. "I know, I know, but she is so...so..." His hands made a gesture of bounty that left little to the imagination.

"That may be, Your Majesty, but she did scheme with Spain to have her son recognized as the true heir. And now you have admitted her back here to, er, refresh yourself. How would one expect the queen consort to take that?"

Henry shrugged and nodded. "True. Women see the world differently than we men. I intended to send Henriette home after last night, but Marie's lady spotted her and told the queen all. And to make matters worse, she saw me with little Jacquette, too, and in a less-than-innocent circumstance."

"The sight of the young and flawless Mademoiselle Chaillou en dishabille might move any wife or mistress to an ugly passion."

The king wrung his hands and looked to the door again as if Cerberus himself might burst through it. "They are both hot on my heels. Advise me."

"There can be only one course. A tactical retreat."

"Live to fight another day, eh? I agree."

Without another word Béthune walked to the wall and pushed on a panel beside the marble mantle. It gave way on well-oiled hinges to reveal a narrow passage. Henri's sad face lit up with a relieved grin.

"This is why I keep you by my side, Maxi. You always have something in reserve."

He ducked through the opening, whistling a happy peasant tune. The instant Rosny closed the door Treville and d'Artagnan tried to flee the room lest any more affairs of state be revealed. But before they got to the door it burst open again and once more they were bowing low, this time for Marie de' Medici and her cloud of hangers-on.

"Where is he?" the king's wife demanded in a shrill Italian voice. Her head swiveled as she began peering behind tapestries and even beneath the furniture in search of her wayward husband. Unlike Henri, she came dressed to intimidate, leaving no doubt of her station. Barely thirty years old, two decades younger than the king, she had a pleasant round face with a pale complexion. Though the fashion was to apply cosmetics with a trowel, Marie eschewed that in favor of a more natural look, knowing that her lovely Florentine skin had no need of assistance. Her light brown hair was heaped atop her head in mounds of tiny curls, decorated with an amber jewel the size of a baby's fist. About her neck a spectacular lace piccadill surrounded the royal head like an immense and intricate snowflake, accented by a double strand of white pearls at her throat. More pearls depended from her shoulders and were gathered at her bosom with another amber gem, even larger than the one in her hair. The blood-red gown, covered in silver leaf brocade, overwhelmed the eye with its full sleeves and fuller skirt. A great round farthingale made the queen look like an enormous drum below her long, pointed waist. Even without the eight attendants and guards she had brought with her, no one would have mistaken her for a washerwoman or housewife.

Rosny rose from his perfunctory bow and faced her with the calm of a man confronted with a huffy child. "Could Your Majesty be more precise?"

"Don't you patronize me." Marie pointed her white feathered fan at him. "We followed him here. It wasn't difficult. I can track the man by the stink of garlic without even calling on my hounds." She sniffed. "It still lingers."

"If you mean the king, he only just departed. I believe he means to take a nap before lunch."

Marie rolled her eyes. "Oh, is that the new term for it now?"

Her entourage giggled at her witticism. Treville recognized most of them. Two were guards in deep blue doublets and tall boots, members of the queen's Gens D'arms, men of the sword at her command. The Forty-Five had a peppery rivalry with them that occasionally ended in light dueling. Both groups consisted of young men from the minor nobility (in Treville's case vanishingly minor), which meant short tempers and long blades. Though they were technically forbidden to fight each other, they all knew that their masters secretly wagered on the outcomes and that any chastisement was mostly for show. Three of the others, chattering in a corner, were attractive, low-ranking ladies-in-waiting to the queen, known for submitting to the king's desires just long enough to get him to reveal some tidbit of information that Marie could use in her underhanded political machinations. In the Louvre intelligence was worth more than gold.

At Marie's elbow stood a dark eyed Italian woman in a sleek green dress and tight ruff. First in influence of the queen's ladies, perhaps five years older than Marie, Leonora Dori was reputed to be a witch. It was said she commanded white magic and used her skills to defend her mistress from attacks by enemy sorcerers. She certainly possessed enough potency to remain immune to the king's advances, to the gratification of her husband. Leonora had made herself wealthy by selling her eldritch abilities in countering curses, but chiefly by taking bribes for granting access to her queen. Much of that wealth went to supporting the ambitions of her husband, Concino Concini, a creature of the Duc du Épernon who lingered in the hall, half hidden by shadows. A handsome brooding man of thirty years, he was clad in a doublet and cape made of scarlet fabrics far above his station. Together they showed the promise of rising far.

Yet she had a weakness. Treville had seen her collapse in a foaming fit more than once. Marie had implored her priests to end such spells by exorcism, but the task has proved to be beyond them. Now Marie had placed her under the care of her personal physician, the narrow and pinched fellow with a pointed beard who stood near the trio of gossiping maids. Elijah Montalto's talents as a doctor meant that the court could overlook his being an unrepentant Portuguese Jew. In an age where faith was destiny and having the wrong one might mean death, Montalto wore his unpopular religion like a naked rapier, daring anyone to object.

Lurking near the door, the final member of the group boasted a regal bearing without having the proper bloodline for it. But she could claim something more tangible in Henri's court than a pedigree: Henriette d'Entragues, Marquise de Verneuil, had spent more time in the king's bed than the queen had, having been his principal mistress for two years before the Houses of Bourbon and Medici had been joined in holy matrimony. She came by her skills honestly: her mother had been mistress to King Charles IX and her sister had just caught the king's eye. It was a sort of family business. Being the man that he was, Henri had felt no urge to set her aside after marrying; indeed, his urges were of an entirely different nature.

So attached was he to his Henriette that he had been unwise enough to have promised her marriage. When dynastic concerns, not to mention financial ones, had forced him to marry the well-bred and better-moneyed Marie, Henriette had made her displeasure known ever since. Striking without being truly beautiful, her powdered face looked as if she perpetually sucked on a fresh lemon. Only twenty-six, her strong nose and fierce eyes caught the attention, as did the blonde hair piled high and strung with gold chains and green gems. But just in case her natural attributes might fail, she also liked to dress as if she were in Marie's place in a more than unofficial capacity. Today she wore a tight rose bodice with white diagonal stripes trimmed in gold and a diaphanous ruff that stood out four inches from her slender throat. More lace adorned her cuffs and the handkerchief that she wrung between angry hands. Unlike Marie, her farthingale was sleek and made her seem the delicate and alluring young woman that she was.

Naturally, Marie hated her for that. But her distaste for Henriette was born of something even more primal. As a Medici married to a French king, she understood mistresses were a royal man's prerogative. Resenting such behavior would only make her miserable and change nothing. It had always been thus. Marie had been able to console herself with the royal heir she had borne to Henri four years before. Yet the triumph of little Louis had been short-lived. Only five weeks later Henriette had been delivered of a son of the king's. The father had been so impolitic as to observe that the bastard was a prettier baby than the legitimate future king of France and declared him legitimate, too. Since then he had been plagued by a shrewish wife and an intemperate mistress.

Treville's daydreaming ended as the former's voice became as brittle as glass. She was upbraiding Béthune as if her were one of her teenaged servants. It became so unsettlingly vituperative that Treville and d'Artagnan exchanged glances and gazed longingly at the exit, only to see it blocked by those Marie had brought with her. None of them seemed the least bit upset by the profane rages of their mistress. Henriette simply crossed her arms, sighed, and waited for the scene to play itself out so that she could perform her own part.

When the queen consort finally paused to take a breath, so red in the face that it seemed likely that steam would rise from it, Rosny leaned in close to her. No one could hear them. As the king's most trusted minister spoke at length to the queen, her complexion drained from claret to chalk and Treville's eyes widened into dinner plates. When the little private speech ended, Marie de' Medici stood up, summoned all the dignity that a woman of her station could command, snapped open her fan with a violent sword-striking motion, and swept from the room, taking her hangers-on behind her like a ship of the line being followed by its corvettes, leaving only Henriette.

Silence reigned, thick as congealed blood.

She glided across the Turkish carpet with slow grace, almost as if on wheels. Fierce dark flame smoldered in her blue eyes. Advancing upon Béthune, she looked more terrifying in her silence than Marie had been with all her shrieking and histrionics. Shoulders back, hands clenched in fists, she stopped before him and fairly trembled with emotion. He braced himself for another feminine outburst. And when it came, it was truly dreadful.

Henriette cried…buckets.

It seemed as if she had intended otherwise. Her face set itself for a glorious tantrum, but then her pretty lower lip trembled, her eyes quivered, and veritable cascades of salty tears gushed down her fair cheeks, cutting channels in her face powder. Soon the room's twenty-foot-tall ceilings echoed with her hoarse sobs. Bits of complaint were gasped in between them: "Mother of his son…treated like a servant…promised to marry me…" Maximilien Béthune, Marquis du Rosny, head of His Majesty's government and bold warrior on his behalf, was utterly nonplussed. Thrice his bearded mouth opened, then closed in confusion as he realized that he had no idea what to say to this demonstration. Counter-attacking the queen's viciousness had been simple in comparison.

An unlikely ally saved him. D'Artagnan appeared at the young lady's side like some handsome angel dispatched from heaven. Whispering something inaudible to her, she turned to bury her noble nose in his shoulder. The young gallant embraced her with a tenderness that surprised Treville. Like some antique portrait of courtly love personified, they remained there in front of the desk for a long minute, bathed in golden sunlight from the great window.

Finally the king's mistress sniffed and pulled away slightly. "Many thanks, monsieur. I confess that I do not know your name."

"Bertrand d'Artagnan," he told her with a chaste kiss on the fingers.

"The words sound like a fight of doves. I shall not forget them."

Alarm churned up in Treville at seeing the looks they exchanged. Little good could come of that with the king's mistress, particularly one already punished for plotting against him. *No! Forget them! Forget him! And you, young idiot. Find yourself a bit of skirt less likely to get you drawn and quartered.*

The same thought seemed to occur to Rosny. He dashed around to the front of his desk and thrust himself between them before the ember could become a conflagration. With practiced efficiency he took Henriette's arm and escorted her to the open door before she knew what had happened. Stopping there, he said some low supportive words to her – lies about her importance to the king, no doubt – and sent her on her way. He seemed not to notice the figure hidden behind a statue of King Charles VII.

Concini. And what he had observed put a gloating smile on his lips.

5

PARIS: TREVILLE'S LODGING

"THE LADY OF THE HOUSE SEEMS TO BE AFRAID OF MY CANNIBAL TENDENCIES."

"What did old Maxi say to the queen, do you think?" asked d'Artagnan when they had finally managed to escape the plotting mess in the Louvre. They strolled through the noisy, filthy streets toward Treville's rooms, d'Artagnan ogling every wench and staring down every bravo they passed. Armored soldiers with lances, chaste nuns in black habits, nobles on sleek horses, and almost-feral children passed them, creating racket and dust that overwhelmed the senses.

"I don't have to think. I know," Treville said, stopping at a vegetable cart so he could take a sly glance behind them. After the unfortunate events in Ostend it was his practice now, more than before, to see if he was being followed.

"Yes? Enlighten me, then, great magician."

"No magic required. My granny was deaf and dumb."

"Unfortunate, but hardly relevant."

"Au contraire. I learned a valuable skill from her."

D'Artagnan proved his quick wit once again. "You dog! You read his lips!"

"I did indeed."

"And what did our great and good master tell Madame de' Medici that made her flee as if pursued by Lucifer himself?"

Satisfied that they were not being pursued, at least not by amateurs, Treville resumed his walk home. D'Artagnan caught up with him and repeated his request. Treville waited until they were in a pocket of relative emptiness amidst the market crowd. No sense risking any eavesdroppers.

"You had best consider your position here, my lady." Treville had a well-honed knack for languages and accents and he imitated Béthune with uncanny accuracy. "I have heard the king tell you that you are here as a brood mare and nothing more. Let me again remind you of that. Keep your Italian nose out of our French politics, produce and rear the heirs, and all will be well. Continue to scheme and to make yourself a nuisance, and you will have much more to worry about than your empty bed."

D'Artagnan winced in feigned discomfort. "Ooh! She'll need an apothecary's salve after that tongue-lashing."

"I gather that she's used to giving those, not receiving them."

"Not to defend her, but having to rear the royal bastards alongside your own kids must be a hard cross to shoulder."

"All part of the job. She should've known such would be the case, coming from that family of hers."

"True enough. The Medici are hardly monks, though they've bought the papacy three times."

"And look about to do it again, with Clement passing only three weeks ago, generously aided by our king's own contribution, just to twist Spain's nose. "

They arrived at last at Treville's lodging, a three-story affair owned by a jolly lady from Picardy who rented apartments to men who worked at court. As one of the Forty-Five, Treville could have claimed a residence in the Louvre, as many did, to be near the king. But he had seen how easy it was for some of his comrades to become embroiled in political messes there, to the cost of their positions and even their heads. So he preferred to pay for a pair of rooms on the top floor here. It also made it more difficult for enemies to get at him, as there was only one narrow stair and the owner kept a keen eye on it.

After pausing to submit to the landlady's attentions – she liked to fuss over him like a doting mother – and assuring her that the pagan red man was not likely to steal her soul, Treville led the way up to his door. There he knocked in a complicated pattern, so that Chipay would know to open it. He admitted them immediately, as if he had watched them approach from the window.

"Good morning, Fantôme," Treville said as he entered and removed his sword. "All well? No trouble?"

"Nothing worrisome," the doctor replied, locking the door behind them, "though the lady of the house seems to be afraid of my cannibal tendencies."

"That would be a better menu than much of what she serves us. Is my poultice ready?"

Treville lay face-down on his bed and let Chipay treat his wound with gentle and practiced hands. In surprisingly little time most of the ache had ebbed. In fact, so comfortable did he become that he fell into a doze. While continuing to minister to his patient, Chipay asked d'Artagnan how their interview at the palace had gone. The youngster helped himself to his friend's wine and told him of all that had happened, being sure to make it as entertaining as his Gascon character could manage. As he did so he practiced several clever but underhanded shuffling tricks with a deck of cards. By the end of the tale the normally bland-faced Chipay had actually cracked a smile.

"That is how our old men would tell tales, back in the village. We younglings would gather round to hear a clever story and before we knew it we had been taught something important."

"We Gascons are fond of talking, drinking, and fighting. I can't deny it."

"Is not your king also from this Gascony?"

D'Artagnan thumped the bottle down onto the table. "By St. Peter's beard, so he is! I'd forgotten that! And I forgot to include women on my list. A grave fault, that." He guzzled more wine and wiped his mouth on a sleeve. "And the woman I met today. Oh, Fantôme…"

He depicted Henriette d'Entragues as a pious Frenchman might paint a visitation from the Holy Virgin, only lingering upon her earthier virtues a bit longer than would ordinarily be expected. A sacred image was created that might have required a chorus of a thousand angels to do it justice. Chipay listened to it with patience, then frowned.

"My people say that it is better to love that which you can hold instead of that which you must describe."

"Agreed, but describing is all that I can have. Holding her would be difficult after the king orders my arms and legs torn off by wild horses."

"Perhaps a man of your years and station should set his sights a bit lower at first?"

"You mean I should settle for a mere countess?" laughed d'Artagnan.

He settled for embracing the bottle of Burgundy. Soon he was snoring in harmony with Treville as Chipay cleaned and repacked his medical tools. An hour later both young men awoke as if by prior arrangement. They were delighted to find that their friend from the New World had prepared them a proper Old World lunch.

"You needn't serve us, you know," Treville said as he munched on beef, cheese, and bread. "I can hire a fellow to do that. Been meaning to do it."

"As you wish," Fantôme shrugged. "I do not mind. One should keep busy and perform the tasks that need to be done. Honest work should not be deemed to be beneath a man."

"Agreed. But you are a healer and should spend your valuable time at that. You know, our master the Marquis du Rosny asked to meet you. Perhaps he could find a position worthy of your talents."

"Just so long as I do not become a curiosity. That has been my experience in great palaces before."

Treville ceased chewing and looked at him with interest. "Really?"

The physician nodded. "I was briefly at Phillip III's court in Valladolid. Treated like a pet, trotted out like a performing monkey. 'Look at the charming aboriginal. He learned our language. Adorable, no? But not truly human, for all that.' They did not trust me to treat any of them as patients, save for a few servants. Afraid they might catch a disease from me, perhaps. Their great painter used me as a model for Saint Francis once. El Greco, he was called. A visitor from afar, like me. That was less offensive. The subject of the picture was a man I could respect.

"And I spent some days with a man who was writing an awfully long story about a poor old fellow who loses his wits and thinks that he is a noble warrior from long ago. He did trust my healing talents. The poor man had been grievously wounded in a grand sea battle many years before. His left arm was useless and gave him much pain. I helped him with it. In return he told me beautiful stories, invented on the spot. Cervantes would have had much honor for that in my village back home."

"You said palaces," d'Artagnan observed, "as if you have been in more than one."

"For a time I was in the household of the Dutch Stadtholder, Maurice. They took my medical aptitude seriously, being a small nation at war. I treated many wounded men. Some I saved. But, again, too often I was paraded for visitors like an exhibit. Why are Europeans unable to see a man when they look at me or my brothers? At home they would often hunt us as if we were deer. And when we naturally fought back they called us savages."

Treville wiped his fingers on a napkin and moved to stand before Chipay. For a long moment he looked into the dark calm face. "I can't speak for all those other fools, but I see a man. An equal. Perhaps a superior, from what I've observed so far. A man who makes the world a better place just by being in it."

Chipay shook his head. "Your adoration may be misplaced. The scales of my past misdeeds are far from being balanced in that regard." Placing his hand on Treville's shoulder, he said, "But you do me honor and I accept it as it is intended. Would you do me more?"

"Of course."

The doctor opened his bag and plucked out a small leather pouch. By the wear on it and the reverential way he held it, the thing was a personal talisman of some kind that he had made sure to keep with him in all his many travels. "I made this during my vision quest. In it are objects made sacred and meaningful by my ordeal. Bits of stone, bark, feather, Mother Earth, tears, blood, hair, sweat. It contains my honor and trust, my power and submission."

Chipay grasped Treville's hand, pouch between their palms. "In this way we become brothers, though not from the same womb. A brother by choice is an even greater bond than that of nature. When we make such a commitment, it is not done lightly, and to break it is the most terrible calamity."

Treville squeezed tight. "Let it be so then. D'Artagnan?"

With a boyish grin the younger soldier leaped from his chair. "Hell, yes! But let's do this properly." He pulled his rapier from its scabbard, hanging on the back of his chair, and wrapped his hand around the forte of the engraved blade.

"What does it say there?" Treville asked.

"Who knows? It's in Latin. I won this beauty in a dice game. You're the one with the posh schooling, you tell me."

"Unus pro omnibus, omnes pro uno," Chipay read aloud to the amazement of his companions. "All for one, and one for all."

"I like that!" D'Artagnan set the sword across the small table and lay his left hand upon it.

Chipay and Treville did likewise. Then they joined right hands above the rapier, which rested against a wine bottle, the money, and the deck of cards, like a parody of some arcane secret society's ritual.

"All for one, and one for all," the trio chanted together.

"Well, there it is," d'Artagnan announced with finality. "You're all stuck with me now." He poured wine into glasses for his friends and held the bottle up in a toast. "But just to make sure, let's seal the bargain the proper French way."

Glasses clinked together and went to three mouths. While the other two drained theirs, Chipay merely touched the rim to his lips and set it down.

"If you will pardon me, friends. It is not my custom. Too many of my people back home were victims of this."

D'Artagnan shrugged. "As you wish. I won't force a brother to do anything against his will. And I admit that many of us should probably say no to the grape more often." He snatched up the full glass and winked. "But not today."

·

6

PARIS: CIMETIÈRE DES INNOCENTS

THIS ISN'T A DUEL, IT'S AN ASSASSINATION.

Treville and d'Artagnan spent the rest of the afternoon examining the documents that Béthune had given them. They hoped to come up with a plan of action so that they could make sensible preparations in the coming days before departing for the United Provinces. As they did so they included Chipay, both because he was now powerfully allied with them and because he had lived there recently and knew much that they did not. It became clear that they would have to depend upon him as a guide not only for traveling the safest routes, but also for negotiating the complexities of that foreign society and its ever-shifting politics.

"It looks like we can dispense with Ostend," Treville said as he perused the secret papers from the Louvre. "As much as I'd like to get back in there and throttle whoever ordered my stabbing, none of these contacts seem to be there. Mostly Amsterdam and The Hague."

"Ah, I have some lovely contacts of my own in Amsterdam," sighed d'Artagnan fondly, booted feet resting on the table.

"You'll get some lovely pox that way," Treville told him. "Fantôme, do you have a cure for that?"

"I do," said the physician, leaning back in his chair, arms crossed, "but he would not like it much. It requires mercury and a narrow steel-bristled brush."

Wincing, the young fellow made a horrified hissing noise and covered his lap with both hands. "So those tales of fearsome Indian tortures are true!"

"So if I were you," Treville said, "I would rely on my other rapier while you're there." He tapped the paper before him. "The Dutchman who faced his own torments at Rosny's hands said that his principal contact in Holland, whom he solely communicated with in writing, was a spy he only knew as Krijger."

"Means warrior," Chipay said.

"Probably an alias then," mused d'Artagnan. "Sounds made-up. Not likely a spy would use real name anyhow. Where would we find him?"

Treville squinted at the paper. "Has a cover identity. Operates as a cheese monger on the King's Canal. He frowned. "The Dutch don't have a king."

Chipay helped him. "Interestingly, it is named after your King Henri, in honor of his aid to the Dutch against Spain."

"You don't say? Well, it seems we'll be paying this warrior cheese monger a visit."

"I like cheese," announced d'Artagnan, practicing with his cards again. "Goes well with wine."

"According to you, hemlock would go well with wine."

"Well, wouldn't it? If you were forced to drink poison, would you want to swill it straight?"

"You go ahead. You're most likely fated to hang anyway. Or to be run through by a jealous husband. Remember?" Treville pointed to the document. "The unlucky Dutchman kindly gave us the sign and counter-sign. Let us hope that they didn't change them when he got himself caught."

Chipay asked, "What precisely is this person supposed to tell us?"

"It says here that he's a double-agent, pretending to work for the shadowy group that Rosny told us of. The people planning some sort of big showy attack to shake up the European system. How they could create more chaos than we already have now is a mystery. Somehow they hope to profit from that. He actually is in the pay of Maurice of Nassau, the general and *Stadtholder*, who is the most powerful man in Holland right now."

"I gather that we want to use Krijger to help us join them, so we can pick their brains from the inside?"

"That would be the best plan."

"And the most dangerous," Chipay noted.

"Welcome to the exciting world of espionage, my brother."

The doctor chuckled. "Not as risky as treating Spanish battle casualties when their officer is threatening to cut your throat you if you fail."

They continued planning their expedition, determining the best false identities, equipment needs, and contingency plans in case of discovery or some other unforeseen event. Something always went wrong, Treville knew. And as he was now partnered with the volatile and inexperienced d'Artagnan, as well as the capable but largely unknown Fantôme, he fully expected problems. Best to assume that they would happen and have a plan to recover from them, or at least to limit the damage.

As it grew dark outside d'Artagnan announced with a wink that he had an appointment and might be out all night. While the lad brushed his gray doublet and tall boots and buckled on his sword belt, Treville warned him to take care. They were known to be officers of the king, even if d'Artagnan was not officially sanctioned yet. That made him a potential target for embarrassment or worse.

"Don't do anything foolish," Treville advised. "You have a mission for the state to undertake. Much rests on that."

"Yes, granny," sighed d'Artagnan, plumping up the feathers in his hat. "I understand. Don't talk to any wolves in the forest."

With that he stomped down the stairs and vanished into the Parisian night, leaving Treville feeling unexpectedly old and paternal. But as there was nothing to be done, he pored over the documents with Chipay for a while longer and then took to his bed.

The old dream returned, reminding him of his shattered family: mother murdered, infant sister abducted, the laughing man in a long-beaked carnival mask leaving a seven-year-old boy for dead in a burning house. That crazed hyena laugh. *I shall never purge it from my soul.* Treville's sleep brought little rest, as usual.

Pink dawn was just beginning to creep into the window when a vigorous knocking brought Treville upright with a gasp. Still groggy, trembling from the dream that refused to die, he did not know where he was or even what day it might be. Apparently unaffected by the sudden waking, Chipay opened the door. Treville noticed that his friend held a cudgel behind him in case this was an unfriendly visitation. His plump landlady burst in, panting with the exertion of climbing the steps from her ground floor rooms. She wore an old dressing gown and a shawl, her hair hidden in a lace nightcap.

Madame Tatillon fidgeted with the hem of her woolen shawl and said breathlessly, "Oh, Monsieur Treville! A dreadful thing! The young gentleman…"

She stood aside to allow two men, strangers, to enter. The first one, apparently the leader, was past forty and from his rich but not gaudy attire looked to be a great man's retainer. Just visible beneath his cloak was an exceptionally fine sword hilt. Behind him came a harder fellow with the aspect of an army veteran fallen on tough times. Treville spied at least two daggers and a pistol on him, in addition to his rapier.

Fully awake and alarmed now, Treville slid from the bed onto his bare feet, slyly placing himself near his own sword. "What has happened? Is it d'Artagnan?"

Of course it is. The juvenile idiot has got himself arrested…or worse. They probably want me to identify the body.

"A thousand apologies for the rude intrusion," said the first man, removing his hat and running long fingers through sleek graying black hair. "My name is Doucereux. This other gentleman is Tranche. I greatly wish that we could meet under better circumstances. Your friend begged us to come and fetch you."

"Why? Is he arrested? Wounded?" Treville began pulling on his hose.

"Neither…yet. There has been an unfortunate incident at the Maison Amusée."

Treville recognized it as a notorious gambling den and brothel, precisely the place he had hoped that d'Artagnan would avoid. Things were becoming all too clear.

"Let me guess. Your patron took umbrage at losing and wants a fight."

"To be precise, my patron took umbrage at losing to a cheater and wants to fight."

D'Artagnan's assiduous training with his deck of cards all evening leaped to mind, forcing a sigh from Treville. *If the boy were any stupider I could replace him with my horse.* He pulled on his linen shirt and reached for his canioned Venetian breeches. "Naturally, you have abundant witnesses and this can all be confirmed?"

"Alas, monsieur, it is an unfortunate certainty." To Treville's mind the fellow's voice held a soupçon too much pleasure. And his brutish friend was all but smirking.

"You are both your master's seconds in this affair?"

"We have that disagreeable duty."

"Then, of course, my friend and I shall attend on Monsieur d'Artagnan. Where is he?"

"We await your pleasure at the Cimetière des Innocents."

That nearly forced a smile from Treville. The medieval graveyard and its environs would be mostly deserted such an early hour. "Your master has a droll sense of humor." As he threw on a serviceable old brown doublet and began lacing its points onto the breeches, he glanced at Chipay. "It's all right. Get dressed and meet me downstairs. Bring your bag." To the others he explained, "My friend is a physician."

Doucereux looked at Chipay as if he were vermin, but quickly masked it. "Excellent," he said, "I confess that we did not think to engage one."

Madame Tatillon escorted the visitors back down while Treville donned his tall boots, sword belt, and short cape. He took his hat from its peg, the same headgear he had worn in Ostend. Just like then, he stuffed the steel skullcap into it.

"That will be necessary?" asked Chipay, nearly dressed already. The man was almost annoyingly efficient.

"If it comes to a duel, the seconds are all too often drawn into it. And something stinks about this one, so we'd best be ready for anything." He handed a loaded pistol to his friend. "Stow that in your bag. I know you've sworn off killing, but the choice may not be given to you. Besides, you can always toss it to me if it's against your principles."

Chipay gave the matter brief thought, then thrust the weapon in with his healing tools. The cudgel he slid inside his doublet. As they reached the door he also took an ash walking stick that leaned against the jamb. Treville tucked a dagger into the back of his belt and led the way to the street. Once they had joined the men of the opposing party, the quartet proceeded in silence the half mile to the chosen dueling ground, meeting very few people in the misty dawn.

The Holy Innocents Cemetery was ancient, having been in place for around seven hundred years. It was attached to the church of the same name, lying to the east of that building. Surrounded by a high wall, it had a tired appearance and a sickly smell. It had often been used for mass graves of plague victims, as well as suicides washed up from the Seine and the pitiful victims of simply living in the Court of Miracles nearby. Along the southern end ran a galleried charnel house, where the clean bones of those once interred in the earth were stacked, to make room for the newly deceased. Occasionally anatomists would study those bones to learn better medical techniques. Inside was an enormous mural of the Danse Macabre, just in case visitors felt too cheery about touring a meadow for the dead. Though mostly open space, the cemetery did have a handful of mausoleums, including a multi-story tower.

Treville squinted into the rising sun as they passed through the narrow gate beside the church. Shadows were long and eerie, resembling giant ghostly claws reaching for him. And he fancied that he even smelled brimstone as he passed beneath the buttressed church roof. He mastered any emotions that might interfere with self-defense, choosing to note how best to use the sun's beams should it become necessary. Inside the graveyard there was little light at man height yet, as the surrounding buildings still blocked much of it. Ground mist lingered, bloodied by the morning light so that the landscape became something from a horror tale.

Under the charnel house gallery stood d'Artagnan, looking sleepy from being up all night but not otherwise damaged. He seemed remarkably cheerful for a young man about to fight a duel. In fact, he laughed and performed card tricks. Treville hoped that his mood would be infectious and the others with him could be talked out of conflict with sweet words.

When he arrived, however, Treville saw from their grim faces that any attempt at reconciliation was likely doomed. Four men surrounded his friend, three of them as stern of manner as the humorless Tranche. None of d'Artagnan's pleasantries made their faces unbend. In their eyes Treville saw the same look that he had seen countless times on battlefields, in men about to charge musket and pike. But they were only hired blades. It was the sight of their master that convinced him that there would be red work this morning.

The offended courtier was Maximilien II de Béthune. Rosny's ne'er-do-well son.

Bloody hell! This can't be a coincidence.

At that moment he recalled the brimstone odor near the church. It had not been any fiend from the pit, but a sharpshooter on the roof, crouching behind a buttress while keeping the match of the harquebus alight. Reflexively he cast his eyes about, trying not to be obvious. Was that the glint of a gun barrel atop the tower? And he thought he spied a prone form on the eastern wall. A third musket man, counting on the low sun's glare to make him hard to spot.

Another trap. Rosny will have my head.

Treville controlled his expression, not giving anything away. So gifted was he at it that he generally won on the few occasions when he chose to play at cards. It was one of the skills that made him such a good actor, such a good spy. Pasting a cheerful grin onto his face, he bowed to the assemblage, taking care to give it an extra flourish for Béthune. The lad was even younger than d'Artagnan, and nearly as handsome. Hatless, he let his curling dark hair run wild in a display of aristocratic nonchalance. Beneath the high pale forehead were cold blue eyes, an arrogant nose, and small, almost feminine lips. His beard was thin, wispy, that of a boy barely able to produce one. He wore an absurdly lavish doublet, more suitable for a formal court reception than for drinking, whoring, and fighting. Of white satin with gold brocade touches, it was pinked with small diagonal slashes lined in scarlet. A plush velvet blue sash with embroidered roses ran across his torso. To his throat clung a starched lace collar that the queen herself might have envied. His long cloak's gold embroidery made the garment hang heavy as lead. Almost more jewelry than weapon, his spectacular rapier looked to be of German design. Its hilt was of graceful, blackened steel sweeps and rings, inlaid with flourishes of bright silver. *Without a doubt it cost more than I am paid in a year.*

To Treville it all but shouted one thing: I envy my father, I can never live up to his example, so I will waste his money and reputation.

"Good morning, my lord," he purred, as if he respected the fledgling. "Captain Jean-Armand de Treville, of the King's Household. This is Monsieur Chipay, physician to the Spanish court and Dutch Republic. I trust that he will be satisfactory to you?"

"Of course," said the young man, his voice polished, educated, but high and thin. "Has Doucereux informed you of the situation?"

"To a degree. He claims d'Artagnan was caught cheating at cards, thereby committing fraud against your noble self."

"Exactly. Nabbed in the very act. No doubt about it." Béthune eyed his six cohorts. "Yes?"

All of them hastened to affirm the crime, though to Treville it looked just a bit too rehearsed. "I see. Did my friend confess? Offer restitution?"

"Neither. The whelp dares to proclaim his innocence."

The humor of this near infant calling anyone a whelp nearly made Treville snicker, but he mastered the laughter and merely nodded. "Let me speak with him. Hopefully, a peaceable arrangement can be made."

With Chipay, he moved over to d'Artagnan, who leaned against a pillar in a casual manner that almost served as an affront to the others. To annoy them further, the deck of cards danced in his clever fingers, performing fascinating maneuvers that only made him look all the more guilty. Impossible one-handed shuffles, palming of cards, making a particular card vanish and reappear in the other hand…it all gave him the aspect of a man who could make his opponent foolish while stealing his money.

"You're hardly helping your case," Treville told him.

"What, this?" The youngster fanned the cards, then collapsed them into thin air. "I didn't cheat the little twit. Didn't have to. He doesn't know how to bet or how to bluff. Nose twitches when he has a good hand. This is just to rub that noble snout in it."

"So you're completely above-board here?"

"I am…this time. My horse could beat him." He plucked the vanished deck from Treville's hat and lowered his voice. "The whole affair stinks worse than this charnel house. They marked me the minute I walked in, like they'd been waiting for the chance. Something's not right. Béthune manufactured this whole fight."

"Actually, I believe you." Treville told his friends about the marksmen. He was unsurprised to note that Fantôme had also spotted them. "You were probably followed the whole way. Somebody at the Louvre has decided to get rid of us. They went to all this trouble to make it look like a legitimate disagreement. Want to keep their dainty hands clean."

"The same spy who set those Dutchmen on you."

"Most likely."

Chipay advised them, "Gentlemen, they will not be persuaded out of the engagement. They actively pursued it. We must devise a course of action."

"I thought about it the whole trip here," Treville said. "Three-to-one is long odds, but here is our best chance."

He told them his plan while making the conversation appear to the others as a heated argument with d'Artagnan, who caught onto the ruse immediately and played his part. The scheme would require delicate timing and as much choreography as a court masque. And they would have to manage it in poor light and on treacherous ground. But there was nothing for it but to roll their dice and hope for the best. When he finished speaking he waited for their response.

D'Artagnan grinned and held out a hand. "All for one…"

Laying his own atop it, Chipay nodded. Treville did the same and all three said, "…and one for all."

"My friends," Treville told the waiting aristocrat and his dangerous associates, "it appears that Monsieur d'Artagnan remains unswayed. He maintains his purity in this matter and is resolved to make good his claim on the field of honor."

Béthune almost beamed with relief. Clearly he was eager to fight. He shrugged off his cloak into Doucereux's waiting hands and stepped out from under the gallery onto a flat patch of ground. It did not escape Treville's notice that the move exposed d'Artagnan, and him, to the fire of all three musket men. But he had anticipated that in his plan. Also not surprising was how Béthune's six friends casually moved to not be in the line of fire. More disturbing was how they lay their hands upon their sword hilts in a manner that, while not overtly threatening, made a quick draw easy. Chipay stood amongst them, surgical bag in hand, leaning on his cane in feigned lameness, pretending to be oblivious to them. Treville wondered why the bag was already open.

Doucereux let his master's cloak slide into his off hand, all too ready for use as France's most expensive parrying device if he joined the melee. Behind and beside him, Tranche narrowed his eyes and set his jaw. The other four flexed their fingers. Treville saw it all and sighed.

D'Artagnan's right. They mean to pile in. That was always their intention. This isn't a duel, it's an assassination.

As Doucereux reminded the combatants of the dueling code and the consequences for transgressing it, Treville loosened the knot of his short cape while reaching beneath it to pull his rapier an inch out of its scabbard. D'Artagnan may have been clever with the cards but Treville had a few little tricks of his own, courtesy of Rosny's inventive quartermaster. From the look of the situation he might need them all.

The two duelists drew swords and saluted one another perfunctorily. Treville doubted that Bethune's parasites would permit him more than a single pass for form's sake. Their duty was to preserve his skin, not let some teenaged yokel damage it. Then again, Treville had not yet seen d'Artagnan handle a blade. His inexperienced friend might have no more sword skill than he had common sense.

At Doucereux's curt "Allez!" the two advanced with caution, feeling one another out. Bethune adopted a textbook guard, dagger well forward for defense, rapier low and covering his center line, obviously trained by the best fencing masters his father's money could buy. Whether he had the will and courage to do more than that with real killing points remained to be seen. For his part, d'Artagnan lumbered up to him with only the barest semblance of any guard at all, as if he had just been informed which end of a sword to hold. His dagger hung at his side, practically useless, and the rapier point was level with his knees. Béthune's lip curled with pleasure at the sight.

Treville's heart sank. His scheme depended on d'Artagnan holding his own, not being skewered on the first pass. He looked at the rising sun, now cresting the eastern wall. Perhaps he and Chipay could make a run for it while the others were congratulating the young lord on his easy victory.

The overdressed challenger feinted a rapier thrust at his foe's handsome face, and when that earned the expected flinch he launched a picture-worthy thrust at the Gascon's heart. Straight and true went the point toward the inevitable death blow.

But it struck only air.

Still moving with country clumsiness, d'Artagnan managed to slip his torso sideways. Bethune's killing stroke missed his chest by the width of a blade of grass. Gasping with relief, Treville silently screamed at his friend to get out of range and then try an attack of his own. The psychic plea went unanswered. Instead, the awkward boy stumbled forward and to his right, weapons still out of proper position. Béthune could resume his assault with little effort, which was precisely what he did, flicking the main gauche out at his prey's throat.

And yet again he just missed.

This time d'Artagnan almost seemed to wrap his upper body around the dagger blade, taunting it with his vulnerable neck but making it slide away as if he had been greased. Still, it had been wrenchingly close and Treville wondered what d'Artagnan thought he was doing, staying in range like that with his defenses down. That was a wonderful way to end up dead.

Then the glorious light of awareness struck him, brighter than the morning sun. Far from being a dolt, d'Artagnan had slyly placed himself where the muskets were least likely to be able to shoot him. His rightward dance and proximity to his opponent had blocked two of their lines of fire with the bodies of the aristocrat's men. Only the man on the eastern wall had a clear shot now. And Treville had a bit of trickery literally up his sleeve for him.

Béthune's lackeys realized that they now obstructed the view of their man atop the church and began to move. Chipay went with them, still playing the role of merciful physician. Opposite them, Treville sidled left toward the charnel house gallery and its protective stone without seeming too deliberate about it. D'Artagnan may have protected himself, but his two pledged brothers were still easy targets.

That was precisely what d'Artagnan had turned out not to be. Béthune had grown visibly enraged at being unable to hit the lout before him. After the fifth missed opportunity he began sending signals with his eyes to Doucereux for aid. This was no longer idle sport. Plus, the sun's rise was exposing them all to detection. Soon someone in the church would grow alarmed and call for the officers of the Maréchausée. Béthune's father would take a very dim view of his only son being taken for public dueling.

His five accomplices took the hint and gave up all pretense of innocence. Tranche's blade appeared in his hand so quickly that witchcraft might have been blamed. More astonishing, he touched it with his empty hand and created a second sword. Treville's eyebrows shot up. Cased rapiers! A pair of blades in a single scabbard. Tricky. This Tranche would bear watching. The quartet beside Chipay boldly tugged on their own swords, eager to join the fray and put down this upstart who so embarrassed their master. But try as they might, they could not persuade their weapons to leave the scabbards. Frowning and cursing, they looked down to see what the trouble was.

All their sweeping hilts had been surreptitiously tied to the belts with catgut sutures.

The doctor who had so cleverly performed that surgery while they had been distracted nodded to them as if meeting them in church. Red-faced in shame and ire, the two nearest Fantôme yanked their daggers free and lunged at him. They had no more luck than Béthune was having. Their slashes only wounded the dawn mist, as if Chipay's nickname were a factual description. One collapsed to the dirt with a gasping sigh as the heavy leather bag smashed his temple. Letting it drop beside him, Chipay met the second onrushing fellow with hand and cane, blocking the dagger arm with a palm while delivering a devastating ashen smack to his ear. An outstretched leg tripped the falling villain, directing him face-first to the ground. When he insisted on trying to rise again, a boot heel to the neck convinced him to stay down. A heartbeat later a third man mustered the nerve to try his luck, rushing Chipay with dagger held high for a downward jab. But he only managed three steps. Fantôme snapped his arm out as if flinging a magic spell, stunning the assailant with the flung cudgel hidden up the doctor's sleeve. The fourth held back, his resolve evaporated by Fantôme's skill, seeming to have rethought his participation in this affair. A moment later he was gone.

That, however, freed the matchlock men from the worry of hitting their own allies. Treville had been watching for that, though, and rushed from cover to jerk him aside. Dust splashed up where the physician had been standing. The marksman in the tower had been uncomfortably accurate. *Must have a rifled barrel. But that will slow his reloading. Now to worry about the other two.*

Béthune abandoned his fruitless attempts to engage the slippery d'Artagnan and dashed toward the church, crying out, "Kill them already!" Smoke puffed from the Holy Innocents' roof, missing d'Artagnan as he had flung himself onto his face when his foe had shouted. Chipay dashed for the cover of the charnel house. He waved for Treville to follow, but that gentleman was standing fast, holding his hand up as if saying hello to the gunman lying on the wall. No doubt that fellow was sighting on one of them and was about to squeeze the lever that would drop the match onto the powder. D'Artagnan and Treville were both trapped in the open. Behind them Bethune and Doucereux laughed in triumph.

Only no shot came. For the musket man caught the light of the sun in his eyes as it reflected from the tiny looking glass in Treville's glove.

The sharpshooter jerked back as the blinding rays struck him. To

Treville's immense joy that proved just enough to overbalance him backward on the narrow ledge and the man fell over the wall, landing on the far side.

"You're a sorcerer, you are!" crowed d'Artagnan as he scampered to his feet and sprinted for the charnel house. He made erratic changes of direction as he went to spoil the aim of anyone else who had a mind to send a lead ball his way. It proved to be a wise decision, for two bullets whistled past him from the tower in the six seconds it took to reach the gallery and get behind a pillar. Seeing that, Treville also made haste and dove behind another column.

"What the devil?" complained d'Artagnan. "Did he haul half a dozen loaded guns up there?"

"I doubt it," Treville answered, drawing his sword and pulling the cord of his cape. The latter slid into his free hand. He looked longingly at Chipay's bag and the pistol it contained, but the thing lay out in the open. "Even with a loader handing him another musket he could never have got off two aimed shots that fast. And there's only room up there for a single man anyway."

"Well, whatever he has, it spits out musket balls like water from a fountain. We'll have to find a way around him."

They had a more pressing concern, however. The men Chipay had put down were getting to their feet, groggy but recovering. Using daggers to free the tied swords, they advanced upon the gallery, roaring profane oaths and declaring that hell would soon receive 'that pagan bastard' and his friends. Tranche and his two blades led them, too calm and relaxed for Treville's liking. His manner spoke of long brutal campaigns and much nasty bladework in festering alleys. Bringing up the rear, Doucereux had been shoved into the fray by Bethune, who was already donning his rich cloak and preparing to vanish. No doubt he had already concocted a plausible story for his father and any guards who might appear.

"Watch that one!" advised Treville, pointing his sword at Tranche. "He looks damned capable."

Mindful of leaving themselves open to musket fire from the tower, the man on the roof not having a good angle into the charnel house unless he changed position, the king's men retreated farther into the recesses of the gallery and let the assassins come to them. Fantôme had a grimmer time now than he had before, as his foe not only had four feet of steel against the wooden cane but was cautious after his earlier drubbing. It occurred to Treville that if his friend's scruples had permitted mortal arguments then they would have three less opponents. But he had done enough killing of his own to have already lost the taste of it. *Hard to blame the fellow for mercy, I suppose. I expect that d'Artagnan won't be offered the choice against Tranche and his partner.*

His silent reflection had to wait in a quiet corner of his mind, for one of Chipay's other victims rushed in with Doucereux. Fighting a determined man with a rapier was difficult enough. Taking on two was dangerous insanity unless the option to flee was unavailable. Luckily Treville had been forced into that situation with disturbing enough regularity that he did not panic. The secret was to maneuver oneself to take them on singly, if possible, using the first to block the second. Blood-fury made his wound's pain vanish. He swept Doucereux's face with the cape to drive him back, while thwarting right and thrusting his sword point at the other's belly. Though it was parried with a dagger, it stopped the charge. Doucereux's retreat satisfied Treville perfectly. Now the aristocrat found himself behind his comrade and unable to aid him. Turning to stab d'Artagnan in the back seemed to appeal to him for an instant, until he saw that the Gascon had dropped one man already and was capably managing the grim Tranche.

Doucereux had little time to linger in idleness, for Treville invited his friend in with a feigned stumble, then flung his cape over the fellow's head and gave him a nasty thigh wound. As the man sank to the stone floor Treville disarmed him with two kicks and turned to face Doucereux. Bethune's lap dog tried to lunge at him before his opponent could fully come on guard, but Treville had expected that and caught the thrust on his dagger, flinging it aside with a wrist snap while jabbing his rapier at the other's knee. It just missed, as Doucereux pivoted to remove the target, then leaped back out of range.

Blood pounded in Treville's head like galloping hoof beats. All about him the stone gallery rang with the harsh echoes of steel on steel, grunts of effort, cursing, and feet sliding along flagstones. The morning light was turning from rose to gold, but did not yet fully seep into the charnel house, which remained murky and disturbing. Amongst the artfully arranged heaps of bones and skulls, the painting of the Danse Macabre made for a lurid spectacle. With its haunting images of Death Triumphant, the grinning skeletal figure escorting victims to their graves, the mural only made the gruesome situation even worse. Treville had a moment to contemplate all of that before Doucereux sidled left, looking for a vulnerable opening. When he found none he kept circling, forcing Treville to counter until they had nearly swapped positions. Now Treville faced the depressing mural, his back to the archway.

Exposed to the tower.

As Doucereux gave a signal with his dagger Treville threw his shoulders right in a feint, then dove left behind a sheltering pillar. He felt the hot breath of the musket ball tickle his ear. Poor Doucereux felt much more than that. Surrendering a hoarse cough, he stumbled back against a stack of hip bones. His head swiveled loosely and he dropped his dagger to clutch at the fine doublet, just beneath the ribs. With a gurgling sigh he slid down the wall, taking bits of skeletons with him until he lay, grimacing, beneath the smiling image of Death.

Safe behind cover, no swordsman near him, but unwilling to risk another bullet from the rapid-firing man in the tower, Treville relaxed somewhat and surveyed the action in the gallery. Chipay's foe had managed to hold his own all this time, uncowed by the expressionless native man. Though he had not scored any hits, he was still on his feet, which was quite the achievement, based on Treville's experience with Fantôme. But possibly the physician had merely been wearing his opponent down, for now he gave ground and let the man rush him. When the angry fellow rushed forward, Chipay put him on his back with the simplest of tactics.

He dropped his cane.

Perhaps it would not have worked on grass, but on smooth stone the club turned into an admirable roller. The front foot of the charging man landed on it and shot up as high as his head. He crashed onto his back in a tangle of blades, all his wind knocked out with a pained oof! Before he could recover his wits Chipay's foot pinned the rapier to the floor. When the assassin remembered his dagger and tried to raise it, the doctor punched his forearm with the heel of a hand, causing the weapon to tumble from numb fingers.

Nearer to Treville, and even more marvelous, d'Artagnan's clash with Tranche was a wonder. Far from being ignorant of fencing, the young Gascon demonstrated that his earlier clumsiness had been a sham. Not only had someone thoroughly schooled him since childhood in rapier employment, but the boy had inherited natural speed, grace, and agility that a tree-living monkey might have envied. Despite Tranche's evident experience and calculating manner, d'Artagnan not only still survived, but was pressing the ruthless minion hard. Already the left-hand rapier had been knocked from Tranche's hand. As hard as he tried the elder man could land no strike, however cleverly prepared. Either d'Artagnan anticipated it and neatly parried, often with a simultaneous attack, or he managed it dodge it with inhuman reflexes. Treville found himself relieved that he was not fighting the youth himself.

At close to twice d'Artagnan's age, Tranche was now showing signs of inevitable fatigue and the concern that came with it. All his allies were down and his master had fled. His enemy's fluid patinando, starting slowly then bursting into a terrifying lunge, nearly transfixed him. Only a sloppy and desperate dagger parry, while flinging himself backward, enabled Tranche to recover. Gasping now, but refusing to surrender, he settled back into his guard and advanced again, the cold resolve on his scarred face announcing his intent to dispatch this upstart puppy and salvage some honor from the morning's debacle. Cunning lived in his eyes, as well, prompting Treville to shout a warning.

"Careful! He has a sneaky look. Might have something up his sleeve."

D'Artagnan laughed. "Isn't that how we got into this predicament?"

Behind Tranche, Chipay made a move to assist d'Artagnan so that they could all go home before being arrested. But Treville held up a palm and shook his head. Their friend would never forgive them if they interfered without his call for aid. Besides, Treville wanted to see what the lad was made of. If they were to all be partners in dangerous pursuits for the king, best to know now if the Gascon could not finish off a tough opponent. As Tranche tried to beat d'Artagnan's rapier out of line and then deceive the dagger parry for a thrust to the belly, Treville risked a peek at the marksmen. On the church roof he spied a figure sliding down, musket in hand. *The fellow's abandoning his post. He must've seen something he didn't like.* Up in the tower a barrel could still be seen poking from the niche. *That one's holding fast, though. But my odds are better now.*

Sheathing his dagger, Treville hefted his rapier and sprinted into the open. After three steps he made two angled turns to spoil the man's aim. It worked, as the bullet zipped behind him. Before the next shot could come he snatched up the physician's bag and dove behind a heavy marble monument. He dug the pistol out of the satchel, cocked it, then used a wave of his hat to draw another miss and dashed toward a small mausoleum halfway to the tower. That safe spot he reached without drawing another musket ball. Treville glanced back to see d'Artagnan and Tranche still trading thrusts. His comrade had lost his dagger somehow – a small success for Tranche -- and was now relying on agility. At one point he laughed and hopped upon the ledge holding a stack of skulls, kicking one at Tranche.

The musket barrel still protruded from the tower window. Again he waggled his hat over the top of the structure. This time no lead ball came. Frowning, he looked up again. Somehow the angle of the weapon was wrong. It was not tracking him. In fact, it seemed to be aimed at nothing.

He's making a run for it.

Just in case it was a ruse, Treville's final race for the tower included many sudden changes of direction. Reaching the door without another shot being fired, he checked his pistol again. Behind him he heard Tranche curse. The last enemy swordsman clutched his arm, the rapier clattering near his boots. D'Artagnan yelped in victory and pursued him as he ran for the church gate. When Chipay stirred to assist him in bringing Tranche down, Treville waved them off, signaling that they should come to him instead. Feet could be heard inside the tower, making an iron staircase ring as the musket-wielder rushed to make his escape. Treville stood close to one side of the door and aimed his pistol at it. In the other hand his rapier hung low, in case of a misfire. But he hoped to not employ either weapon. They needed a prisoner who could explain all of this.

At the very moment that d'Artagnan reached the tower, the door was jerked open and a panting body burst from it. The man's toe caught the flat of Treville's sword and he stumbled for two steps before losing all balance and flying into the arms of the waiting Gascon. D'Artagnan had all that he could do to control the screeching beast that punched, scratched, and kicked him until the fellow finally exhausted himself and hung there, gasping through a black kerchief mask.

"We'll have guards breathing down our necks any moment," said Treville, sheathing his sword and handing the pistol to Chipay. "We need to make ourselves scarce. But first let's see who this irritatingly-fine shot is."

He approached the prisoner, the mask bringing back ghosts from his nightmare. With one tug of thumb and forefinger he exposed the face of the deadly marksman. Astonished noises came from Treville and his friends.

Their captive was a young woman.

7

CIMETIÈRE DES INNOCENTS

"MAGNIFICENT! I DON'T KNOW
WHETHER TO MARRY HER OR SHOOT HER."

Tall for a woman, with fierce eyes, a slender freckled nose, and wide mouth, she was older than she at first appeared, perhaps only three or four years shy of Treville's thirty. Strands of golden-brown hair peeped from the brim of her cap. Her rough clothing was that of a male laborer. Despite the masculine disguise she was undeniably pretty in a careless sort of way. That she could be a casual murderer for hire was not at all apparent.

While they all gaped at her with open mouths, their prisoner acted. D'Artagnan yelped and released her, sucking on a bitten hand. Before he could recover she had spun away and shoved him into Treville. They tangled and fell in a heap of limbs and curses. The girl sprinted for the gate at the church, where no doubt her employer waited to take her away. In a few moments she would be beyond catching.

Instead of rushing after her, Fantôme merely bent over to rummage through his medical kit. He stood up and spun his arm overhead, releasing an odd object at her that resembled some exotic animal. It wrapped around her legs like a serpent's coils on a mouse, sending her tumbling face-first into the dust. She was berating him with language that would have made a Spanish sailor blush as he threw her across his shoulder and returned her to the base of the tower. Halfway there she reached into her boot and snatched out a small poniard, but the doctor had anticipated that and snapped it from her grasp before she could stab him. He dumped her on her backside next to d'Artagnan. A search of her person turned up two more knives, a garrote wire, powder and shot for the gun, and a tiny wheel-lock pistol.

The Gascon laughed and clapped his hands. "Magnificent! I don't know whether to shoot her or marry her." A flood of raw expletives made it clear what her opinion of him was. When Chipay tied her hands behind her back, that earned him the same abuse. "Such language!" d'Artagnan chided. "Do you kiss your mother with that mouth?"

"She's dead and in heaven, pig!" she spat, struggling against the bonds on her legs. Despite the insult, her voice spoke of some education. "I expect you'll never have the chance to see her there."

"You may be right. I don't live the life of a saint." He blew her a little kiss. "But I have so much more fun that way."

That prompted an even more vitriolic stream of profanity. If the priests in the church had heard it, they might have fainted dead away. Chipay chuckled and unwrapped her legs. The weapon he had used was three bits of linked leather with a stone ball at each end. Naturally, she tried to kick him, but he slid behind her and hauled her onto her feet before she could land a blow.

"That's a charming item," said d'Artagnan. "Brought from the New World?"

"Yes. Our people sometimes hunt with them, though they are useful in war, as well. Where is our missing friend?"

D'Artagnan raised his chin. "Upstairs. Wanted to see what she was shooting at us with. I think he's envious of her toys."

On cue Treville walked from the door with a curious musket in his hands. "That I am. Look at this beauty."

It was a masterpiece of the gunmaker's art. The varnished mahogany stock was inlaid with ivory in complicated geometric patterns. Chased silver decorated the polished steel firing mechanism and barrel. But what made it unique was the odd swollen bit in front of the firing pan. Treville twisted it and it rotated on a central pin with a click.

"This cylinder thing holds eight bullets. She preloads the powder and ball into each space and twists her wrist for the next shot. Can reload in two seconds instead of thirty."

"That's diabolical," said d'Artagnan. "My future wife impresses me more every moment." He looked her with a sad face. "But this is worth more than a good house. Where did you steal it?"

She told him what he could do with his request, in the rudest way imaginable. With a laugh he yanked her mask up into her mouth and gagged her.

"I like my women with some sauce, but there are limits."

"And we've reached ours," Treville announced.

They all followed his gaze to the gate, where a dozen armed men in the livery of the Royal Provosts were entering, swords drawn. Their job was to police members of the army, and to respond to serious outbreaks of trouble in the city. All too often well-connected aristocrats suborned them, up to and including the queen, to be personal bully-boys and score-settlers. On more than a few occasions Treville and his comrades in the king's service had traded thrusts with them. The leader, a broad swarthy fellow with a black beard and a blacker scowl, spotted Treville's group at once and aimed his rapier in their direction. Half of his force immediately advanced toward the tower.

"Ah…the Maréchaussée smell blood," sneered d'Artagnan.

Treville nodded at the girl. "What will you wager that this one's blue-blooded boss sent them here, no doubt with a believable story of how we foul ruffians set upon him and his loyal comrades?"

"I won't take a fool's bet. But I will wager that two can play at that game."

"Brazen it out, you mean? Sounds good to me. As much as I'd like to bloody Colére's nose, I'm too tired to fight any more."

Rather than wait to be arrested, they marched toward the oncoming knot of swordsmen as if they were the kings of the world. Treville threw the fancy musket over his shoulder and d'Artagnan propelled the girl in front as a royal captive. Fantôme hung back to not draw attention to himself. By the time the king's men were within speaking distance of the marshals, he had somehow vanished utterly.

"It would seem that he deserves his nickname," said d'Artagnan, unable to spot the physician anywhere in the open cemetery.

"Probably all for the best," muttered Treville. "These dolts would just use him as a target otherwise. Isn't that Coupé? Quite the bully, that one." He forced a broad smile onto his face and hailed the newcomers. "Good morning, gentlemen! How are we doing this fine day? Are you the honor guard for a funeral, perhaps?"

"Only if it's to be yours," answered Coupé, a much-too-suave blonde sporting a sparse chin beard.

"I regret that we cannot oblige you." Treville pointed to the charnel house. "However, there is an unfortunate soul in there who may require such service. His wound looked grievous. Did you perhaps bring a doctor?"

Coupé set his hand on his rapier hilt. "No, but we do have scalpels."

Treville sensed d'Artagnan tensing all his muscles at the insult. In another moment he would pitch into the whole pack of them. That wouldn't do. "And I have no doubt that you are fine surgeons. Would that we could assist you in treating that poor fellow, but we have to get this saucy lad to Lord Rosny for interrogation." He indicated the sulking captive in d'Artagnan's hands. "He gave us quite a bit of trouble just now."

The girl proved to be clever. She caught on to the game immediately. Her voice grew low and harsh as she began struggling again, though not so much as to give d'Artagnan trouble. Apparently she preferred her current captors to these new ones. "And I'll give ye a good deal more'n that, ya lickspittle!"

Everyone on both sides laughed. Coupé said, "Hand him over and we'll get more truth out of the little brat than he knows he possesses."

"That would mean my head, captain. There was quite the row here, involving some important personages, and the Marquis expects me to personally deliver this witness."

"Important? Like his fair-haired boy? We just met him. He swore out a complaint against you and this snot-nosed stripling." His sneer at d'Artagnan got the Gascon's blood up again. "Said that you ambushed him and his friends over a gambling affair."

"He would say that," snorted Treville, laying a calming hand on d'Artagnan's shoulder, "seeing as how he ran off with his tail between his silk stockinged legs. Left his poor second bleeding like a waterfall, too. But he was less than honest with you. We were the ones who were ambushed." Treville recounted the whole fight honestly, keeping secret only the sex of the sharpshooting prisoner they held.

Coupé shook his head. "You expect me to believe that the only son of the king's right hand not only picked a scrap with this nothingness but that he went to the trouble to plan an elaborate scheme to assassinate the lot of you? Why? It makes no sense."

"I agree. Which is why our prize catch here is going straight to daddy's office in the Louvre to explain it to him. If he proves reluctant, well…the Bastille has talented persuaders in its employ."

"I think not. As you, too, are involved in the fray, we should take charge of him. He should be in the care of a disinterested party."

"Which is why he remains with us. Young Béthune's purse has left you rather less disinterested than we are."

Before he could catch himself Coupé's hand unconsciously strayed to the leather pouch hanging on his sword belt, heavy with gold. With a low growl he glared at Treville through narrow eyes.

Treville twisted the knife. "Is that your take? Quite generous. But I expect your captain received the lion's share. Bethune must have been worried that he'd gone too far, to spend that much for your loyalty."

Another officer stepped into Treville's face, though he did not intimidate his foe as much as he had hoped to do. "No, now it's you who's gone too far. Outnumbered six-to-one, throwing your royal weight around…"

With a tiny smile Treville shrugged. "Of what use is weight except to use as leverage?" He casually set his palm on Coupé's wrist, locking it onto the sword hilt so that he could not draw it. "Now shut your pie-hole and listen. I am one of the Forty-Five, guardian of the sacred person of Henri IV, God's anointed King of the French, while you are under the thumb of the queen. You interfere with my mission at your peril. And in case you think to take your case to the king, remember this: not only are they presently estranged, but His Majesty is also having some mistress trouble. So consider how well he will receive any complaint from her when he's in that black a mood."

It seemed for a long moment or two that Coupé was willing to try his luck anyway. D'Artagnan's free hand strayed to his rapier in case the order to arrest them was given. Treville, too, had begun to reach behind him for his dagger hilt. The tension between the two groups smelled like the instant before a lightning strike. But the thunder did not crack. Instead, the Maréchaussée blade chose to make a great joke of it all.

"By God, you have the stones of a bull!" he bellowed, laughing. His men relaxed and followed suit, no doubt glad not to have to cross swords with Treville and his dangerous friend. "Come along, gents, let them have the trouble of explaining all of this at the palace. Writing the report alone will waste a day." He led his crew toward the charnel house to investigate the state of the wounded Doucereux. Dead or dying men were easier to handle than Treville.

"Well, that was a near thing," said d'Artagnan as they resumed their walk toward the gate, where the remaining six marshals waited.

"You'll never know how near," Treville told him. "It was all I could do not to knock out all of his teeth with the butt of this musket."

The girl made a pained sound in her throat. "Please don't. It's expensive…and delicate."

"Like my women!" snickered d'Artagnan.

They passed Colére's squad. To Treville's amazement the glowering commander made no move to intercept them. Instead he gave a small ironic salute and waved them toward the cemetery exit.

And once their backs were turned, he tried to kill them.

He might have managed it, too, if the sun had been anyplace else. But the ruddy eastern rays betrayed him. The long shadows of raised swords and pistols danced upon the wall. D'Artagnan whirled to face them, shamelessly using the bound girl as a shield while drawing his rapier. Treville lowered the magical musket, the prisoner's captured pistol cocked and ready in his other hand. They had no chance of surviving such odds, of course, but they could sell their lives dearly and make the Maréchaussée pay for its treachery.

Just as fingers tightened on triggers the iron gate creaked open on rusty hinges. A flurry of black and white robes rushed in amongst the combatants. Before death could explode there, small pale hands grasped masculine arms. Women's imploring voices begged for peace. The cluster of nuns inquired if there was any sacred service they could provide to the noble marshals. And what of those dreadful gunshots a few minutes before? Was anyone harmed? To think that such a thing could happen at the house of the Lord!

Someone tugged at Treville's sleeve. He saw Chipay at his elbow, wearing a self-satisfied smile. Behind him stood an elderly, white-robed abbé who looked quite concerned about events in his cemetery. Uncocking the pocket pistol, Treville pulled d'Artagnan and the young woman past him and back through the gate. He remained there, watching the nonplussed Colére and his men trying to shoo away the nuns, who were mostly young novices, while sheathing their weapons.

"Another time, captain." Treville touched the brim of his hat. "Though it's pleasant to see you finally immersed in good habits."

It was fortunate that Colére's deadly stare could not translate into bullets. "Make jokes while you can. You won't always have a shield of innocents to save you."

"No. But one does wonder why I suddenly need saving. How did I manage to get into your new patron's bad graces?"

"Orders are orders, Treville. You know that."

"Whose orders, though? That's the question."

"You're on your own there. I'm not fool enough to get my throat cut enlightening you."

Treville backed through the gate, asking the deacon to lock it for a quarter of an hour so that they would not be followed. He joined d'Artagnan, Chipay, and the girl. She was shuffling along with them; hands still tied, mocking their low parentage. The young man thought she was more entertaining than a troupe of actors.

"Have you ever heard such creative imprecations?" he wanted to know. "This one doesn't settle for your run-of-the-mill insults. Even in Gascony we can't match her foul mouth."

"I think that priest nearly died of shame," said Treville. He slapped Chipay on the back. "Speaking of cleverness...you, sir, have a touch of the genius in you. Things were about to go very badly back there."

Fantôme nodded. "I trusted that not even hardened assassins would slay teenaged girls."

"You're lucky that it was Colére in command and not that dog Coupé. He might have done us all in anyway. Well, we're out of that stewpot, no matter how. But eventually we'll have to explain all of this to Rosny and I don't look forward to that. Before we do, though, we need to have a long chat with this charming lass. Better not do it at my place. Our Maréchaussée friends know where it is, as does that vile little Bethune."

"Off to my lodgings, then" said d'Artagnan. "I'm of no interest to anyone."

"Ah, those days are over, I fear. That rapier of yours spoke all too loudly today."

"Truly?" The Gascon patted his sword hilt. "I thought she was merely whispering."

None of the quartet noticed the sleek shadow that followed them.

8

PARIS: D'ARTAGNAN'S LODGING

"I'M DYING TO KNOW WHY THEY THOUGHT I SHOULD BE DYING."

After paying a street urchin to ask Madame Tatillon to misdirect any suspicious persons who might come looking for him, Treville followed d'Artagnan to a decidedly-seedy quarter of the city near a tannery and abattoir. The foul smell made their eyes water. His partner's single room on the ground floor of a ramshackle boarding house matched the neighborhood's squalid atmosphere. Rodents outnumbered the human tenants and black mold oozed down the walls. In comparison Treville's lodging was a royal palace.

"It's awful," d'Artagnan confessed, hastily clearing laundry from the bed so that his visitors could sit. The only other resting place was a pair of chairs at the single tiny table. "But I came here with nothing and His Majesty's government has yet to favor me with so much as a sou."

It struck Treville that this was why his friend had been so rash as to gamble with dangerous men. "I'll favor you with much more than that if it will get you out of this stink-hole. That plague pit in Ostend would be a healthier choice."

Their prisoner coughed and made a face from her perch on the very edge of the bed. She was trying to touch as little of it as possible. "All of the bugs I see are dead. That can't be a good sign."

"What's your expert opinion, doctor?" Treville asked Chipay while untying the girl's hands.

Chipay gave the room the sort of inspection he might have given a man dying of scurvy. "Fire. Fire and then quicklime." He shook his head at d'Artagnan. "You truly eat and sleep here?"

Their host shrugged. "Only when I don't have a better offer." He winked at the girl, who made a disgusted face and returned a rude gesture.

Treville made certain that the door was locked and returned to the bed. "The smell of that tannery alone is enough to melt the plaster from the walls." Curing animal hides required dog droppings, urine, even cattle brains. Such businesses were always relegated to the undesirable outskirts of towns. That was how even the impecunious d'Artagnan could afford to rent the room.

"That's why I volunteered to infiltrate a Spanish garrison town. I was hoping that my nose might get shot off."

The girl made an impatient noise. "Can somebody please shoot my ears off? I'm tired of listening to all of you blather."

Chuckling, Treville pulled her hat off and dropped it in her lap, exposing short, tangled hair. Now she looked less like a tough street rat and more like a timid child. "Did anyone ever tell you that your charm is positively infectious?"

She shuddered with theatrical affectation. "Less infectious than these sheets."

"Hold on!" complained d'Artagnan. "I just had those laundered."

"Where? In a prison outhouse?"

Treville raised his voice like a parent silencing squabbling children. "Enough!" He dragged one of the chairs over and sat on it backward, facing her. "The sooner you tell us what's going on, the sooner we can all move to more fragrant accommodations."

She snorted in derision. "Like I'd tell you anything."

"Why not?"

"Because I'd end up dead in a ditch, that's why not."

"How do you know I won't do the same if you don't help us?"

"Because you're all noble and such. Act like you were raised on tales of chivalry. Think you're on the side of the angels."

"You nearly introduced me to the angels with that exotic musket of yours."

"Nothing personal, Forty-Five. The money was too good to pass up. Besides, they didn't give me much..." She caught herself mid-sentence and clamped her mouth shut.

"Much choice? They forced you to shoot at us and paid you handsomely? That's odd."

She muttered to herself, staring down at her hat. "The whole bloody thing's odd."

"How's that?" When she didn't answer he tried another tack, moving over to the bed to sit beside her. His voice was gentle now. "What's your name?"

"Abandonée."

"No mother calls her baby that."

"Mine never gave me a name at all. Died birthing to me, she did." Her bravado had evaporated, replaced by old pain and loss.

The familiar hollow feeling churned inside Treville, the wretched sensation that lingered whenever he woke from his nightmare. "I lost my mum, too."

"At least you have some actual memory of her. I only have..." Again she interrupted herself. This time her hand strayed to her left sleeve, as if she had something that she treasured hidden up it.

Since that did not seem to be relevant to their present purpose, Treville did not pursue it. "Actually, I have only the faintest recollection of her. Flashes, shadows. Golden hair and smooth hands." He chose not to mention the screams and the blood. No sense in dissolving into a puddle of misery in front of everyone. Instead, he grasped her hands in his before she could shrink away. "Abandonée it is, then."

"Oh, are we all assuming a nom de guerre?" asked d'Artagnan. "Let's see, we already have Fantôme and Abandonée. You should be Penseur, since wheels and gears are always turning in that head of yours. I ought to be ---"

"Stupide?" suggested the girl.

"Catastrophique?" said Chipay from the window.

"Temeraire," Treville offered, with finality, "since you're so reckless."

D'Artagnan pretended to pout. "Well, I'd prefer Guerrier, or Héroïque, or ---" He raised his eyebrows at Abandonée. "Amant." When she shook her head he sighed in false despair. "She cuts me. Love is cruel. Temeraire it is, then. It does sort of leap from the tongue like a song."

"I may leap from a cliff like a suicide," she whispered to Treville. But her words held a bit less disgust toward d'Artagnan than they had before.

"Before you do," said Treville, "try leaping into the story of how you came to be in that tower."

"No. I told you that my life would be worthless if I did. They'd disembowel me in my sleep...if they're feeling charitable."

"You might as well talk. Because if they're as ruthless as you claim, they'll be coming for you anyway." She frowned, not grasping his meaning. "They saw us take you. Naturally, they will presume that we have thrown you into the Bastille, and that your tongue will eventually loosen. Everyone's does there. With their obvious royal connections, they may manage to get someone in there to dispatch you before you can do them much damage. Perhaps one of the torturers is in their pay already. If not, they will hunt you down nonetheless, probably to leave a warning on your cold body so that others will not let themselves be captured."

"This is supposed to make me cooperate with you?"

"I'm merely laying out the unpleasant facts of your line of work."

"And now you're about to tell me something less gruesome that will encourage me to giggle and spill my secrets to the king's men?"

"I'm guessing that you have few friends, if any. Probably ran away from whatever orphanage or foster family took you in. Was the man of the house starting to look at you in the wrong way, perhaps? Now a life in the shadows, performing distasteful tasks – thievery, forgery, even outright murder -- because that at least keeps you from becoming a brothel girl. But now you're deep in the quicksand, aren't you? Took a job from the wrong people and they've left you to sink."

"I don't need you to tell me how low I've ---."

"No. What you need are allies. Someone to grasp your arms and drag you from that mire before it's too late."

"Throw my lot in with the king's men? And when I've given you what you want you'll toss me into the Bastille after all."

"I could do that now and wash my hands of you. Get my intelligence elsewhere. I'll wager that you're already known to them as a petty criminal."

"Why don't you then? It has to smell better than this place."

"Call me starry-eyed. I think you're worth saving."

"Ha! That's just what he said."

"Who?"

She paused for such a long while that Treville thought that she would not speak at all. But after looking into the eyes of all three men, she apparently decided that they were less likely to kill her than her erstwhile employers. "The serpent who got me into this mess. Tried to cut his purse, but he was a quick one. Snagged my arm and had me dead to rights. Trussed me up before I could use my knife."

"Where was this? Here in Paris?"

"No. Amsterdam. Paris was a trifle too hot for me at the time. Thought I'd have a bit of a holiday."

"How long ago?"

"November, I think."

"And what did this fellow look like?"

"Tallish, broad-shoulders. Muscles. Big black beard and mustaches. A veteran soldier, that was certain, though he was dressed like a courtier then. Eyes like a zealot from the Bible. That fit, because all he talked about was Christ and the Pope and 'answering their call.' Got awfully thick after a while."

D'Artagnan grumbled while cutting himself a hunk of cheese. "Damn! I hate all this religious business. Why can't people kill one another for honest reasons, like money, women, or power?"

Treville ignored that. "This man who caught you. Does he have a name?"

"I heard somebody call him Guido once. Made him see red. Said, 'Stick to the code names or I'll cut your tongue out.'"

"Guido...that's Italian."

"His name may be, but he's English born-and-bred, to hear him talk."

"An English Catholic?" d'Artagnan complained. "I like this even less now. They're mad dogs with prayer books."

"Amsterdam is where we're already headed," Treville mused. "This confirms that we made the right choice."

D'Artagnan picked up a wine bottle, making a face as he shook it and found it nearly empty. "Good beer there."

"Do you know anyone named Krijger?" Treville asked Abandonée.

She wrinkled her brow in thought. "No. Sounds made-up, too."

"It most likely is. A spy of some sort. Apparently a double-agent. He's said to be dangerous in a fight. That's all we know." He left the bed to stretch and pace the narrow little room. "You undoubtedly know more. Enlighten us as to your part of their plan. I'm dying to know why they thought I should be dying."

Abandonée hesitated, as if reconsidering her decision to cooperate. Treville fancied that he could almost see the debate swirling in her mind. If she told him all that she knew, holding nothing back, then she would have no cards left to play. Her only value right then was as the keeper of knowledge. Once that had left her vault, what was to prevent them from turning her over to the authorities? After all, she had tried to shoot one of the king's personal bodyguards. Even worse, she had possibly killed a retainer of a great lord's son. That she had been aiming at Treville hardly made her plight better. Yet the intended victim seemed to bear her no ill will. Remarkable. In her experience attempted murder was rarely overlooked. Were these men truly what they claimed to be, selfless servants of the state?

Treville recognized her torment and played his own hand. He opened the door and stood aside, leaving her a free escape. Seeing that, d'Artagnan stopped his snack in mid-chew. Chipay remained at the window but missed nothing inside the room.

She cocked her head like a confused dog. "What's this?"

"An assurance of my sincerity," Treville told her. In his hands was her remarkable musket. He offered it to her while waving at the open door. "Here. If you can't trust us, then anything you say would be suspect. I can only use honest intelligence, not clever lies. Your way is clear. None of us will stop you. But if you remain, it's as one of us."

Abandonée popped up from the bed and flew to the door, snatching the weapon from him as she passed. Treville remained where he stood, as did Chipay. D'Artagnan slid from the edge of the table where he had been eating and freed his hands for action.

The young woman looked out at her potential freedom, then back at the three men. She opened her mouth to speak, but closed it again and shook her head. Again she gazed outside, taking a step through the portal. Treville felt certain that he had lost his gamble, that she would flee back to her old life. He began considering alternative ways to accomplish his mission. Instead of bolting, though, she laughed. Then she turned the musket's cylinder to line up the one remaining full chamber with the barrel. Before anyone could react she jerked back the lock and cocked it. An instant later the muzzle covered every man in the room, unwavering and deadly.

9

D'ARTAGNAN'S LODGING

"HE WORE A SILVER NOSE.
SOMEONE CUT HIS REAL ONE COMPLETELY OFF."

Without even looking at him, Treville reached back to stop d'Artagnan's advance with his palm. He had felt the young man's body tense and heard his hiss. At the window, Chipay stirred a bit but remained impassive. Abandonée gave them all a puckish little grin.

"Negotiations are a funny thing," she said, looking out at the foul neighborhood again, "Interrogations, even more so. Back and forth, give and take. Threats, cajoling."

Treville forced a smile of his own. "Which is this then?"

She glanced at the gun. "This? None of them."

The stock flew to her shoulder and her finger felt for the trigger. Treville dove behind the table, pulling it over as a shield. His hand fumbled for the little pistol again. D'Artagnan seized the empty wine bottle by the neck and raised it to throw. Only Chipay made no reaction. In fact, he crossed his arms and leaned into the corner.

But no boom came, no white smoke or smell of powder. Just silence.

Eventually it struck them that murder was not on her mind. At any rate, not the murder of anyone in the room. Treville risked a peek around the table's edge. Abandonée had whirled to point the musket out of the doorway. She rested the barrel against the jamb to steady it, lifted the muzzle toward the sky, squinted at her target, let out a long breath, and pulled the trigger. Sparks and flame spewed up from the pan, followed an eye-blink later by the sharp roar of the main charge. Her whole body jerked back with the weapon's kick. But Treville was impressed by how steady she stayed. He had seen women knocked onto their backs by muskets.

This he thought as he rushed to the door to see what she had fired at. D'Artagnan went to the window at the same time, crowding alongside Chipay. All of them saw a man atop a roof across the narrow mud street, windmilling his arms to try to keep from falling. But it was much too late. The heavy bullet had struck the decorative tile he had been leaning on, exploding it into tiny shards. His hat leaped from his head, preceding him as he pitched forward and plummeted three stories. It might have meant certain death, but he had the good fortune, depending on how one considered the question, to land in a pile of fresh horse manure that had been readied for transport. An instant afterward a wooden object slid from where he had been hiding and tumbled after him, smacking into his rump just as he tried to rise.

"What was that?" asked d'Artagnan.

Abandonée lowered the musket, a thin stream of smoke floating from the barrel. "Crossbow. Someone followed us. Good at it, too, as none of us noticed. This time they wanted a nice quiet assassination."

"Well, you certainly ruined that," said Treville. "Half of Paris will have heard that shot of yours."

"Does this strike you as a district where people are curious about such things?"

She had a point. No one so much as poked a nose out of a window to see what had just happened. The fallen bowman thrashed about in his vile landing site, cursing and trying vainly to clean some of the ordure from his face. As he managed to get onto his feet, d'Artagnan rushed to the door to capture him. But Abandonée blocked him from leaving the room.

"Wait." When he held up his hands in confusion she nodded toward the street.

A black carriage with no markings rumbled from the next corner and lurched to a stop next to their man. He flung himself into it, much to the apparent disgust of the driver, who was masked with a heavy scarf. The fallen man also had his face covered. Two other faceless men with bows raced from cover and piled into the vehicle. Before the doors could close the two horses had been whipped into motion and it vanished back toward the center of the city.

D'Artagnan smiled at her. "You aimed to miss him, didn't you? That tile was your target."

She nodded. "Wasn't being paid to kill him. Besides, it was more entertaining that way."

He looked at her the way religious men adored statues of saints. "Is it too early to propose marriage, do you think?"

Her eyebrow raised. "Careful. That might be the death of you." Her voice held a faint offer of another sort of death.

"What was that all about?" Treville wondered, pulling Abandonné back inside and shut the door. "Do you know them?"

"Never saw them before," she protested, laying the gun on the bed. "The carriage nor the men. Our work was all with pistols and muskets. Could be some other part of the gang I was never told about, I suppose. "

"Your work," said d'Artagnan, righting the fallen table. "It's time that you explained just what that is."

Treville sat astride his chair again. "I doubt that you trained for months just to take potshots at us."

"No, that was a sort of practice event," Abandonée admitted as she began to clean her musket of its fouling. "We were hastily assembled and sent over to the cemetery so that our masters could get us some experience beyond shooting at paper targets and old bottles."

"But why shoot at us at all? What's going on? And since you chose to aid us just now rather than taking flight, I expect honesty."

"And you shall have it. I warn you, though, that I know less than you may hope. They are clever enough not to let anyone be privy to their whole scheme."

"I'll take whatever you can offer. We know next to nothing, except that we're apparently in someone's way."

"Guido took me to a farm in Picardy, along with two other street rats he'd snared. As far as I can tell he never noticed he had a girl in his employ. I didn't think it would wise to enlighten him. The others were too busy with trying to impress our slave-master, for that is what he was, to pay me any attention. He kept us locked up when we weren't going to school. I suppose you could call it that. Every day we learned how to assemble and disassemble every type of pistol and musket. We were whipped hard for the slightest mistake. Yet, at the same time we were given generous pay, though not offered any opportunity to spend it. Slaves on salary. Once we had mastered mechanics, we moved on to the firing of them. More than once I thought of blowing Guido's brains out and running, but he took care to always have control of us. Several other men were there, armed to the teeth, ready to intervene if we tried anything. It occurred to me to do it anyway and let them kill me. At least I'd be free. But an awful thing began to happen."

"You started to like it, despite yourself," Treville suggested.

"True enough, to my shame."

"I've heard of it happening to galley slaves and other captives who spend a long time in such situations. Against their will they come to look upon their captors as a sort of family. Their old identities fade and they adopt the beliefs of their jailers."

"It is true," said Chipay from the window corner. They all startled at his voice, since he had gone so long without speaking. "Twice I met some of my brethren who had been enslaved in the galleys of the Spanish and the French. Prisoners from wars in what you call the New World. On both occasions I had the means to arrange or even buy their freedom. But they refused. So long had they been rowing there, living with the other captives, eating strange food and taking orders in barbaric tongues, that they thought of themselves as no longer Cree. I even tried to force them from the ships, but they held back, even struck out at me." His eyes glistened with tears. "I had seen it happen with those of other tribes who we had taken and reared as our own. Yet we are so similar in blood and in our shared ways that it hardly seemed odd to do that. This, though…to abandon the beliefs of your fathers for something so foreign. It made my soul ache."

D'Artagnan frowned. "Yet you have forsaken your own people to become almost a European yourself."

"You speak the truth. Yet I have reasons for remaining here. Unlike the poor wretches in the galleys, I know where I belong. Someday I can return to my people. But right now that is…impossible." For half a second sorrow flitted across his usually serene face, then hid itself beneath the mask again.

Treville burned to know Fantôme's secret, but other mysteries craved his attention more. He looked back at Abandonée. "So you spent several months at this place in Picardy?"

"I did. Near Amiens, it was. I could see the towers of the cathedral, the one that is so much bigger than our Notre Dame. When the bells rang I wanted to go there. It reminded me of my childhood, of being schooled by the nuns. Then it would strike me that there was little difference between then and my current plight, other than the killing part. Both were violent. Both demanded faith and obedience. Both made me love them despite myself." Abandonée's voice caught, as if confessing a secret shame to a priest. Perhaps that was what she felt that she was doing.

"What was the purpose of it all? Who was your target?"

"They never told us. Said that if we knew, then we might ruin the whole plot if captured. Someone important, though, that was obvious. No point in going to all of that trouble and secrecy to murder a grocer."

"French?"

"I think not. They seemed to be planning an international conspiracy. Many languages spoken, money from all over Europe."

D'Artagnan ran his dagger across a whetstone. "Some Spanish general or visiting potentate? Amiens is close to the Spanish Netherlands. No love lost between London and Valladolid after that Armada business."

"Or just as likely a Dutchman," Treville countered. "Sounds like they're Papists with a grudge. They'd love to exterminate a Protestant, sow some chaos in Amsterdam or The Hague." He asked Abandonée, "Their whole plan depended on three young people picked up on the streets? Doesn't sound sensible, given what you've told us about their professionalism." Perhaps they were more expendable than the others, easier to dispatch if things got too hot? A thought struck him and he showed her the drawing of the Dutch trading company tattoo that his intended assassins had borne.

"Have you seen that anywhere while training with your happy band of cut-throats?"

Recognition flashed in her eyes. "That was on some of our supply barrels."

Treville nodded in satisfaction. Another link added to the chain. "Did you see anyone else there while you trained, besides your tutors?"

She nodded, checking the spring on the lock of her gun. "Plenty of swordsmen hanging around, practicing with their shiny toys. They seemed to be guards of some sort. Perhaps they were to go with us whenever we went on our final mission."

That word 'final' lingered in Treville's mind. *It almost certainly would be your final mission. These people wouldn't leave any witnesses to assassination or treason.* He chose not to mention that to her. "Did any of them stand out, particularly?

That made her think, but only for a moment. "Well, there was one who the rest of them were afraid of. Not only was he fast and accurate, almost able to pick a fly out of the air with his rapier point, but he liked to hurt people. His fellows would stop short if they an opponent's pierced defense in practice. He would make sure to leave his partner with a nasty gouge to remember him by. Nearly all of them had slices taken out of arms, thighs, cheeks. When they complained he sneered and said that the enemy would do much worse and that they would remember the mistakes all the better from his painful reminders. Eventually Guido ordered him to stop. Bad for morale."

Now she had d'Artagnan's full attention. Here was an opponent worthy of his skills. "Would you recognize this paragon again?"

"I should say so. He reminded me of you a little, in his fighting and general movement, at least. Not quite as pretty as you, though."

He preened. "Well, of course not. Few could equal my ---"

"It's not because of Mother Nature's gifts. Perhaps at one time all the girls might have chosen him over you. But his blade skills hadn't always been perfect. He'd lost at least one fight."

"Yes? How could you know?"

"Because he wore a silver nose. Someone cut his real one completely off."

10

PARIS: D'ARTAGNAN'S LODGING & THE LOUVRE

"WE HAVEN'T FOILED AN ASSASSINATION PLOT
IN NEARLY TWO WEEKS. ABOUT TO EXPIRE OF ENNUI."

"Probably uses it to blind his enemies," mused d'Artagnan.

Treville cocked his head at him. "That was your first thought?"

"What can I say? I'm a slave to my art."

"Why wouldn't it blind him as well?"

"Perhaps he's clever at squinting."

"Perhaps you were dropped on your head as a baby."

"Oh, that's certain. My mum used to show me the split flagstone where I landed."

Seeing no profit in humoring him, Treville turned to Abandonée. "What is he called, this fellow with the precious proboscis?"

"La Haine, I think."

"Hate? That's no name, that's a nom de guerre. What else do you know of him? Did he sound French?"

"He spoke it like a native. But there was another tone to his words, as if he'd spent a long time elsewhere. An odd music to it. Nothing European."

"From your description of this crew, that's no surprise. The plot sounds wide-ranging and cosmopolitan. All the way to the Spice Islands, I expect. That makes it more dangerous, but it also provides us with more chinks for penetrating its armor. I don't care for the religious aspect. Fanatics about faith are always more unstable than mere patriots. Harder to buy off, nearly impossible to seduce away from the cause. Is this La Haine a true believer, do you think, or a mercenary out for gold?"

"I never heard him speak of God, except in some foul oath, but I never heard him disparage religion in front of his masters, either."

"So he, at least, might be open to creative bribery. Most likely his men, as well. That's good. No doubt Rosny will be eager to give us a few sacks of coins to try that route if we can get close enough. Are they still in Amiens?"

"No, when I left they were already moving the men and wagons out. It was mostly all gone three days ago. The center of their operations was shifting north and east, back into Holland. Paris was just a sideshow, they said."

"Why such a long detour?"

She shrugged. "Who knows? But once one of their money men visited. He was too far away to get a good look at his face, but he was a great lord of some sort, by the way he dressed and how they all bowed to him. Definitely French, though I couldn't catch any of the words."

"Perhaps he had a score to settle and decided to use his new toys for it."

Maybe. I never saw him again."

"So it is to Amsterdam we go, after all. But before we do, let's see if we can pounce on any of your old friends who might be lingering. You must have had a base here. Where did they keep you while waiting for an opportunity to shoot at us?"

"A house on Montmartre, near the Royal Abbey. Secluded, but easy enough to find."

Treville knew that what they would find would be an abandoned building with no clues, but it couldn't hurt to look.

D'Artagnan rubbed his hands together. "Let's go find it, then. All of this conversation is putting me to sleep."

That made Treville look at him with disbelief again. "It's hardly the talking. You've been up all night, my little card sharp."

"Sleep is over-rated. A waste of precious time." The Gascon put on his hat and checked his weapons. "Don't you know that we begin to die the day that we're born?"

"That hardly requires you to rush into Death's arms by falling asleep mid-battle. Particularly if I'm depending on you to watch my back." Treville prepared to depart himself, prompting Chipay and Abandonée to follow suit. "We'll go to the Louvre to report and start gathering supplies for the trip. I'll convince Rosny to send some soldiers to Abandonné's Montmartre hideout. Perhaps luck will be with us and we can catch them before they flee Paris to join their comrades. And then we'll all get a full night's rest, for once. We leave for Amsterdam in ten days. Until then, watch your backs."

*****

The great lord Maximilien Béthune, clad in an ominous black robe, scowled while he listened to Treville's account of the duel and its aftermath as he sat at his vast desk, fingers drumming. In particular, he glowered upon hearing of his only son's behavior in the affair, though the attempted assassination of one of the Forty-Five and a promising potential recruit to that august body also clearly angered him. He seemed not to notice that the latter young man was slumped in the corner chair near the door, head nodding, three-quarters asleep.

"Outrageous! The king will have some heads for this!" As he spoke Rosny's long beard shook like a terrier worrying a rat. With a deep breath he mastered himself. It would not do to behave without restraint. His position demanded that he examine all possibilities. "How certain are you that he was involved, that he knew of the intended murder?"

"Perfectly," said Treville, seated across from his commander in his best doublet, a blue beauty with slashed sleeves, a diamond pattern in silver, and high collar. They had stopped at his lodging to deposit Abandonée with his landlady. Fantôme remained in Treville's apartment, ostensibly to prepare for the Netherlands journey. In fact, his assignment was to ensure that the girl did not escape Madame Tatillon and vanish into the warrens of Paris. Duty dictated that Treville turn her over to Rosny for trial as a would-be murderess, but something told him that there was more to her than he had discovered so far, and that she would be useful on their mission. After all, she had spent more time in Amsterdam than he and would be invaluable as a guide and to identify any of the conspirators they might encounter there. For those reasons, and an indecipherable feeling that tingled his mind, he preferred to keep her close to him rather than have her rotting in a dungeon.

The Marquis looked at him hard. "Perfectly? How so? Because I must be frank, he stole a march on you and has already been here to give his side of the story, which differs markedly from yours. And he can provide witnesses to corroborate."

"As can I, m'lord."

"A red Indian and..." Béthune frowned at the drowsing d'Artagnan, "...that?"

"Chipay's honor is beyond reproach, sir. And the boy... I trust him with my life. Indeed, I did so this very morning, and in Ostend. As for your son's friends, could he say the same? Could you?"

That drew a grumble of defeat from Rosny. He leaned back in his chair, fists clenching and unclenching. "Gambling...whoring...dueling. Beating the servants. Lying. Stealing. He even mistreats his dogs, for God's sake. The whelp is barely eighteen, even younger than that snoring pup over there. Lost his mother when he was still soiling himself, barely old enough to walk. I was always off killing whoever Henri thought needed it. To atone for that I made sure that little Maxi was reared like a prince. Clearly that was foolish, an error born of guilt. Bad enough to encourage that sort of thing in a real prince. You've seen how they behave." His satin-clad shoulders shrugged. "And now I'm stuck with him. An heir with his nose stuck in the air."

"He's your eldest, then?"

"To my great annoyance. The only other son is just seven. So no getting around it. I must put a leash on this one. He never got on with Rachel, my new wife. The usual attitude of 'you're not my real mother.' Treats her like a servant when I'm not there to stop him."

Treville sighed inwardly. He had not come to the Louvre to hear about his master's family squabbles. But he had always known that the palace contained more immaturity and intrigue than a schoolyard. There was real work to do, enemies of the state to frustrate. This blubbering about a wayward son could not aid him in that. "You've tried taking a hard line with him, of course?"

"Oh, naturally. Cut off his funds, bashed him around a bit, threatened to put him in the army as a private soldier. None of it worked. Because he knows that when it comes down to it, I'm obligated to cover his debts and keep his scandals private. The king is trying to build a new France, struggling to reconcile two warring faiths. I'm his chief instrument in that. Wouldn't do to have that instrument dulled by any disgraceful behavior, even indirectly. That would give the feuding parties all the more reason to remain uncooperative, particularly as I'm a Protestant."

"Have you considered the opposite approach? Give him real responsibility, a seat in your council. Perhaps he wishes to emulate you and has no idea how to manage it."

Hearing that brought Bethune upright again. "Now that makes sense. Then I could keep a close eye on him while hopefully shaping him into a man worthy of our name. I'll consider it. Well done." With that load removed from his mind, Rosny seemed ready to take on another. "Give me all of the particulars about this plot you've stumbled onto. It sounds similar to some other schemes I've heard about, but there are some disturbing twists."

Taking care to keep Abandonée's involvement, even her existence, hidden for now, Treville outlined what had taken place since he had last sat in Rosny's office. His tale was mostly true, with a few creative flourishes. It did permit Treville to organize the situation in his own mind. D'Artagnan had been targeted by unscrupulous friends of the young Béthune and manipulated into a duel, with the object of luring Treville in as his second and dispatching them both by treachery. When that failed they had employed a secondary stratagem of having the Maréchaussée kill them during a supposed arrest. Again the king's men had managed to escape. At d'Artagnan's residence more men had appeared to do them harm. But those scoundrels appeared to be unaffiliated with the other groups. They had been sent packing. Treville had carefully examined the records that Rosny had given them and decided that contacting Krijger in Amsterdam was their best choice, particularly after interrogating the wounded sharpshooter whom they had been fortunate enough to capture. Alas, the fellow had expired and was not able to be subjected to the Marquis' own questioners. Before succumbing to his wounds, however, he had confirmed Rosny's own intelligence about a disturbing and wide-ranging conspiracy to unsettle Europe with a *coup de main*. Apparently it involved skilled marksmen and men of the blade from many nations. The clues all pointed to the Netherlands as the staging area for the plot, which seemed to have a religious odor.

Rosny listened as he always did, with the focus of a predator stalking a kill. Occasionally he nodded or frowned, but in general he let Treville tell his story as he wished. When his man had finished he settled back in the chair again, a sour expression clouding his face. "This is deeply troubling, of course. Did you get any impression that my son knew of the wider implications of what he was doing?"

Treading carefully, Treville labored to put the best possible face on things for the troubled father. "Difficult to say, m'lord. Having never met him before, I would have trouble saying with certainty that he was apprised of the full details of this conspiracy. Perhaps he had merely been duped into provoking the duel by some unscrupulous agent who knew that he could be seduced by the thought of tweaking your nose." That was a charitable lie. Treville had seen that Bethune had known precisely what was going on, had clearly given orders to the musketmen. But the father need not know that yet. Better that the son hang himself than Treville be the one with the rope.

"Well, I need to know. He may be my son but France is my mother. If it comes down to a choice between them..."

"Understood. I will undertake to discover the identities of all the ringleaders. If he is truly among them, I will not spare your feelings."

"That's as it should be. If there's rot in my corps, I need to cut it out."

"I agree. And rot there is, plainly."

"How so?"

"Too many well-armed people keep appearing to dispatch me, with entirely too much convenience for their ambitions. I am more than usually competent at spotting a pursuer, yet still these men are always waiting for me and d'Artagnan. In Ostend. The false duel this morning. Then at d'Artagnan's place after that."

"Someone in the Louvre is reading my mail, so to speak?"

"You did consider that likely when last we spoke."

"True. But I haven't had time to run any rats to their nests. That will be my priority this afternoon while you're preparing for your jaunt to Holland. I have a few likely ---"

He interrupted himself to glower past Treville to d'Artagnan's chair. It was empty.

Treville shrugged. "Probably looking for a commode. But I'd better find him before he gets into trouble. Though generally it finds him first."

With a bow he took his leave of Rosny and went into the forty-foot-wide hall. D'Artagnan was not in sight, though a few paces to the left Concini, wearing a red leather doublet with black lace, was exiting from a narrow panel that served as door to a tiny convenience room. When he saw Treville he made a small, startled jerking motion that he instantly transformed into an oily courtier's nod to a presumed inferior. The overdressed Italian wore a look on his twisting lip that advertised entirely too much careless charm. He closed the door and strolled away, spurred boot heels snapping and ringing on the tile floor, as if he had just won the Louvre in a dice game.

Suspicion clanged in Treville's mind, the very thing that Leonora Dori's husband no doubt hoped would not happen. But Treville had not been plucked from obscurity to be one of the Forty-Five, and its preeminent spy, on a whim. After waiting for Concini to vanish around a distant corner, Treville popped into the privy to see what the plotter might have been up to.

He had hoped when he began his search that the missing d'Artagnan might have been there, though that was clearly impossible since Concini had already occupied it. Perhaps his friend had found it locked and was hunting for relief further afield. Other than near Rosny's office and the king's private quarters, the Louvre reeked of urine and worse. Courtiers and soldiers tended to take care of their business in any convenient corner.

At any rate, Treville's suspicions were aroused enough that he opened the door with care. The nook was so small that he could stretch out his arms and touch both brocaded walls. It was no more than ten feet deep. Covering the floor was a fine red Turkish carpet. At the far end sat, beneath a small window that provided the only light, sat a polished oaken close stool. Beside it on a little table was a chinaware basin filled with rose water and a stack of soft cloths. As spots for answering the call of nature went, it was most royal, befitting the locale. A pungent stink of ammonia pinched his nose. Treville had smelled much worse, though, be it army sinks or fetid holes in African taverns. Locking the door, he gave the place a thorough inspection.

His work was rewarded almost immediately. In two different places – beneath a loose board under the carpet and behind a cleverly-made false decorative panel in the wall – he discovered messages. The former was in a masculine hand and was written in cipher, while the latter had been penned by a woman in plain French. While the code would have to wait for some patient attention, the wall message seemed clear enough. 'Behind the Luxembourg at sunset; wear a white feather.' Instructions for a rendezvous.

Having been lucky twice, he hardly dared hope for more. But that was precisely what happened. Experience had taught him to look in the place least attractive to a searcher. So, after exhausting all other surfaces, Treville lifted the stool's lid and felt under the rim. He nearly expired from the stench, but such was the price of serving one's country. Just as he was about to admit that he was wasting his time in a disgusting effort, his fingers struck something that should not have been there.

A small funnel. And suspiciously clean.

With a frown he tugged at it until it came free. It weighed more than it should have and was difficult to pull out. When he managed to get it into view he saw why. It was attached to a leather tube the diameter of his thumb that ran down into the stool and beneath the floor. He put the funnel to his ear. Bethune's voice could be heard in the room Treville had just left, giving instructions to one of his secretaries about finding the spy in their midst.

"Bugger me," Treville muttered.

His first thought was to tear the thing loose and present it to his master. But he caught himself before committing that error. Far better to leave it in place and see who used it and why. The same applied to the pair of notes. He would copy them and then return them to their places so that no one knew that the treasons, if such they were, had been discovered. This incredible bounty of intelligence had to be exploited.

Treville rinsed his hands in the basin, tucked the notes into his breeches pocket, and snuck out of the room, making certain that no one saw him leave. He proceeded down the hall in the same direction that Concini had gone, hoping to find d'Artagnan. Not for the first time did he marvel at his place of work. The vaulted ceilings were so high that a fall from them would prove fatal. Enormous windows of Venetian glass, installed at mind-boggling expense, ran the length of the corridor and nearly up to that curved height. Sunlight made every surface gleam and warmed the air almost to the point of discomfort. Everywhere bas reliefs and free-standing statues proclaimed the glory of French artists. King Henri was determined to not only unify his broken nation but to make it a force to be reckoned with in all arenas.

Most of the doors he passed were closed, silence reigning behind them. Enough intrigue lived in the Louvre, both the officially-permitted kind and the illicit sort, that those who lived or worked there made caution a habit. That made Treville's discovery of three clear signs of spying – three! – in a single jakes even more remarkable. He had a good mind to search every comfort closet in the palace.

He turned the same corner that Concini had and found himself on a great stair at the intersection of two wings of the palace. So awe-inspiring and ornate that Heaven itself might have envied them, he half-expected to see angels floating up and down the white stone steps. Unlike Rosny's hall, this place was busy with all the traffic of a great palace and government center. Soldiers, clerks, various departmental functionaries, ladies of the court, and numerous job-seekers made their way to appointments. Treville imagined them to be a hive of splendidly-overdressed bees. Velvets, brocades, leathers, gold chains, glinting gems, and intricately-hilted rapiers caught the eye. But Treville's gaze went directly to three figures in plainer garb, chiefly because they were not moving. They stood on a landing in the center of the commotion, leaning against the balustrade while keeping watch on all who passed. Their languid manner betrayed a keen professional observation, for they were fellow members of the Forty-Five.

"Careful," Treville said to them with a smirk, "if you don't move every now and then someone'll mistake you for the statuary."

Gaston, the tallest, wearing a garish silver-trimmed green leather doublet and an enormous black moustache that matched his love of high living, not to mention his great Gallic nose, barely moved his head to acknowledge his comrade's presence. Many birds had given their lives for the explosion of plumage in his broad-brimmed hat. "Oh, look, it's the Marquis' pet. When you tire of kissing his upholstered backside, you might try doing your actual job and guard our king for a while."

"Why, when you're clearly doing such a tremendous job of it all by yourself?"

"True, we haven't foiled an assassination plot in nearly two weeks." He addressed the shorter man to his left. "About to expire of ennui, aren't we, Antoine?"

The elegant Antoine, who dressed like a minor prince in gold and black velvet stripes and seemed almost too fragile to be an elite royal guard, stroked his pointed blonde chin beard and nodded. "I'm getting entirely too much sleep standing here. I'll toss and turn all night." He had once trained to be a priest. At his throat was a gold cross worth half a year of his salary. Another almost as expensive adorned his flat cap.

Beside him, the glum Louis sighed. Older than the others, his dark full-bearded face Despite his rough appearance, he really was an aristocrat. Some unfortunate incident back home had led him to abandon his lands for the life of a soldier. Now he dressed and groomed carelessly in well-worn, faded leather and dueled at the slightest provocation, as if eager to leave the world. "Toss and turn you may," he muttered with a rumbling voice, "but it won't be from too much rest. More likely your bed will have too many occupants."

"Envy doesn't become you, Lou-Lou."

"And the pox doesn't become you."

"Gentlemen," laughed Treville, "if I might interrupt before you cross blades…" He knew that they were all actually the best of friends and that the only stabbing they were likely to indulge in would be of the king's enemies. Around the palace they were known as Les Épuisants, the Exhausting Ones, and a fiercer and more loyal group of rascals would be difficult to find.

"Looking for your stray pup?" Gaston asked.

"Among other things. He came by here?"

"Everyone comes by here. Do you think we lounge about on the stairs merely to elevate the tone of this establishment?"

"Well, it is sadly in need of elevating. Such a shabby building."

Antoine snickered. "A squalid hovel."

"Only a few hundred rooms," Louis added. "Shameful."

Treville held up a hand. "Now that we're in agreement that your glorious presence is required to save the state from architectural humiliation…which way did d'Artagnan go?"

Gaston aimed his prominent nose up. "That way. He was following the Vice-Queen like he was one of her little spaniels."

Most of the guards called the Marquise de Verneuil the Vice-Queen or something even less respectful, as if she held an actual government post. Not in the king's hearing, of course. He might currently be having a tiff with his mistress, but that did not mean that he would tolerate his troops disparaging her.

The news, while not surprising, made Treville pound a fist into his palm. "Damnation! That brainless fool will get himself drawn and quartered before he's twenty."

"Well, if one has to die for one's country, that beats being blown to bits in a Spanish trench," Antoine observed.

"I'd better drag him away from her. Sad to say, I need him for actual serious business." Treville started to climb the immense stair, then turned back to them. "While I have you here…I found some astounding things in Rosny's comfort closet just now."

"Ah, you pet spies!" Gaston exclaimed in mock envy. "Always snagging the glamorous jobs for yourselves."

"It's not all romancing foreign temptresses, you know. Sometimes you get to rummage about in piles of royal shit." He made a point of clapping his friend on the shoulder as he spoke.

Gaston seized the wrist and pulled the hand away from his expensive sleeve with two fingers. "I do hope you washed up afterward."

Louis, always the serious one, asked in a quiet voice, "What did you find?"

Treville had them gather around to shield the documents from spying eyes. He showed them the brief assignation note first. They all agreed that it was clearly in a woman's hand, though just which woman was anyone's guess. The palace was entirely too full of likely candidates. While they debated her identity Antoine snatched the paper from Treville's hand and sniffed it like a hunting hound.

"Rose…lily…something musky…hint of orange." He held the paper up to the light, squinted at it, then rubbed it between thumb and forefinger. "Royal paper, but not quite the best. Most probably the queen's maid."

Stuffing it back into his pocket, Treville shrugged. "I'd already suspected as much, since I saw her snake of a husband slink out of the room moments before I found this. Doing her errands. But thanks for the display of cleverness. One does wonder how you came to have Madame Dori's scent up your nose so well that you had it memorized."

"A magician never revels his secrets. But you, however, are here to do just that. Show us the other one."

They peered at the coded message, which was rather more to their taste than perfumed love notes. It was written in a blunt soldierly style, just the opposite of the other, in block letters that gave little hint of anyone's handwriting. The paper was the common barracks type. And the only detectable scent was the lingering pungency of the place where it had been found. No attempt at disguising its nature had been made, since the document had been hidden and not meant to fool a casual observer. All the letters, which seemed to be random gibberish, were arranged in careful rows. In fact, faint lines could be seen where a grid had been laid in with some sort of stylus. Two dozen rows up and across, it contained hundreds of letters.

"Well, that'll be a treat to crack," laughed Gaston. "Lay in plenty of meat and wine. You'll be at the table for days."

Louis asked, "A tough nut. You say you found this in that little necessarium next to the Marquis' office?"

"That I did," replied Treville, stowing the paper back in his pocket. "In a neat cubbyhole under the carpet. The lady's invitation was in the wall."

"Popular place for mischief," Antoine chuckled.

They all looked at him, waiting for an explanation. "Do tell," Gaston prodded.

"Actually, don't tell," said Treville. "I don't want the image of one of your sordid amours to interfere with my elimination the next time I'm in there on business."

Antoine gave them all a sad head shake. "Your salacious imaginations are all too predictable. I'll have you know that I don't carry on my amours in such places. What I mean about mischief is that a great many plots seem to be hatched there, if my observations about who goes in and out are any indication."

"Such as?"

"You've seen that Signor Concini frequents it. One of the more overt schemers here, and clumsy, to boot. Thinks he should be a great lord of France. I haven't determined if his wife is pushing him or if he's merely a specimen of that odious sort of bored husband who looks for something to set him above his successful wife."

"And Madame Dori?"

"She's been in there with him, of course, but also with Doctor Montalto and once with the Duc du Épernon himself."

Treville's eyes widened. He had overlooked the possibility that the scheming former enemy of the king, a fiery Catholic through-and-through, might be a force in all of this. But the courtier had once been caught plotting with Spain against his own nation. "Erpernon? The Admiral of France? Seriously?"

"As I live and breathe. Amazed me, too. Normally he prefers to run his treasonous affairs via intermediaries. Whatever he was discussing must have been so sensitive that he dared not trust it to a lackey."

"How do you know all of this? Do you make it a habit to linger about Rosny's commode closet?"

"No, but after I stumbled upon a couple of suspicious rendezvous and learned of several more, I set up a rotating squad of women disguised as cleaning staff to do the lingering. No one pays attention to servants. They say the most indiscrete things around them, as if they are dumb animals. I receive regular reports."

"The Marquis gets those reports, of course?"

"Absolutely. Has he not mentioned them to you?"

"Not that I recall. But the subject will most decidedly come up in a few minutes when I show him these letters. And when I inform him of the third bauble I picked up in there."

"Third?" exclaimed Louis. "Does anyone actually go in there merely to void himself?"

"Apparently not." Treville told them about the eavesdropping tube secreted in the close stool and how it made every word near Rosny's desk audible. His friends giggled at the news.

"Beats reading the Bible while you're sitting, I suppose," Gaston said.

"Any idea how long it might have been there?" asked Louis.

Treville shrugged. "None. But it looked new. No wear or grime on it."

"Fairly simple to discover who put it there," mused Antoine.

"Start feeding false information from the office and see who reacts? That had already occurred to me. Used in conjunction with your spies, it won't take long. Can I depend upon you all to be behind the Luxembourg at sunset tonight? I have to prepare for a trip to Amsterdam and have too much else to do."

Gaston rubbed his hands together. "We'll acquire some white feathers and attend the ball."

"Excellent. Try not to kill anyone. This requires stealth, not a brawl."

"Yes, we heard all about your splendid use of stealth at the cemetery. Quite the role model, you are."

Treville lazily saluted them as he mounted the stairs in search of d'Artagnan, unwilling to let them ensnare him into any more conversation. That Gaston could talk the ears off a donkey and the boy had already been missing long enough to get into great trouble in so sensitive a place. His whereabouts were surprisingly easy to determine, for the second door that Treville tried turned out to be a small geographical reference library. He just had time to make note of the impressive globe and the atlases chained to the shelves when he saw the queen's personal maid, Leonora Dori, lying on her back on the floor. She moaned and cried and twisted her body.

D'Artagnan lay directly on top of her, pinning her arms down.

11

THE LOUVRE

"STAND ASIDE AND LET ME BALANCE HER HUMOURS."

Cursing himself for having wasted so much time with the Épuisants that he had let this happen, Treville pounced upon d'Artagnan with a growl. He seized the young fellow by the scruff of the neck and hurled him across the library, where he clung to the great globe with an astonished and hurt expression.

"What are you doing?" the Gascon demanded.

"What are **you** doing?" Treville echoed with some heat, anger reddening his face.

"Trying to help a lady in distress!"

Treville turned to point at her. "The only distress she's in is from you taking advantage ---"

Amazement choked off his words. Madame Dori – Madame Concini, to be precise – had not ceased her animal-like noises and thrashings. Foam bubbled up from her lips. Her eyes rolled up until only the whites showed. Fists clenched, drawing blood in the palms. She arched her back until only head and heels touched the floor.

D'Artagnan recovered himself and approached her again. "She's having one of her fits. I was trying to settle her so she didn't do herself an injury."

"What did you do to set her off?"

"Nothing. I was twenty feet away from her, talking to the Marquise, and she started shaking and frothing. Speaking like some ancient oracle. Then down she went." He knelt beside her and pushed her shoulders down. "Something for her head?"

Treville glanced about, spied a small pillow on a divan, and brought it to the tormented woman. He slid it beneath her skull and helped d'Artagnan to restrain her. Though small and slender, the Italian lady nearly bucked them off like an unbroken horse. Beneath her green silk dress, muscles of iron flexed. When he tried to uncurl her fingers, he found himself unable to manage it.

"I'd thought she was pretending somehow, to distract you or gain some advantage, but clearly not."

"That occurred to me, too, until the fit went on and on and she started foaming like a rabid hound. Court gossip did tell of this. I never believed it."

"I think she's beginning to come out of it."

Dori's passion was, indeed, starting to subside, though slowly. Treville could feel the granite sinews beneath his hands softening a bit. He took the opportunity to gather more intelligence before she came back to her senses. "She spoke as the attack took hold? What did she say?"

"Gibberish. Sounded like 'il leo…nay…um, intra…po..larcy mol…lay in aut…unno.' Is that even a language? Latin, maybe?"

A deep foreign voice spoke from the door, making them start. "Not Latin. Italian." Concini approached them, towing Dr. Montalto behind him. "When God grips her soul, babyish syllables from childhood often leak out, squeezed from her mind like dishwater from a sponge. I used to write them down, believing them to be prophecy. But they are nothing." D'Artagnan moved aside so that the husband could kneel in his place and caress the distraught woman's cheek. As much as Treville loathed the man, thinking him a traitorous schemer and an enemy of the state, he was impressed by the touching sincerity of the gesture. For that moment, at any rate, politics was forgotten.

Treville surrendered his own spot to the doctor, and for several moments they attended to the stricken Dori. The fighting men retreated to a corner near the globe, where the eldest upbraided his cadet.

"Are you mad, pursuing the Marquise? I see only the one empty head on your shoulders. You have none to spare."

D'Artagnan looked hurt at the impugning of his judgment. "I wasn't pursuing her."

"Then how did you come to be alone here with her?"

"Alone? That poor lady was with us the whole time."

"And hardly in her right wits."

"She was perfectly sensible until the moment she fell down."

"And what happened to the king's mistress?"

"Ran to get help. How do you think the doctor and her husband happened to appear?"

With a sigh, Treville waved that aside. "How did this conversation, if that's what it was, come about? And what was the topic?"

"I was looking for a comfort room. The one next to Rosny's office was locked. They frown on us soiling the palace floors, you know, though the ones wearing velvet do so with glee. Those three poseurs on the landing sent me up here, said I'd find relief on the next floor. I did, and just in time, too. But two steps out of the room Madame Dori snagged my sleeve and asked me to step into the library to hear something to my advantage. No sooner was the door shut than the Marquise de Verneuil appeared from behind the shelves."

"And did you, in fact, hear something to your advantage?"

"Hardly. They wanted me to turn spy."

"Bloody hell! Spy on whom?"

"You, of course. And Rosny. And to generally keep my ears open when around anybody important."

"Well, this is just delightful. How much were they offering for this duty?"

"Enough to buy my parents' house in Pau ten times over."

"Amateurs. They tipped their hand. That was far too much. Now we know that something big is afoot. What was your reply to this munificence?"

"Why, I agreed, of course."

Treville boxed the lad's ear and grinned. "That was precisely the right thing. Now we have an agent in their camp."

Though rubbing his aching ear, d'Artagnan basked in the praise. "So I thought. But what do I do with the down payment they gave me?" He hefted a clinking leather pouch.

"Give it to the church. Rescue orphans. Found a hospital." Treville snapped his fingers. "But before you do any of that, get yourself a decent place to live. I refuse to visit that abomination again."

"That makes two of us."

At that moment, the door opened and the Queen of France entered.

Accompanying her were several of her court ladies, the royal astrologer, and the Épuisants. The latter had obviously been pressed into service in case their particular skills might be needed in the emergency. Everyone in the room bowed in the automatic reflex of any European palace. Even the two men on their knees ministering to Leonora Dori dipped their heads as they worked. Treville did not lower his own so far that he could not keep an eye on the room. Marie was a vision in green and gold brocade with pearls and emeralds, and her attending ladies were only slightly less resplendent. Concern for her maid and confidant knitted the queen's brow. Lurking in the doorway but proceeding no further, the lovely Marquise du Verneuil also wore a worried look, but hers seemed to have more layers of complexity to it. D'Artagnan made a happy purring sound when he spotted her, which earned him a sharp elbow in the ribs from Treville.

At a gesture from Marie, the astrologer – the splendidly-named Cosmo Alabastro – moved forward to assist in treating Dori. He was the archetype of his breed: an alchemist and planetary seer in a floor-length black robe, matching skullcap, a white ruff the size of a wagon wheel, and waist-long gray beard. Brass-framed spectacles, hinged at the center, hung atop the bridge of his very Gallic nose. Everything about him was calculated to radiate wisdom and powerful learning. The only person in the library who remained unconvinced of this was Dr. Montalto, who fairly sneered as he approached.

"Leave her be," the physician warned, blocking access to his patient as if the alchemist held a dagger. "Your false science can do her no good."

Alabastro continued as if the other had not spoken. "She suffers from delusions and tormenting visions." He held out a smooth stone that resembled veined jade. "This green jasper shall ---"

"---Shall do nothing! Stand aside and let me balance her humours."

"Humours! Surely you can't be serious. This is the modern age."

Concini could endure no more. "Gentlemen, stop! She shall recover in a few minutes without the dubious aid of either of you." He addressed the queen. "Your Majesty, my apologies, but your sages have never cured her before."

Marie seemed about to insist, then looked at Dori again and relented. "As you wish, Signor. Everyone, get her onto this divan, please."

The men of the Forty-Five, glad to have a task that required only strong backs, leaped to it. While they were carrying her to the makeshift bed, the queen took Concini aside for a private conference. Always on the lookout for intelligence, Treville slid into the stacks of books to eavesdrop.

"Did she say anything, do you know?" asked Marie with an interest beyond the merely medical. "We must be on our guard."

"I confess that I was not here, my lady. But the cadet there claims that she did." He repeated the sounds that d'Artagnan had heard.

Marie pursed her lips as she turned the phrases over in her mind. "Enigmatic, as always. We almost need a new Delphic oracle to untangle that. What does the lion represent? Have you any idea?"

Just as Concini was about to speak to that, Treville's arm brushed against one of the chains tethering a volume to the shelf that he hid behind. The Italian caught the whispered tinkling and held up a palm to the queen. "I shall give it thought and report to you later today. Right now I should be with my wife. This…visitation…was particularly stressful."

"Of course. Selfish of me. By all means, remain with her. Need you anything else?"

"No, Your Majesty. Once she is entirely herself I shall take her to our rooms."

"As you think best. Do not hesitate to call upon anything that I can provide." She raised her voice into that soft but imperious tone that only royalty, generals, and schoolteachers could command. "The rest of us shall all withdraw." When everyone hastened to obey, she moved to the door, telling Louis to leave a man on guard in case the lady relapsed.

While bowing again, Treville saw that the Marquise had vanished. He had intended to linger, but Marie turned in the hall and made sure that he and d'Artagnan left the room. Accepting that his hand was forced this time, he departed with head high, reminding her that he was one of the Forty-Five. It did not escape him that the Maréchaussée was her puppet and that she had possibly given the order for Colére's bit of attempted murder in the cemetery. He had no power then to do more than display some pride as he passed her, but he intended to get to the bottom of the mess upon returning from Holland. If the queen were intriguing against her husband, Treville would not flinch from reporting it to him.

All that could be done at that moment, however, was to report to Rosny instead, informing him of all that had happened in the busy hour since he had left his master's office. After giving him a detailed accounting and displaying the secreted documents, Treville received a satisfied smile that made him feel as favored as an archangel. Both papers were copied and returned to their hiding places, where hopefully the authors would be none the wiser about the discovery. Code-breakers would get to work on the cipher immediately. Leonora's mystical babblings were written down, as well, for Rosny's experts to ponder. That left only one bit of business.

After replacing the messages in the wall and beneath the floor of the comfort room, Treville opened the close stool again and seized the little funnel. He pushed and pulled it with some force, hoping to rattle it at the other end. When he heard the triumphant voice of d'Artagnan come through the tube, he tucked it away and returned to the office. There he found his partner standing on a chair beside the fireplace, fiddling with a bit of decorative plasterwork.

"Come look!" d'Artagnan urged. "This is cleverly done."

Treville replaced him on the chair and examined the white floral design. He saw that it was not plaster at all, but starched and sculpted gauze, a cunning replacement. Though seemingly solid, it was quite porous. Behind it a funnel, larger than the one in the close stool, captured conversations in the office and sent them via the leather tube to a listener in the comfort room.

"You can't help but admire this," he declared, "criminal though it be."

"It actually works?"

"Oh, yes. I heard your voice on the other end." Treville climbed back down and peered at the wall. "Who has access to this office, my lord?"

"No one but I," Béthune assured him.

"Truly? How is it cleaned? What guards check it on their nightly rounds?"

"I have one key and the Captain of the Guard has the other. It remains around his neck at all times."

"We'll have to investigate that. Men have been suborned by gold, religion, or silky skin before."

"I trust Captain Honnête with my life."

"I don't doubt that, but stranger things have happened. There is also the possibility that somehow it was copied without his knowledge, while sleeping or bathing. Some thieves are magicians that way."

D'Artagnan slid behind the desk to the corner panel, just left of the offending faux flower. Pushing it open to reveal the secret passage that King Henri had used to flee his ladies, he said, "Or some magician knows about this."

"Impossible!" Rosny insisted, though his expression was not nearly so confidant. "That leads directly to the king's bedchamber."

"And who has access to that?"

The Marquis du Rosny sagged, then slumped into his chair. His words held almost comical measures of despair and doom. "Half of the women in France."

12

THE VEXIN

"LE COUP, YOU ARE A DIABOLICAL GENIUS!"

"I hate this!" Abandonée complained from the wagon, loudly enough that she might have been heard in Rome.

"Hate it all you want," said Treville, "you'll dress like a proper woman for the duration of this trip."

She swore like the rudest of sailors and tugged at the tight ruff around her slender throat. "I'd rather be in the Bastille."

"Easily arranged. I did give you the choice."

Her rude male garments had been replaced by the sort of dress that a traveling woman of business would wear. A chestnut brown sleeveless bodice over a white shift, a matching wool shirt with a padded hip roll, and wide straw hat proclaimed her a respectable young lady of modest means but no peasant. Her male companions were similarly attired as of the same class, to pass as family escorts accompanying her on a long market journey.

Abandonée was not done grousing. Her fingers poked at her ribs. "Whoever invented stays should be drawn and quartered. I volunteer to do him that honor personally."

D'Artagnan laughed from his horse as he rode beside her. "So sensitive! How did you manage to live rough on the streets all of that time?"

"Sleeping in ditches is a downy delight compared to this."

They were ten leagues north and west of Paris, on the road to Le Havre. All about them was the glory that was the Vexin region, site of much bloodshed between the French and English in days past, as it was the route from Paris to England's Channel ports. On their left ran the Seine River, with some attractive hills overlooking it. To the right lush fields and forests rolled. The trees had few buds yet, but to judge by the warm weather and fresh smell of the air, spring was decidedly in the offing. Behind them lay Pontoise, the splendid town and ancient capital of the Vexin, where they had spent the night – taking turns keeping heavily-armed watch at their inn -- after departing Paris the day before. Still visible in the distance was the flamboyant tower of the Church of Saint-Maclou. For practice, in a test of their disguises, they had sold their bolts of wool and linen at the market in front of the church, using the nom de guerres they had jokingly come up with in d'Artagnan's room. It had gone well enough, despite Chipay's exotic appearance attracting attention and Abandonée's inability to stop fussing with her hated clothes.

Their pretense was that they were a family of mercers, cousins from Paris who had taken over the business after a fever had carried off all their parents. Resolved to see something of the world before settling down in their shop, they were headed to Rouen and Le Havre, then by ship to Holland, England, and perhaps even Germany. The canvas-topped wagon was full of their wares, all manner of cloth, mostly expensive. In hidden compartments in the side it also contained enough weapons and other war gear to fend off attack by a determined regiment.

It had taken some doing to get out of Paris without being obvious. The Louvre had turned into a madhouse with Treville's comfort room revelations. Such things were impossible to keep completely secret, particularly when Rosny's agents began poking into the darker corners in their hunt for code-writing spies and clever eavesdroppers. When esteemed ladies of the court were questioned about the Luxembourg assignation note, the lid had truly come off. Queen Marie threw an inkwell at Rosny himself for daring to suspect her coterie of disloyalty.

Blissfully unaware of all of that, Treville's group had spent the rest of the week sequestered in his rooms, firming up their travel plan and preparing for the inevitable cock-ups. Again and again they had gone over likely scenarios, establishing contingencies and rally points in the event something went wrong. Out of Abandonée's hearing they also decided what to do if she proved to be an enemy, after all. Despite having a certain amount of confidence in her, he dared not entirely trust himself to someone who could well turn out to be a clever double-agent.

It was not until Treville had visited a secluded corner of the Bastille that he learned of all the palace uproar. His armorer, a mysterious little bald fellow who called himself Le Coup, shared the gossip while explaining the workings of a couple of new toys that he had just built for Treville.

"Truly, sir, the king was nearly as outraged as the queen at the interrogation of the ladies. Granted, for different reasons. They say he, er, talks in his sleep."

"That would be a concern," Treville admitted, examining the new rapier on the workbench. He wondered if Rosny had been forced to rent a theatre to hold all the women with access to the king's bedchamber and thus the passage to Bethune's office. "How does this one work?"

"Ah, simplicity itself. Merely twist the pommel, give it a sharp tug, and voila!"

Treville did as instructed and was gratified to see a wicked little stiletto in his hand.

"Le Coup, you are a diabolical genius!"

The armorer feigned embarrassment. "The gentleman flatters me."

"Give me more reason to. What else have you? The caltrops worked perfectly, by the way."

"I am gratified to hear it. This item may be of some service."

Le Coup produced a large door key. At a distance it was unremarkable save for its size. It might have been the key to the Louvre's front door. When Treville brought it close, however, he cackled in amazement. Its shaft was hollow and near the bow were a tiny flint and trigger.

"It's a bloody pistol! How did you ever manage to make it so small?"

"With much patience and even more profanity." Le Coup pointed to a complicated device that held an enormous lens. "The new equipment from the king helped. He is greatly devoted to the sciences."

"You amaze me. Dare I ask for more?"

"I am pleased to say yes." Le Coup handed him a length of stiff wire.

"What's this for? A garrote? I have several already."

"Nothing so murderous. The wire has bits of diamond in it."

"So it's an expensive garrote. I still don't –aha! A secret saw!"

"Correct. In tests it cut through an iron bar thicker than your thumb."

Treville wrapped it around the crown of his brimmed hat, tucking it beneath the band until it was invisible. "I almost hope I am captured, so that I may try it out."

"Please do not, sir. I would miss our little chats if anything untoward happened to you."

"And you'd miss the money I lavish on you even more, you rascal."

As they rode through the Vexin, Treville reached up to make sure that the wire-saw was still in place on his hat. Le Coup had favored him with one or two other items besides the rapier and key. To his right Chipay drove the wagon, with the grumpy Abandonée beside him. The Canadian native obviously could be no relation to them, so he wore a priest's vestments and some clever eye makeup so that he could pass to the casual observer as a convert from the East Indies. He told the curious that he had been taken aboard a Dutch ship as a child and reared as a citizen of Amsterdam, which was closer to the truth than not. Abandoning his pagan island beliefs for those of the One True Church, he had moved to France, the Catholic faith being in bad odor in Holland. Desiring to see friends there, he had undertaken to act as wagoneer and guide to the young people on their first long journey.

Treville and d'Artagnan rode on either side of the wagon, occasionally cantering ahead to scout the way, as bandits were thick as flies on manure along the old Roman road. The horses were not the splendid mounts worthy of the king's men, as those would attract attention, but were serviceable enough. Their swords were stowed with the wares, as splendid rapiers would hardly be part of a salesman's equipage. But tucked into their saddlebags were a brace of pistols each, to give a warm welcome to any thieves who might accost them. They were getting into a more wooded stretch than any they had yet encountered, with many corners and hillocks for cover, and the enemy's love of sharpshooters loomed large in Treville's worried mind.

A whistle from Fantôme alerted him to potential trouble ahead. The wagon rumbled to a stop. Perhaps a bowshot to the front, a farm cart lay on its side, one wheel still spinning. Its horse had not fallen, but was too alarmed to help right the cart. Its owner, a woman, was trying to calm the frantic beast so that it would do no more damage.

D'Artagnan turned back to Treville. "Should I go see?"

Treville waved him ahead, but he did not like the situation. It was too convenient for trouble. "Yes, but be prepared for an attack. Don't let any pretty faces distract you. And be sure to only use our travel names." He reached into one saddlebag and cocked a pistol, keeping it hidden. Behind him, Chipay did the same with the blunderbuss beneath his seat. In case the entire scene was a distraction so that they could be flanked, Abandonée twisted so that she could watch the rear. In a mere moment she could dive into the back of the wagon and snatch up her marvelous musket if an assault came from that direction.

Assuming his guise as a helpful young merchant traveler, d'Artagnan approached the scene at a walk while Treville carefully scanned the wood line for trouble. When he drew near, the Gascon saw that the frightened horse was one of the most pitiful specimens ever seen. It was as yellow as a buttercup, with a nearly hairless tail, and was older than d'Artagnan. How it had managed to pull the cart more than half a league was a mystery.

"Good morning, madame," he said with a touch of his hand to his hat brim. "Nasty accident. May I be of service?"

"That you may, young man," came the reply from the stocky red-faced woman of middle age. Her low hoarse voice carried alarm and worry. "My son's caught under the cart."

A glance confirmed that this was true. The fellow's head and shoulders jutted out from beneath the vehicle. He moaned in pain, as anyone would in such a situation. A bit past d'Artagnan's age, he had black hair and a sparse beard.

"Fool horse shied at nothin'," explained the mother. "We take this same route every week without a problem, but today…"

"We shall get him free, fret not," d'Artagnan assured her. "No good Christian could do less, Madame…?'

"Forgeron. That there's Jacques, my youngest. Bless you, kind sir."

"The name's Temeraire. And it's my pleasure."

D'Artagnan was eager to help, but not completely a fool. He dismounted, inspected the cart and its surroundings, and made certain that no fatal surprises were in the offing. When he saw no weapons, hidden confederates, or ambushers in the trees, he waved for Treville to approach. "We'll need help to get it off him. My cousin Penseur has a strong back."

When Treville cantered up to him, d'Artagnan quickly summarized the situation and said that it looked safe enough. No obvious traps awaited. They had reason to be wary. False accidents were a favorite ruse of bandits in the Vexin. While a good Samaritan was busy giving aid, those supposedly suffering would fall upon him with their hidden confederates. Once he had made his own survey of things, Treville nodded and motioned for Chipay to come up with their wagon. He preferred to have all of them together for this, no matter how innocuous things appeared.

While the other vehicle approached, he slid from his horse and knelt beside the unfortunate Jacques to assess his condition. A bit of blood bubbled from the victim's mouth and his groans grew louder. "We'll soon have you free of this. Can you feel your legs?"

"Yes, sir," he muttered through clenched teeth, "though they do tingle some."

"And you can breathe well enough?"

"So far. I landed in a hole, so the full weight isn't on me. But it still hurts like the devil." He ceased speaking and roared through clenched teeth.

"Stay strong, lad. You'll be out in a trice."

Fantôme hopped nimbly from the wagon, much as he must have negotiated forest obstacles in his native land, and held his hand out to assist Abandonée in getting down. Her cumbersome clothes much impeded her normal ease of motion. But d'Artagnan had anticipated him and was already there, lifting her down by her slender waist. They remained in that position even after her feet had reached the earth, prompting Treville to sigh and remind his partner that a man was in distress. With sheepish looks they hastened to the wrecked cart.

The men all put their shoulders to it, heaving with a long mutual shout until Abandonée could drag the whimpering Jacques out from under. His mother cheered and cried. Having calmed the horse enough to tie it to a tree, she dashed to her injured son and covered him with kisses.

"Bless you, monsieurs! And mademoiselle. The good Lord surely sent you to us this day."

"Happy to be of service," Treville said, already looking to get his people back on the wagon and through the woods before anything else untoward could happen. "Let's get your cart all of the way back up and you can be on your way again."

The five of them managed that feat easily. As the ridiculous old horse proved to be uninjured and amenable to pulling it home, all seemed to be well. But when Jacques tried to stand and get into the cart again, he gave a sharp cry and bent over, arms across his belly, blood gushing from his mouth. Clearly he had damaged something inside him. Fantôme examined him, marked his reactions to prodding, and announced that he would have to be taken back to Pontoise. He might die without a physician's care.

Treville cursed under his breath. More time lost. But there was nothing for it but to escort them back to town. Fortunately, it was not far, perhaps an hour. Once Jacques was in a doctor's care they could resume their journey. His mother sat beside him in their cart, which d'Artagnan drove, his horse tied behind it. Fantôme resumed his duties as driver of his wagon again, leading the other vehicle back from whence they had come. Bringing up the rear, Treville kept twisting in his saddle to ensure that no one followed or prepared an ambush from the woods.

No attack came. They cleared the forest and entered the safer geography of open fields. Farmers and shepherds worked there, but none turned out to be disguised murderers, intent on interfering with Treville's mission. Likewise, no one in the outskirts of Pontoise assailed them. Everyone they passed smiled, nodded, and bid them good day. The town was an old place on the River Oise, full of timbered houses and some pale stone structures. Its church tower dominated the view, as did the twin spires of the cathedral in Paris, visible in the far distance through the bit of haze not yet burnt off by the morning sun. Its main street was rutted and muddy from late winter rains, jolting poor Jacques in the back of the cart. He never cried out, as most would have. His mother held him close, whispering to him the whole time. She only spoke aloud to direct d'Artagnan as to which turns to take to get to the doctor's house, which turned out to be in a cul-de-sac with only one other dwelling near it.

"The physician likes his privacy," observed Treville.

"Keeps the neighbors from hearing the screaming," d'Artagnan retorted.

They all stopped before the two-story house, Abandonée hopping down to help the injured man from the cart. His mother took his other arm. Between them they moved him with tender care to the front door. The older woman knocked in an odd way, a pattern of three, three, and two.

Which was when the shooting started.

13

THE VEXIN

*OH, BLOODY HELL. IT'S GASTON, LOUIS, AND ANTOINE,
COME TO RESCUE ME. I'LL NEVER HEAR THE END OF THIS.*

White powder smoke blasted from two upstairs windows. One ball struck the side of the wagon near Fantôme's foot. Wood splinters exploded, alarming the horse even more than the gunshots had. Chipay snapped its reins and got the wagon turned so that the rear end faced the danger. Abandonée swore and dove into the back, fumbling for her musket. The other bullet passed between the ears of Treville's horse and nicked the cuff of his left gauntlet. As his mount reared, he yanked its head about and galloped away from the house, seeking the safety of the only other building on the dead-end lane, an old farrier's shed. In contrast, D'Artagnan whooped for joy and urged his horse forward, dashing behind the house, pistol already in hand.

Luckily, the men who had fired at them did not have muskets, only less-accurate handguns; otherwise, they might have dropped their targets instead of just missing. Before Abandonée or Treville could shoot back, their attackers withdrew to reload. Treville relaxed, since it would take a few moments before bullets stated flying at him again. He waved at the wagon to come toward him, where they could regroup and get away from the trap.

Then the grievously-injured Jacques stood up straight, laughing, as if Christ himself had just laid healing hands on him. He plucked the bit of blood-filled calf's gut from his mouth that had, along with his gift of performance, fooled even the physician into believing his injuries had been real. In disgust, Treville recalled the all-too-convenient depression in the ground beneath the wagon and cursed himself for a gullible fool. His self-loathing only increased when Jacques' distraught mother shrugged off her dress to reveal a man's clothes, for she was no more a woman than Treville was.

What did they do, hire the best actors in the Vexin?

"They're shamming!" Treville bellowed to the oncoming wagon. "Mama and her boy! Led us straight into this like lambs to slaughter."

The pretended mother tugged a brace of pistols from his belt, tossing one to Jacques. Rather than immediately blaze away with them, they took to the bushes and scrub trees along the lane, working their way toward the shed like trained soldiers. They never exposed themselves long enough for Abandonée to get a clear shot. To make things worse, the two men upstairs reappeared, taking aim so that Treville had to pull back behind the corner. Three more burst from the front door, armed with pistols and swords, and began maneuvering through the vegetation. Chipay steered the wagon around until it, too, sat behind the cover of the small building. He set the brake and hopped down, helping the girl out of the back. She had her musket cocked and ready.

"Seven of them," grumbled Treville. "Blast it! Where'd d'Artagnan go to?"

"Rode behind the house like he was on a holiday," Abandonée said. "If there are more of our new friends there, he's likely lost. Serves him right. Temeraire's the perfect name for him."

Chipay frowned, peering into the trees. "We should exercise discretion. They have too many advantages."

"My thought, exactly," agreed Treville. "Our aim is to get into Amsterdam without fighting." He shooed Abandonée toward the wagon. "Up. Get the wagon going and head back to the road we were on when we met these blackguards. Keep your toy ready and discourage anyone who tries to stop you."

She nodded and hitched up her skirt to step back up. Before she could get far another wagon rumbled into the lane, blocking it. Riding on its open back were half a dozen rough men, all with rapiers and lethal expressions. They jumped down, weapons ready, advancing in a disciplined line toward Treville's band. When Abandonée took one down with an almost casual shot, the rest shouted and charged at a sprint.

"Did I somehow anger God today?" Treville complained. "Everybody into the shed. We'll hold them off until the noise of the fight alarms the town."

The front of the building boasted a large double door for admitting vehicles, as it was a blacksmith's establishment. They were unlocked – the only bit of good luck that Treville had seen all day. But a small exultation died in his throat when another four swordsmen were revealed to be hiding behind them. Now they were outmanned sixteen to three…four if d'Artagnan still lived.

All complaining about life's unfairness would have to wait until the crisis passed. Fantôme snatched the musket from Abandonée and brained one of those lurking in the shed before the fellow comprehended the danger. A second lost most of his teeth to a lusty swing of the butt. The remaining pair retreated out of range of the makeshift club. When Chipay handed it back to its owned and she aimed it at them, they ducked behind support pillars and heavy benches.

"Leave them!" Treville barked, sword in one hand and pistol in the other. "We need you back this way."

He fired at the charging knot that blocked their escape, missing his man when the target jerked aside at the last moment. With his other pistol still on his horse, Treville dropped the empty one, drew a dagger, and prepared to meet the rush, fully expecting it to be his last fight. Even with the repeating musket, they would be overwhelmed from three sides. To reinforce that point, pistol balls blew past his head from the rear as the three from the house arrived out of the trees. And the men in the windows had also resumed their fire. To judge by the sounds coming from the shed, Chipay was engaging the two in there. Treville risked a glance and saw that one was already down and the other was busy fending off the unarmed doctor. But there was no time to retreat into the shed and get the doors shut. Their enemies were now atop them.

Taunting laughter spat in his ears as the two forces converged on them. One more fell from Abandonée's musket, but now they were too close for that to be of any more use. She doubled another over with a barrel thrust to his belly, but the man beside him seized the gun and yanked it from her. That earned him a kick to the knee for his trouble. Treville ran him through the body before he could recover, slashing the first man with his dagger at the same time. Abandonée clambered back up onto the wagon, surprisingly nimble in the irritating dress. Once there she employed the whip to keep at bay anyone foolish enough to try to follow her.

Treville wanted to help her, but he was assailed from the rear by Jacques and his false mother. Their shots had just missed, and rather than stop to reload they had moved in with daggers. Far too clever for Treville's liking, they made a coordinated attack to make his defense more likely to fail. The man who had worn the dress took Treville's rapier in the face, but as he shrieked and recoiled he clutched the blade and tore it from its owner's grip. At the same moment Jacques avoided the main gauche and tried to slip under Treville's arm to thrust his knife between the ribs. He only missed because the king's man flung himself to the right, seizing one of the swordsmen who had come from the end of the lane and shoving him at Jacques. That bought a moment's respite, but the men from the house were now on the scene. To make Treville's disgust complete, another man had picked up Abandonné's musket and was preparing to shoot her with her own weapon. She was occupied fending off another fellow and did not notice the danger. Too far away to assist her, he shouted a warning. But in that instant the gun boomed.

The man with the musket coughed and fell to his knees, blood gushing from his mouth. No smoke surrounded him. Realizing that he had not fired the shot, but had been the victim of one, Treville looked for the source. But he had no time to locate Abandonée's benefactor, for Jacques and the man who had collided with him had sorted themselves out and were coming at him again, backed up by the other three. He backpedaled toward the wagon, unwilling to leave the girl. Perhaps he could put it between him and the deadly quintet. One of them yelped and pitched forward, taking another with him, his legs tangled by Fantôme's odd throwing device. With the other enemy in the shed downed, the doctor was now free to join the larger battle. Treville doubted that he could turn the tide, however. There were simply too many foes.

Just as his back crashed into the body of the wagon and he hefted his dagger to at least make someone pay for killing him, the group skidded to a halt. *Really? Am I that fearsome?* They turned as one to meet a new threat, which made the ground tremble. Treville dropped down and backed beneath the wagon as he looked to see who was coming. Hooves passed his face in a blur, kicking up turf as they bore down upon his enemies. Three large horses scattered the seven men still fighting him. They drove past and into the shed, where their laughing riders leaped from the saddles, swords in hand, and pitched into the crowd with gusto.

Oh, bloody hell. It's Gaston, Louis, and Antoine, come to rescue me. I'll never hear the end of this.

The Épuisants wore expressions of glee at the prospect of an outmanned fight. Overdressed as always, the hulking Gaston grinned as if he had just been told the funniest joke the French language could offer. Antoine, slim and elegant, wore the polite smile of a man listening to some droll drawing room quip. Beside him, the grim and business-like Louis' mouth was tight and hard, with just one corner turning up at the delight of the affray. Faced with such determined and experienced opponents, their adversaries' faces held no such looks. Rather, they blanched with alarm and frantically parried thrusts and cuts that were undoubtedly much more dangerous than their masters had led them to believe they might face. Steel, shouts, and sparks filled the air as the space before the open shed became the scene of a desperate struggle.

A pistol ball slapping into the wagon above him reminded Treville that there were still marksmen in the house. He crawled out to tug the musket from the dead fingers of the fellow who had nearly used it on Abandonée. Blindly, he heaved it over his head to her waiting and eager hands. She thanked him and prepared to return fire at the windows. Chipay appeared, apparently content to let their saviors manage the rest of the heavy fighting, and offered his hand to pull Treville upright. They tucked themselves around the corner of the shed to safely watch Abandonée do her work.

But she had little chance to do so. As she drew aim on the left-hand window, where an arm with a pistol was visible, the man leaped from it as if he had suddenly tired of life. He crashed into the shrubbery below, where he clutched a broken shoulder. Not far away, the other marksman already lay unconscious, seemingly having also jumped out of his window.

"What the devil ---?" cried Treville. "Are they mad?"

"Not mad," Chipay informed him, "merely unwise. They should have locked the doors behind them."

Sure enough, another figure appeared in the first window. Abandonée was about to shoot him when Treville knocked her barrel down. "No! Look."

A charming boyish face beamed at them. D'Artagnan gave them a cheerful wave and a wink.

"He leads a charmed life," complained Abandonée, a little smile escaping her despite the irritated tone of her words. "They'll burn him at the stake some day for having such luck."

His good fortune was not shared by the remaining assassins who were still fighting for survival against the Épuisants. Two were already down, staining the lane with their blood. Those who remained standing looked to be the most competent with a blade. They had tried to escape into the trees, but had been cut off and forced back toward the shed. Now victory was their only hope, as they were being pressed into the building itself, with the king's men blocking the door. No help would come from any of their compatriots, as those not dead or wounded had already absconded to fight another day. With his own adventuring apparently over for now, Treville edged around the corner to collect his fallen rapier and watch how the duel unfolded. Based on experience, he had little doubt as to the outcome.

The fencing styles of his friends matched their dress and demeanor. Bluff, bragging Gaston enjoyed sweeping, extravagant moves that intentionally opened him up to attack. When the opponents tried to take advantage, they discovered that it had all been a ruse to lull them into doing the very thing he had wished them to try in the first place. They also found, to their shame, that he was not nearly the buffoon that his clothes and boasting taunts proclaimed him to be. Despite outnumbering him, he always managed to place himself so that they could never both attack him at the same time. One was always in the other's way.

Contrarily, Antoine handled his blades like a surgeon, with tight precision and deft parries. His elegant dress and manners were reflected in his blade play. No motion was wasted, he was never caught in an awkward position. Like a chess master, he anticipated his enemy's moves and was rarely surprised. And the whole time his fair moustache twitched with a wry smile as if he were privy to some great joke that the other man could not possibly understand.

In the corner, Louis' stern outlook on the world, his sullen and cynical belief that little was worth the candle, led him to simple, almost crude tactics. He seemed to value his own life less than that of the pair of men he was trying to slay. In fact, he scorned using a dagger for defense, relying only on his sword. Thrice he took thrusts through the sleeve of his leather doublet, eventually getting pinked in the hand and dropping the rapier altogether. When his adversaries cried out in triumph and pressed in for the kill, they became aware, to their cost, that Louis hardly needed a sword with so much other rich material available in the blacksmith's shop. A heavy hammer served to parry one fellow's killing thrust and three rusty horseshoes tied together broke his partner's face.

Now the odds had been reduced to one-on-one, bad tidings for the remnants of the great horde that had ambushed them. Gaston sang a lusty drinking song about bowlegged women, then achieved success by the simple expedient of tossing his sword to his foe as if making him a gift of it. Frozen in astonishment, the hapless man took a spurred boot to the belly and a great fist to the nose before he realized that he had lost.

At nearly the same time Antoine parried a shoulder thrust against a support beam, then used his dagger to lever the sword from the other's grasp. Before Treville could move to intervene, the disarmed rascal took to his heels and vanished into the trees. Abandonée's hurried shot was spoiled by a slender trunk that intercepted the bullet.

Still with only the old hammer, Louis had managed to keep blocking attacks as he retreated behind an anvil. There he just slipped a belly thrust that snuck across it. As the attacker was about to pull his rapier back for another try, a mighty downward blow of the hammer snapped the blade in two. All will to fight leaked from him and he turned to flee. This time, though, Treville was ready. The flat of his blade caught the man in his chest, then it slid up to catch in his beard, where it remained until the other's hands lifted in surrender.

"Is that it?" Gaston groused. "I was promised a proper tussle."

Treville frowned. "Oh? By whom?"

"By our noble and approved good master."

"Rosny sent you?"

"Of course. Did you think we came here for the renowned fleshpots of Pontoise?" He noticed Abandonée and swept his hat toward the ground as he bowed. "But I am always ready for a reappraisal of that opinion. Your servant, mademoiselle."

It was not apparent if her smile was because he charmed her or amused her. In any event, she had no opportunity to respond, for a set of worn saddlebags smacked Gaston in his three-acres of brocaded bosom. "Here, servant," said d'Artagnan, "make yourself useful and hold onto that."

The young Gascon grinned at the assemblage, then surveyed the carnage before and inside of the shed. "My, you **have** been busy. And I thought you were sitting in the shade swilling wine while I did the real work."

"We thought you were probably captured or dead," Treville told him, "galloping at the house like that."

"It struck me that the last thing an ambuscade expects is to be charged. The whole point is to shock and surprise the enemy into freezing or fleeing. Rushing at them like a demented fool upsets their rhythm."

Abandonée snorted uncocked her musket. "Well, you certainly achieved realism in your impersonation of a demented fool. Utterly true to life."

"Love talk, so early in the day?"

She raised one eyebrow. "Careful, this corset has already made me choleric."

Gaston interrupted the banter and held the saddlebags up. "Just what am I supposed to do with this?"

"Search them," d'Artagnan advised. "There might be clues as to why they were so eager to kill us. I took them from one of their mounts behind the house."

"Anything in there?" Treville asked, as he followed his friend's suggestion and went through the clothing of one of the dead men in the lane.

"Four unfortunates, rather cooler than they were before I met them. Plus, the two idiots with the pistols who were too stupid to watch their own backs."

"Yes, we saw them fall. Very entertaining."

"I just grabbed their ankles and put my shoulder into them. No trouble at all."

"It took you quite a while to get up there. Did you have more trouble with the others?"

"Some. The first two lounging behind the house were easy. They thought I was one of their friends until I rode them down. The two in the hall were tougher. Had the sense to keep level heads and cooperate. But eventually they saw reason and, well, died."

All of them reached for swords and pistols as someone broke through the trees. They relaxed when Chipay held up a palm. "The firing has alarmed the town. A force has been sent here to investigate. We should leave." At that moment, the man who had just surrendered dashed behind the shed and escaped before any of them could react.

"Damn! Well, pick up one of the other wounded and truss him up in the wagon," Treville ordered. "We've lost enough time with this business already."

14

ROUEN & LE HAVRE

"I HAVE A GIFT FOR SPUR-OF-THE-MOMENT SCHEMERY."

With d'Artagnan riding ahead to scout a route out of the town, and the Épuisants using the cachet of King Henri's name (and some creative mendacity) to allay the fears of the pursuing townsmen of Pontoise, Treville's disguised band managed to get back on the road to Le Havre without serious risk of arrest. In the back of the wagon they stowed a securely-bound prisoner, the most callow-seeming of the fight's surviving enemies and the one most likely to be intimidated into revealing whatever he knew. Only when they were securely through the patch of woods where Jacques had snared them with his undeniable thespian talents did Treville inquire about how Gaston had put the hounds off the scent.

"It seems that the good citizens of Pontoise have had the misfortune to host a dispute between two Satanic covens today," the giant fellow said with nearly a straight face.

Treville cackled so loudly that he nearly spooked his horse. "Really? That was the best story you could concoct?"

"Can you think of a better one? It's our standard ruse in such situations. Mention witches and people's brains seize up. It's so horrifying to them that they don't stop to consider the likelihood. 'Our community must be cleansed of this scourge!' they say. And off they go with their torches and pitchforks, hunting for non-existent demons instead of the real evil in their midst."

"So they took one look at your honest face and took the tale on faith?"

"Of course. But scrawling pentagrams and such on the wall of that shed helped seal the deal. I keep a stick of charcoal with me for those sorts of needs."

"Clever. But it worries me that now they'll find some poor half-mad beggar and burn him in their foolish frenzy."

"Admittedly a possibility. But that luckless unfortunate would probably be high on their list at any rate. This would only accelerate his fate, not be the origin. Besides, when we have need of this recourse, we make sure to send in a picked judge who will find the defendant innocent. Exorcise the guilt into a pig, perhaps. Then they get a witch-killing and a feast all at one go."

"I'm of the mind that you are the one practicing witchery. That's diabolical thinking."

Gaston shrugged, twirling his moustache. "What can I say? I have a gift for spur-of-the-moment schemery. My drunken father was fond of bruising me from head to toe and distracting him with a good story was often the only escape."

"Tell me another, then. How did you happen to arrive at the precise moment that we were in most need of reinforcements? Just decided to exercise your horses in the Vexin today?"

With a laugh Gaston regaled all of them with the details of what had occurred since Treville's group had left Paris. While the latter had prepared themselves for the journey to Amsterdam, the Marquis du Rosny had set himself to acting on the windfall of intelligence that had landed in his silken lap. A painstaking yet surreptitious watch had been set on the comfort closet, the identities of all who frequented it being recorded. France's most brilliant code-breakers were put to work on the cipher.

Béthune had heaved a great sigh and visited the king to discover the identities of all the lovelies who had companioned him in the previous two months. Apparently the list was the length of a Bible. Trusted men were placed in the secret passageway to his bedchamber to intercept any covert conversations there. Madame Dori, Concini, the Marquis de Verneuil, Dr. Montalto, and even the queen herself acquired discreet spies. Most watched of all was the Duc du Épernon, Admiral of France, that crafty old courtier whose only loyalty was to himself. As he was an old hand at evading detection, only Rosny's best teams had that duty, employing frequently-changing disguises and revolving personnel.

"How long did it take him to escape them?" asked Treville with a twinkle in his eye. "I wager four hours."

With a sigh Gaston answered, "Close. Six. They are searching half of France for him."

"He'll be in the other half," predicted d'Artagnan, having dropped back now that they were in open country again.

"No doubt. Or in Spain."

Treville nodded in agreement, having lost the man more than once himself. Holding onto a greased eel would be an easier job. And the man's allegiance was just as slippery. It had not surprised him that the nobleman's lackeys had been among those who had just tried to kill them all. The odd VOC tattoos and young Bethune's seal had also been discovered in the search of the dead and wounded. How Épernon fit into a plot involving religious fanatics, Rosny's disappointing heir, and a Dutch merchant company was still unclear, though he loved to cause Henri any trouble he could, almost as a reflex.

"Which honorable task were you three assigned?" he asked.

"Us?" said Antoine, interrupting his flirting banter with Abandoneé, who was experiencing the novelty of male attention now that she was in a proper lady's garments. "We drew duty behind the Luxembourg."

Louis' chuckle sounded like the cocking of a pistol. "We made pretty boy here keep the rendezvous, white feathers and all."

"Thank the Virgin Mary it was dark as the maw of Cerberus there."

"At that moment, anyhow," Antoine said. "It grew distinctly brighter, and hotter, three minutes later."

"Why?" Treville asked. "What happened? Who kept the appointment?"

"Marie de' bloody Medici kept it."

Jaws dropped all around. "The queen?! At night? And unaccompanied?"

"Completely. Well, unless you count the eleven gens d'armes lurking in every niche."

It turned out that Antoine's ruse had worked all too well. Keeping his voice low so that he might be taken for nearly anyone, he managed to entice Marie into approaching the insubstantial figure with the required pale feather in its cap. After only a moment's conversation he determined that she believed him to be Charles d'Albert, Duc du Luynes, a young courtier of Antoine's very age and build, as great good fortune had it that night. The young nobleman was a great favorite of the king's and was being groomed to be the prince's confidant and advisor, much as Rosny was for Henri. Knowing this, the queen tried to boldly suborn him into a bit of treachery while ensuring that her child did not lose this valuable ally. As only she could, she played to the supposed Luynes' more sentimental instincts, begging him to hold fast to his duty to the three-year-old Louis while also swearing his allegiance to the mother, a poor lost foreigner with barely a friend in France. Surely the occasional report on Henri's and Rosny's activities would not be too much to ask?

Treville could see that it could not have gone well. "What was your reply?"

Antoine hung his head. "The wrong one. I foolishly said that I was unsure that her request could be granted by a gentleman so trusted by her husband."

"And naturally her response was...?"

"To have me instantly killed by the all-too-eager Maréchaussée."

"Ah, the lady is predictable to a fault, eh?"

"As is Coupé. He led with the same head feint/leg cut combination as the last three times we fought."

"Never understands how that always gets parried," snickered Louis. "Thinks it's sorcery."

To the boundless joy of the Épuisants, the affair had turned into a glorious melee, one that would no doubt grant them free drinks every time they told of it. The queen vanished into the murk, spirited away by several of her guard. Those left, at least half a dozen, appeared as if the very shadows had come to life. Innocent passersby taking the night air shrieked and dashed between sword blades that caught the light of the moon, which conveniently peeked out of her cloudy curtains for the occasion. Since the king took a dim view of the Forty-Five and the Maréchaussée butchering one another, great care was taken to keep the fracas light, aiming only to wound and thus secure bragging rights at the soldiers.' Even then, tragic accidents could occur, but in this instance all went well. Every gens d'armes found himself thoroughly pinked in short order while, of the Épuisants, only Louis went home with a ruined sleeve.

"You were injured?" gasped Abandonée, displaying a surprising amount of womanly solicitude. "And still you rode here to assist us in another fight?"

Louis tried to wave it off, though he did wince a bit with the motion. "I've had much worse. The doublet suffered more than I did."

"Let me be the judge of that." She snapped her fingers and gave him an imperious glare. "Come here and let me see."

Like a great scarred old guard dog obeying its child of an owner, the gruff soldier did as he was told and rode up to the wagon. He unbuttoned his doublet and slid out of one sleeve so that she could examine him as they progressed along the track.

"I pity poor Luynes," Treville said. "He'll have a tough time explaining that when she summons him back in the Louvre. Won't understand why he's being packed off to some particularly hazardous war."

"He might have already sent himself off to a cozy siege," Antoine chuckled. "I saw him arrive for his rendezvous just as the queen threw her snit and released her hounds. The lad vanished as if snatched away by God. Haven't seen him since. Certainly wasn't at the palace the next day to be upbraided."

"And neither are the three of you. Are you planning to accompany us all the way to Amsterdam?"

"No," replied Gaston, "our penance for dueling is only to nursemaid you onto your ship. Then we get to go back and do something constructive."

"So Rosny got you out of the queen's sight for a while and we gained an armed escort."

"That seemed to be his aim, yes."

"Well, we're always happy to be a little bit less dead than we might otherwise be. Any other choice bits of news we should know about?"

"A trap has been laid for your commode spy."

"Ah! I hoped so. Some enticing bits of utterly false intelligence dropped in Rosny's office for the benefit of curious ears next door?"

"Precisely. I wasn't privy to all of the juicy details, but apparently a delicious plot to arrest the Spanish ambassador's secretary is supposedly in the offing, if one is gullible and sitting on that fancy close stool."

"And since Senor Gonzalez and his duplicitous master are always being watched, whoever brings a warning will be our spy...or his lackey."

"That's the hope, yes."

Little else besides gossip and japery interrupted the rest of the journey to the Channel. No more assaults came. They spent a peaceful night at an out-of-the-way inn that night without any attempted murders. Their prisoner, a beardless dark youth of sixteen seduced by promises of gold and glory into joining the attack against them, proved to not only know little but to be more than eager to change his allegiance. He called himself Flan, an old family nickname, and said that he had been loafing in Picardy when a silver-nosed gentleman had plied him with drink and coins. The next he knew, he was handed an old rapier and thrust into the company of a dozen others of decidedly terrifying temperament. Silver-nose informed them that a nefarious plot was afoot that threatened the very kingdom, and that God had set them the task of foiling it. All they had to do was wait at a certain house and pounce upon a wagonload of spies pretending to be cloth merchants. Flan's job had been to hide in the shed and cut down anyone who opened the doors.

"Imagine my horror, monsieurs," he said, as Abandonée wrapped his minor forehead cut, "when I foolishly engaged your driver there. Entirely unarmed, he thrashed us as if we were kittens. Never have I seen a man move so quickly with so little effort. It was like fighting a panther. When he hurled me into the corner, I saw no shame in pretending to be unconscious. And glad am I that I did, for I saw and heard enough to know that that I had been placed on the wrong side of the issue. Thank the great good Lord that I did not harm any of you."

Treville had seen his type before, a country boy with little talent for dissimulation and who only wanted someone to direct him toward a worthy goal. The king's man had a nose for political troublemakers and smelled none of that in Flan. "Did you see what became of that man with the sparkly nose? We are quite eager to meet him."

"Oh, no, monsieur, do not be so eager to meet your doom. I saw him take apart a pair of rowdies who challenged him. Cut them up like a butcher does a lamb, he did. Seemed to love doing it more than a lad loves kissing his sweetheart. Chilled my blood, it did."

"But was he at the house where you all attacked us?"

"Yes, to set us all in our places. I never saw him after that."

"Nor did I. Did he have any confederates? Did he give his name?"

"The man called Jacques, and Pierre, the one who dressed as his mother to fool you, they were with him when we recruits were all placed together. They called him La Haine most of the time, though I think I once heard Pierre call him Undercroft. La Haine turned black in the face and knocked him down. Told him to never do that again."

"Undercroft?" Antoine said with a frown. "Odd name."

"Not if it's a code name," Treville pointed out. "Perhaps Pierre made a slip. That may be a boon for us."

Flan had little else to tell them that they did not already know. He did corroborate much that Abandonée had related in Paris, which made her more trustworthy in Treville's eyes. To be certain, though, the youth was assigned to the care of the no-nonsense Louis, who was devilishly difficult to fool. The newcomer would work as a servant for the group, at least until they arrived in Le Havre. By then the stolid soldier would have taken his measure and decided whether he was a spy or a mere pawn.

They all took turns standing watch that night, but nothing untoward happened. The next morning Treville roused them all earlier than usual so that they could get to Rouen before nightfall. A day beyond that would see them in the port and on board their ship to Holland. Again no assaults or anything of great concern came at them on the road, which became much more crowded as they approached the cathedral town where the kings of France were crowned. Treville and the Épuisants gave hard looks to everyone they encountered. All seemed innocent, but so had Jacques and his mother. Treville kept a special eye out for any treachery from their new servant. Flan committed no overt sins, but it was sneaky signals or sabotage that worried Treville more. Louis and Chipay had been warned to watch for those. It would take much more skill than the boy seemed to possess to fool them both.

The only moment of concern was when a cluster of riders was spotted on the crest of a low rise near the river. They could have been anyone, and were too far off to inflict harm, but to Treville's mind they showed a bit too much interest in a single wool wagon. One man at the center, richly appareled and riding a marvel of a horse, seemed to command the obedience of all the others, who paid him great deference. Treville wished that some clever fellow would invent a device to let him see detail at that distance. For such a thing he would pay more than he paid Le Coup for his special weaponry. While he vainly squinted at them, they rode off, three to the north and the rest back toward Paris.

"Trouble?" asked d'Artagnan, bringing his horse alongside.

"Could be. Or perhaps they're merely fascinated by your pretty face."

"Yes, it is a curse. I shall endeavor to bear it manfully."

The young Gascon moved over to share his curse with Abandonée, on the off chance that she might stop flirting with Antoine long enough to take notice. Treville replaced d'Artagnan as the advance guard, on the chance that he might spot the mystery riders at a closer vantage. But they did not appear again and all arrived in Rouen that night in apparent safety. Their party took rooms at an inn near the great cathedral, hoping that it would be less likely to suffer attack or espionage than someplace further out. To be sure, though, Treville reminded everyone to use their assumed names and characters. Gaston took his team elsewhere, so that curious eyes would not wonder at the king's men escorting the merchants. He promised to keep watch over them, however.

"Who knows?" he said in a wistful tone "maybe I'll get lucky and another sharp fight will come my way before you leave."

"You have a queer idea of luck," laughed Treville

"Well, no glory ever came of a quiet life."

"That's the sort of glory I can live without, then."

After dinner they all gathered in Treville's room to plan the voyage, leaving Flan in the care of the fussy proprietor, who kept a stern eye on him by making him help her wash plates and cups. They all agreed that as innocent as he seemed, it was too soon to trust him much. Treville laid out what was known and suspected, adding the intelligence that they had gained since leaving Paris. It annoyed him that much of what they knew kept coming from nearly being killed by unknown men.

"Always our enemies, whoever they are, manage to be ahead of us," he said with a sour voice. "I tire of the constant ambushes and surprises. Hopefully leaving France will make it more difficult for them. The greater distance between us and the cesspool of intrigue in the Louvre, the better our chances. That's one reason for us to make this journey on seemingly so little information. This is a fact-finding mission. Remember that. Our aim is to remain disguised and see what this Krijger can tell is, willingly or not. We must attract as little attention as possible."

D'Artagnan played with a silver coin and feigned a pout. "So no seducing tavern wenches or brawling with the night watch?"

"Do that and I may leave you there."

"How about if I brawl with the wenches and seduce the watch?"

"Though that would at least have the virtue of novelty, no."

"All right, then, spoilsport. Once we get to Amsterdam, what will we do?"

"Rosny has a house there for us, occupied by one of our men at all times in case of need. Just off the canal, near the market square. That puts us close to Krijger's shop, but also to the Dutch East India Company. As merchants we can visit both without having to be too fluent in their awful language. They are all used to trading with the French and will speak to us in our own tongue."

Abandonée frowned. "But the Company will hardly share any dark secrets with foreigners."

"True. Which is why Fantôme will be the one to visit them. He is fluent, and having served their leaders as a doctor, he can gain admittance. Since they see him as a servant, they will tend to speak candidly in front of him, as do all bluebloods with their help. If not, he will cheerfully spy on them."

"That's all fine, but what are we trying to find out?"

"Anything that affects the safety of France. This plot that Rosny fears is too hidden. We need to turn over the rock and see what scurries out. From your experience we know that they are training marksmen. We also know that there is some Catholic aspect to the scheme, though they have no difficulty involving Protestant Dutchmen in it. That points toward a mix of religion, politics, and trade. The sort of powder keg that can blow a hole in what passes for European peace nowadays. I wouldn't be surprised to find the smell of Spain all over it, but we should make no assumptions without solid information."

"And if things go wrong?" asked Chipay.

"If captured by the authorities, stick to your cover story until we can use King Henri's name to get you released. The Dutch won't be eager to torture innocent-seeming French citizens too readily."

D'Artagnan made his coin disappear. "And if we are taken by the real enemy?"

"The same. Play the foolish merchant. Displaying your swordsmanship will merely confirm their suspicions."

The coin reappeared in his other hand as if by sorcery. "Their suspicions won't much matter if they're dead."

"True, but cold corpses generally speak little."

They spent the next hour running through contingencies, meeting places, and escape plans before going to bed, with a reminder not to talk about any of it in front of Flan yet. As usual when a mission was about to turn dangerous, Treville struggled through his childhood dream and woke up gasping and sweaty. The too-familiar image of his sister's laughing masked abductor lingered in his troubled mind.

Getting onto the ship in Le Havre two mornings later went off without incident. They drove the wagon and their horses directly onto it, showed carefully-forged papers to the harbormaster, and were off with the tide. As it was cold and foggy at that hour, most passengers were bundled up against the weather. That was why neither Treville nor any of his companions noticed the silver nose of a man who wore his scarf pulled up nearly to his hard dark eyes.

15

AMSTERDAM

"YOU CAN ALMOST TASTE THE MONEY.
NO WONDER THE WRETCHED SPANIARDS WANT IT."

Gaston was disappointed in his dream of another brawl. The Épuisants escorted Treville's wagon to the wharf in Le Havre, all the while pretending that they were doing no such thing, without any entertaining bloodshed. Before they left, Treville arranged to have them inform the Marquis du Rosny of all that had transpired in the past few days. Maximilien Béthune would be greatly interested in the sort of men who had swarmed them. Descriptions of the dead and captured, along with the contents of their pockets and saddlebags, would tell him much. He kept disturbingly-complete files of all enemies, even potential ones, and his clerks might make some enlightening connections. If they turned up anything that Treville might need to know, a special courier service would get news to them via relays of fast horses through a route around Liege that would avoid any encounters with Spanish troops.

The ship was middling large, a smooth Dutch vessel made by men who took pride in their work. Its other passengers were mostly traders and merchants such as Treville pretended to be. Thanks to fortunate winds the journey took only two and a half days, though it no doubt felt longer to the seasick Abandonné, who stared daggers at the unaffected d'Artagnan. The cruel jests he made at her expense only made her feel worse. For the most part they remained in their cabins, except when the young woman was spewing her stomach over the side. Chipay remained in the wagon with Flan, even sleeping there, as a guard against any saboteurs or common thieves. Though they had not met with any assailants or obvious pursuers since the affair in Pontoise, Treville felt that their past luck dictated extreme caution.

He kept a dagger beneath his pillow and wedged a chair against the door when he slept.

Dame Fortune smiled once more and they had no cause to wet their blades with blood. On the second day they arrived in the Zuiderzee, the great inlet from the North Sea that led to the mouth of the River Amstel where Amsterdam was situated. Nearly one hundred miles long, it took them another day to reach the Dutch capital, arriving in sight of it in the mid-afternoon. Spread before them was an impressive and wealthy city ringed by a wide canal. Innumerable docks and warehouses crowded the northern end, at the confluence of the river and bay. Treville had never seen so many ships in one place in his life. Seemingly all the world was anchored there.

Beyond the wharves, the rest of the town of fifty thousand souls resembled Henri's Paris: a medieval city in the midst of modernization. Construction was visible everywhere one looked. Shipbuilding, trading, diamonds, and banking were holy religions. One of the secrets of its success was that this most tolerant of places welcomed people of all faiths and beliefs, using the grateful energy of refugees to fuel itself. Catholics, Protestants, Jews, even former citizens of the exotic Indies could call Amsterdam home. The heady cosmopolitan blend of talents and experiences made for an almost magical money-creating machine. Unlike other parts of the country -- especially poor sacked and ruined Antwerp, which had been the center of trade and finance until the Spanish took it -- Amsterdam thrived.

Their papers were examined in a cursory way and they drove off the ship and into a teeming mass of vehicles, horses, and pedestrians, all seemingly headed for a single spot near the city center along the canal. Abandonée nearly kissed the ground in relief. Treville's band joined the throng, as their objective was the same, the merchant and residential hub. They loaded Flan down with luggage like a bedraggled donkey as a test of his loyalty and resolve.

"Smells a lot better than Paris, eh?" said d'Artagnan with a grin.

"The Dutch are great believers in cleanliness and order," Chipay told him. "Amsterdam especially. They are traders, and the whole city is an advertisement for their success. A foul town would not encourage investment."

Order was certainly evident, despite all the building and renovation. For the capital of a tiny nation hard-pressed by the might of the Spanish army, the town showed little sign of the misery seen in a place like Ostend. One would hardly be aware that a war was raging in the south. The streets were nearly as clean as the halls of the Louvre and the canal water looked potable. Houses were narrow and brightly-colored, with many windows arranged in perfect symmetry. Stepped gables decorated the tops, masking gray slate roofs. Overall, the effect was of good virtuous Calvinism, full of classical restraint and pious sobriety.

"You can almost taste the money," d'Artagnan laughed. "No wonder the wretched Spaniards want it."

A balding, portly gentleman wearing a blue wool gown over black doublet and hose waved at them from the street. His thick white ruff was a spectacular testament to his wealth, extending nearly to his shoulders. Treville nodded a reply and told Chipay to stop the wagon. The pleasant-faced fellow approached and made a complicated gesture with his hands, prompting Treville to respond with a similar one.

"Meneer Beurre, is it today?" he inquired in French.

"As much as yours is Monsieur Penseur," chuckled the other.

The two spies shook hands, causing the rest of the group to relax. With a great deal of huffing and groaning Beurre got himself up onto the wagon, squeezing poor Abandonée between him and Chipay.

"Go where he tells you to," instructed Treville. "We'll follow and make certain that no else does the same. Flan, dump your load in there and go with them."

Wheels squeaking, the wagon jerked forward again as d'Artagnan dropped his horse back alongside Treville. The two riders feigned nonchalance, playing the part of foreign visitors, and gawking at everything around them, while keeping an eye on their rear.

Ahead of them, the masked La Haine smiled behind his kerchief as he peered into a small looking glass and marked their destination without even facing his prey. His lord would be overjoyed to hear this news.

Beurre guided them around a corner to the back of one of the pretty three-storied homes fronting the canal. There they found a private stable and small enclosed yard. In no time the wagon was safely stowed and the horse released from its burden to happily munch grain. Their host unlocked the rear door of the house and they all filed in to the first real comfort they had enjoyed in many days. Though a secret retreat for spies, the place was charming and homey. Attractive rugs covered well-oiled wooden floors. Glass-doored cupboards held blue and white Delft crockery. The hearth was faced with gleaming white tiles that had hunting scenes painted on them. Elegant and slender furniture, family portraits, and curving pewter chandeliers made it feel like a true home rather than a base for intrigue. Treville said so.

"That's because it is a home... mine," Beurre said, shrugging off his gown and hanging it on a brass hook. "I maintain it and stay here year-round. That makes it look authentically lived in and we don't have to wonder if somebody's been poking about, as we would if we only opened it when the need arose."

Treville clapped the jovial man on his broad back. "Marcel...that is, Monsieur Beurre, has been here since before most of us were born. Started in the spying game when just a lad. Younger than you two imps, even. Utterly loyal to France, yet he might as well be a native Dutchman, he's been burrowed in here so long. Anything he doesn't know about the people, the politics, or the rulers is probably irrelevant. Had this house for twenty years."

"Well, it looks utterly adorable," said Abandonée, happy to be on a surface that did not move. After a week on the wagon or the ship, stability impressed her. She plopped herself onto an upholstered divan as if she were a duchess. "As an agent of the French crown, I declare it acceptable."

"As do I," agreed d'Artagnan. He had already found the wine and was uncorking a bottle. "They may be heretical Protestants here, but this is good Burgundy from back home."

Treville sighed. "Don't make yourself too much at home. In two hours we go out to survey the town and get to work. One glass only."

The young fellow obeyed, but made sure it was a large one. Then they all pitched in to unpack the wagon, particularly of the portion of its cargo that merchants were unlikely to carry. When the weapons and other incriminating gear had all been safely stowed in various clever spots in the walls and floors that Beurre made available to them, everyone went upstairs to select bedrooms and take naps. It was a joy to be still, to feel no pitching of wagon or deck. Even more welcome was the lack of screams, shots, and threats. Treville slept as peacefully as a righteous child. His dreadful dream stayed away. A few more such slumbers would be welcome, but bitter experience warned him not to set his hopes too high.

He woke first, to the smell of roasting chicken and potatoes. That was another forgotten luxury, as they had been living on insubstantial road rations, disappointing inn meals, and whatever the greasy swill on the ship had been. Aided by Flan, who looked to be more than familiar with a chef's duties, Beurre had been busy while safeguarding his sleeping guests. Soon the others rushed downstairs to see if their noses told the truth. All of them fell upon the bird – two birds, as it turned out – like wolves upon a farmer's sheep. Little conversation ensued until the bones had been picked clean. Then Beurre was encouraged to tell them all that he knew of the situation on Amsterdam. The fewer surprises, the better.

"The war with Spain has gone on for a lifetime," he said, sipping his wine. "Literally longer than any of you have blessed our good earth. Thirty-nine years, with no sign of an end to it. Started all the way back with Phillip II, the one who sent that doomed fleet against the cursedly-lucky English. Partly over who prays on his knees and who does it on his feet, but more so over taxes and the usual Hapsburg pig-headedness. It looked to possibly being done with now, after Spain lost so much blood and treasure taking Ostend. This northern part of the country is no longer in much danger. Independence is all but assured, though the Spanish have yet to realize it. But the south is still in play, and the sea is a bloody mess. You saw the shipyards on your way in, yes? The Dutch are building ships faster than boys make paper boats. They aim to challenge Spain on the water, a thing undreamed of in my youth.

Money and backbone can make up for a small population, though, as Philip found when he sought to overwhelm Elizabeth.

"Both sides are tired, nearly out of money. Their people want it all to stop. But the boys at the top all hope for a miracle, especially in Spain. Losing to a tiny bunch of heretical upstarts sticks in Phillip III's craw. I expect there to be a truce soon. It will look good on paper, everyone will congratulate themselves on bringing peace. And naturally, Spain will whip its New World slaves all the harder, mine even more gold and silver, rebuild its forces, and have another go. Whether the Dutch will have made themselves a match for them by then is an open question. Their fleet is fast, cleverly-managed, ambitious, and growing every day. They can't compete with the Hapsburg Empire on even terms on land, however. Not in the long term, though there have been successes. So it may come down to allies, as it so often does in Europe. And that, as I'm sure Monsieur Béthune has told you, might very well lead to an immense and costly war amongst many nations."

Treville nodded. "He said that a great war is coming someday, that it would dwarf anything ever seen. That man would volunteer to pull a lion's tooth with his bare hands, but this prospect scares him. I could hear it in his voice. You think it could start here, that this Dutch business might be the catalyst?"

"Not only do we think it possible, our enemy – this mysterious group in league with the Dutch East India Company -- is actively seeking to bring it about."

"Despite the dreadful cost?"

"You know religious zealots, no price is too high for Paradise. Mix in money and power and they'll do anything to look their god in the face. And if a few million unbelievers get their comeuppance at the same time, so much the better."

"We're missing puzzle pieces," d'Artagnan said. "Catholics and Protestants working together toward an apocalyptic war? Why would they do that?"

Beurre shrugged. "If I knew that, perhaps my priest would be out of a job. My guess is that there are rival factions in this group who are swallowing their distaste for the others to accomplish a larger goal. Some may care more for faith, others money, others political domination."

"Unstable," observed Treville. "If that proves to be true, we can exploit it. Break them up from the inside."

"If you can get inside. We've lost several good men trying. These people are extremely cautious. Hard to fool."

"Not impossible. Rosny has already broken one of them who fell into his hands. That's how I have enough information to contact this Krijger here." He pointed his knife at Abandonné. "And we took her away from them. They aren't invincible."

Even as he said it, Treville still considered that she had been caught very easily, that he might have been too eager to take her on. Why was that? Something about her spoke to him. But was that enough to risk all their lives on? Perhaps she was expert enough to play on his feelings that way. Still, so far she had been a valuable ally.

"Does this group have a name?" Chipay asked. As was his fashion, he was at the window, watching for trouble.

Beurre cut himself a slice of bread. "Yes, though we don't know if it is what they truly call themselves or if it is just some of them being sardonic. But Manqué is the term."

"Manqué?" Treville snorted. "Unfulfilled? Referring to their ambitions, perhaps?"

"Could be. Sounds as if someone is trying to be overly clever."

"He must be French, then," d'Artagnan laughed.

Abandonné burped. "Well, I can't say that I'm unfulfilled. Thank you for a lovely dinner, sir."

"You are welcome, mademoiselle. It's the least I can do. All condemned men get a final meal."

"Now that was a French thing to say," said d'Artagnan, laughing louder.

After the plates had been cleared away, Treville went over plans with his team again, then set them to making any preparations they might require. Then he left them to it and went out on his own to scout the area. Entries and exits need to be inspected, as well as buildings that might provide vantage points to attack their house. Once he had satisfied himself as to the various means of escaping another ambush or of launching one of his own, he settled into his character as a proper French merchant and ambled about the center of the city, noting the location of the business district, the banks, the civic offices, and other sites his people would be entering in their pursuit of secrets.

He made sure to speak to as many of the good citizens of Amsterdam as he could, introducing himself as a new arrival to their splendid town. Could the honorable gentleman or lady direct him to such-and-such? Much thanks, and what trade do you practice? Are there any quarters of the city one would do best to avoid? Excellent, and who are the honest people of business and who are the ones with their thumb on the scale? With such polite banter, the sort of skill that made Treville a master at his job, he began to accumulate a deep understanding of the field of play.

Finding Krijger's cheesmongery was easy enough. Nearly everyone he spoke to knew it, as it was a well-respected establishment. Located on the market square, it occupied the bottom floor of a charming limestone building with green and yellow shutters. A sculpted wooden wheel of cheese hung from a large hook above the door to advertise the wares. *Kaas* was painted on it, for the benefit of literate Dutchmen. In the windows the real items were on display, either in wax-covered wheels or already sliced. Some of the former were enormous and clearly weighed more than Treville. His long shadow on the storefront reminded him that the work day was nearly done. If he wanted to find Krijger now he would have to hurry.

The interior was small, cozy, and aimed at a wealthier clientele than the average cheese shop. Not only were the creamy delights sold to stock Amsterdam's kitchens, they also could be consumed on the spot, as three tables occupied one corner for that purpose. Bread, fruit, and wine were available to go with the main fare. Everything was clean, well cared for, and elegant. One customer, a bulky fellow in the black garb of a Protestant minister, was finishing his snack at one of the tables, while the staff were tidying up and preparing to close for the day. A tall fellow swept the floor near the entrance and a small woman in an apron wiped down the counter. Another man, a burly sort wearing a stern expression and suspicious eyes, was preparing to cover the merchandise with protective cloths. He had the look of a spy and assassin.

Treville caught his eye and approached him. The presumed proprietor of the shop frowned, seemingly unsure of this new customer, but ceased work and addressed him. "Yes, sir? We are about to close."

"I see that," Treville said in halting Dutch, with as much charm as he could manage. "My fault, for waiting too long to patronize such a fine establishment. You are well spoken of."

"Thank you. That is the sort of thing all merchants like to hear. May I interest you in a little something. It will have to be to take home only."

The Frenchman pointed to a wedge of yellow Edammer. "That will do nicely." He lowered his voice and delivered the coded identifier phrase that had been painfully extracted by Rosny's men from their prisoner in the Bastille. "The larks are gathering beneath the willows, I see."

While wrapping the cheese the shopkeeper said, "Are they? I'm not much of a bird fancier."

That gave Treville pause. For it was most definitely not the coded response he had expected to receive. Rather than try again and raise suspicion, he paid for his purchase and made to leave. Perhaps the other fellow? He could be more dangerous than he looked. Passing the tall man at the other end of the counter, he complimented him on his waistcoat and uttered his secret sentence.

The assistant chuckled. "Well, that's a damned sight better than havin' 'em fly overhead and shit on you. Right?"

Nonplussed, Treville agreed with him and left the shop in defeat. Had the prisoner lied? Or had the interrogators misheard him? Something was clearly wrong. He would have to return to the house and look at the documents again. Heading along the line of storefronts, greeting passersby with pleasantries, his mind was a tangle. The whole mission depended upon finding Krijger. This was not a good sign. But perhaps Beurre could help.

He ducked into the alley that he had earlier spotted as a shortcut home, making certain that it was empty first. His terrible experience in Ostend had made him cautious of such places. Ten steps into it, however, he discovered to his shame that he had not been cautious enough. A boot stomped onto the back of his knee, buckling the leg and throwing him off balance. Before he could recover a strong arm had shoved him face-first into the grimy wall. The tip of a disturbingly-sharp knife pricked his throat. Just as he was about to throw an elbow and fight back, a feminine voice gave him the proper countersign to his earlier avian phrase…in perfect French.

"And the thrush will soon be nesting with her young."

In astonishment, Treville risked a glance behind him. It was the woman from the shop. She had followed him, unnoticed, and here he was, ambushed yet again.

"Aw, are your feelings hurt, Treville?" she mocked. "Nobody told you that Krijger wears a skirt?"

16

AMSTERDAM

"DON'T MIND HER. SHE DOES LIKE TO SHOCK."

So not only is she good enough to take me unawares, she knows who I am. Lovely.

Despite her tiny frame – only a very few inches above five feet, her head did not reach to his chin – she was strong and knew her business. She knew his, as well. Her free hand slid over to his Ostend wound and two fingers bored in. Though he ground his teeth and tried to remain silent, a pained hiss escaped him.

"Ooh…not quite healed down deep, is it?" she remarked, as if she were seeing the weather. "But your Indian friend did a splendid job on you, I'll give him that. You're supposed to be safely dead."

Since she had not chosen to cut his throat, parley seemed more in order than a tussle. Not that he was greatly interested in the latter anyway. Krijger was clearly well-trained in handling those larger than herself. "Sorry to frustrate your plans. My appointment book was too full. No room for death this month."

She snickered. The knife pulled away and she put space between them so that he could turn around. "You didn't frustrate me. I wasn't the one trying to kill you. Because I wouldn't have botched it."

Moving slowly so as not to alarm the woman, he spun and put his back to the wall. One hand crept behind him, ready to draw the secret dagger strapped beneath his doublet in case she lost her sense of humor. His eyes lowered to take her in. Like most spies, she was not particularly pretty. Except for missions calling for an alluring presence to entrap a victim, beauty was not the ally of a covert agent. It only attracted unwanted attention when one wished to blend in. The double agent looked perhaps thirty years of age. Her nose was too small and her mouth too wide. Sharp and angular, the planes of her face and her jaw gave her a somewhat mannish appearance, though not to the point of robbing her of a certain puckish feminine charm. Posing as a man would have been easy enough. What hair was visible was light brown and wavy. She still wore her plain brown homespun dress, muslin apron, and white lace cap from the shop. But beneath the skirt's hem he saw high-quality military boots.

"You have the advantage of me," he said, making her laugh. "You know my name but I don't know yours."

"Then the vaunted French intelligence service is all canelé and no cream. The Marquis needs to recruit a better class of man." She tucked the knife away, much to Treville's relief, gave him an ironic bow. "Maaike Scheermes, more or less at your service."

"Mary Razor? Really?"

"That's what everybody knows me as. You're not getting anything else."

"Just so long as you save your close shaves for other gents."

"Don't give a reason and that pretty throat of yours will stay intact."

He ventured to step away from the wall, showing her both empty hands. Krijger shrugged and retreated a bit more, her sturdy shoulders relaxing. She led the way out of the alley, head high, as if she were the Queen of the Netherlands. From the deference shown her by those they met in the square, that may not have been much of an exaggeration. Treville noticed that she had the tiniest of limps on her left side and asked if she was in good health.

"You mean the hitch in my step? That's not a new one. Two years ago a sneaking Spaniard got a lucky shot in…with a crossbow, of all things. Wasn't their best marksman. Only got the calf. Still, it tore a nice, ragged hole on the way back out." She chuckled. "The hole I made in him was a lot bigger."

"You killed him with an arrow in you?"

"Wasn't hard. I put on a good act, squealing and shrieking. Made sure to fall behind a big cask. When he came to gloat, I sent him off to whatever vile Catholic hell his kind believes in."

"How?"

"Stuck him in the eye with his own bolt."

Treville was glad that he was behind her so that she could not see his reaction, a mix of horror, fear, and admiration. "Selling cheese must seem awfully tame after that."

"Well, I still get to play with knives. Besides, it's a spy's paradise. Nearly everyone in Amsterdam comes through that shop. Because we are also a little cafe, often the wine loosens tongues that shouldn't be. If not, their documents have a way of falling into my hands." She stopped, half turned, and handed him a small knife. It was the last-resort dagger that he thought had still been in the rear of his doublet. His mortified face must have been a delight to her, for she grinned and winked. "Don't take it so hard. You were too busy with my hand on your ouchie to notice much else."

"I don't know whether to shoot you or marry you," he said, echoing d'Artagnan's jibe with undisguised appreciation.

"Well, let's see how the day goes. No need to rush into things."

They were halfway across the square now. "Where are we going?"

"To meet the rest of your people, of course."

Taking her to Rosny's expensive secret lair hardly seemed advisable. "All right. Let me arrange a meeting at a neutral ---"

"What? Oh, you think I don't know all about Marcel and his charming little house? Aren't you just adorable."

Treville was feeling two steps behind again. That was becoming an uncomfortably familiar sensation lately and he cared little for it. "Should I just go back to Paris and leave you to solve this whole thing yourself?"

Again she laughed. This time it was a warm, pleasant sound rather than the harsh mockery earlier. "Heavens, no! What good is a fine performance without an audience to applaud it?" Maaike stopped and gave him a maternal frown. "Aw! Don't pout. It makes your face all wrinkly." Stepping in entirely too close to him for a proper Dutch lady, she held a hand to his cheek. "And it's far too pretty to mar. Though a little dueling scar would lend it roguish charm." Before he could respond to that, she was rushing off, surprisingly fleet on such short legs. "Hurry up, before that crazed Gascon of yours drinks up all the wine!"

Neither of them took note of the clergyman from the cheese shop, who ambled behind them at a respectful distance all the way to Beurre's home. Once he was sure of their destination, he allowed himself a tight smile as he turned back toward the square and began to remove the makeup from his silver nose.

A few minutes later they stood at the front of the house. Treville had insisted that they do so, to give Fantôme an opportunity to see them and for Treville to signal that he was with a friend. Beurre opened the door, one hand behind him. Stepping in first, Treville whispered in his ear, "Put it away before she hurts you with it."

"Goedenavond, mijnheer," Krijger said in a cheerful voice, nodding to him. "Maaike Scheermes. Lovely home you have. How many spies does it sleep?"

The round gentleman opened his mouth, the closed it without speaking and set his pocket pistol on the foyer table. When she had passed him and made her way into the dining room, he said under his breath, "Why is the cheese lady here?"

"Gouda question," Treville chortled. "Let's go find out."

By the time they arrived in the next room, d'Artagnan and Abandonné had their mouths hanging open in astonishment and Chipay wore one eyebrow up in puzzlement. Apparently Krijger had already uttered another of her outrageous statements. She had a wine bottle in her hand and her boot heels up on the table.

"Don't mind her," Treville said to them all, "she does like to shock." D'Artagnan shook his head. "Mission accomplished."

Not bothering to ask what she had said or done, Treville made introductions, though Maaike clearly knew everyone already. He used her code name and her given one, since he assumed the latter was just as fraudulent as the first. Once etiquette had been observed, they all settled in for a war council. The newcomer immediately abandoned her irritating ways once serious discussion was required, not even touching the bottle she had claimed.

"First of all," she said in enviable French, "I know that you only trust me at arm's length. That's fair. I'm a bloody double agent, after all. You aren't yet certain which side I'm truly working for. The Spanish? The Manqué? Myself? Always hard to tell, especially if the agent's any good, which I am. Be dead long ago if I weren't. But one thing's for sure." She yanked up her skirt and rolled down the left woolen stocking to display an angry white divot in her lower leg. It looked like a great wild beast had bitten there. "As I told your boss here. Spanish crossbow. No love for those swine."

The dress went back down and the right sleeve went up. There she showed a round spot that looked like she had been poked by the finger of God. "Musket ball, courtesy of a Protestant fanatic trying to shoot the man I was hired to protect, the *Stadtholder* Maurice. It seemed that my man's prayers weren't sufficiently pure for him. So I have little use for that end of the God question, either."

Her fingers pulled back the hair on the left side of her head, just above the ear. A fresh red line ran along her skull. "Rapier point. Le Haine thought I deserved this last week, just because it amused him. I laughed right along with the snake, because shooting him in the face isn't my current assignment. He has to believe me a friend or his secrets will be hard to come by. I've spent nearly a year gaining his trust."

"And how did you manage that?" asked d'Artagnan.

"The usual way a woman does it," she told him with an undisguised shudder of disgust.

Treville rubbed the back of his left hand, recalling his own scars. This one was barely visible, so old was it, but it still hurt deeper than the burning of mere flesh. The flash memory of grabbing his baby sister's arm seared like the flames of the burning house had. She had escaped the worst of it, thanks to him, though that limb had been badly scorched. Another moment and she would have been lost to the conflagration. As it turned out, she was lost anyhow, stolen by that murderous masked man. He hoped that her fate had been less dreadful than fire.

"Does he talk in his sleep?" asked Abandonné, "or is that too much to hope for?"

"He does some," answered Maaike, "but so far nothing has been intelligible, more's the pity. I keep hoping he'll spill the beans and I won't have to endure that again. He's not particularly to my taste. Serpents are rarely cuddlesome." She winked at Treville, as if to indicate a clearer picture of what her appetites might be.

Pretending not to notice, he brought things back on track. "If I may...you are remarkably, if not disturbingly, well-informed."

"We have to be, don't we? A tiny clump of dairy farmers, shopkeepers, and fishermen against the whole bleeding Hapsburg Empire. Like a minnow against a whale. It's not sorcery, we just try harder, take more risks, use what tools we have. And since few take us seriously, we can often slip through cracks unnoticed. Our people are everywhere in Europe: buying, selling, or hauling what's bought and sold in our ships. Every citizen's a spy. They keep their eyes and ears open and make sure that what they notice gets back here. It's our organization that makes us so good, knitting all of the strands together into a garment that we can use."

"And are you planning to share some of your needlework with us?" d'Artagnan inquired.

"Perhaps. That's what I was ordered to do. So long as you share, as well. Maurice has no scruples about working with France, at least while she has a king who makes all of the right noises toward toleration of Protestants."

Treville shrugged. "Henri isn't eager to have the Hapsburgs gobble up even more territory and power, no matter how Catholic they may be. Not good to have one giant bear prowling amongst the lambs."

"On that we agree. Just make sure that the Dutch get their own pen...and a good guard dog."

"So...time to share. Though I imagine that it may be a lopsided trade. You seem to have few gaps in your knowledge."

She smirked, biting her lower lip. "Oh, there's bound to be some little thing you have that I can make use of."

For the next hour they swapped stories, rumors, and scraps. As Treville had suspected, his contributions amounted to less than Krijger's. But she had not known about Abandonné's recruitment and training. The sharpshooting business was news to her, for her time with Manqué had been spent with another branch of the operation, which was working with an even deadlier weapon.

"They're making bombs?!" cried d'Artagnan. "This is indisputable?"

"Barrels of gunpowder? Fuses? They make a big boom? What else would they be doing?"

"Where are they training? Who's in charge?" Treville demanded.

Maaike pointed to Abandonné. "Her foster father is the boss, that so-called Guido. Though he's no more a Guido than I'm a Chinaman. Has a lot of experience making mines and such. Was an English mercenary helping us against Spain down south. But I hear that he fought for both sides and is actually a not-so-secret Catholic zealot. Either way, blowing up things was his specialty. We paid him a king's ransom for it, I hear."

"Bombs and sharpshooters." Treville sighed and shook his head. "To what end? Who's the target?"

"We're not sure yet, but it must be somebody whom they want to make sure is all the way dead."

"Any oblique hints that we can start with? What about languages? That could give us an idea of the place they plan to operate in."

"I wish that were true. So far I've heard French, Dutch, English, and Spanish. None more common than the others. That narrows it down to everything west of the Germans and south of the Swedes. Not much use."

Abandonné raised her hand. "What about messages? How are they passed and what codes do they use?"

"Mostly face-to-face, in whispers. What written items I've seen are in a solid block of indecipherable gibberish."

"Like this?" Treville plucked his copy of the Louvre's grid cipher from his doublet. He spread it open on the table for her to inspect.

She peered at it with care. "Just so. How'd you get hold of it?"

He explained the marvelous vagaries of the French palace's commode room, which made her laugh and clap her hands. "You people are never-endingly amusing!" she cackled. "I like that eavesdropper, though. Clever, in its way. Took a bit of daring to install that under your very noses."

"Here's hoping that it works in our favor," Treville said. "We're feeding bogus messages through it now, so soon whoever uses it will take action on the bad intelligence and give himself away." He tapped the cipher sheet with one finger. "How does the Manqué read these? A grille?"

"Yes, but they throw in another step in case the grille is compromised."

"A codebook, as well?"

"That would explain the number in the corner." She pointed to the **ZE1** at the top.

"Could mean anything, though, from a codebook to a common text that's used as the key. Can you snoop around without being too obvious, see if there's a volume that they keep close at hand?"

"You think I haven't? They aren't fools. I'm not allowed in the office by myself. Actually, no one is. They don't even trust each other."

"With such a cosmopolitan crew, I would expect an abundance of such caution." Treville thought for a long moment, then slapped the table with a grin and told her a clever way to force the Manqué's leaders to reveal the book.

Maaike smiled back and blew him a kiss. Everyone else in the room applauded the idea.

"Brilliant," d'Artagnan said. "But how do we arrange it?"

"Leave that to me," replied Beurre, rubbing his hands together. It had been a long time since he'd been in on anything fun. "I know a gent who can help us."

17

AMSTERDAM

"OH, WE HAVE CLIENTS WHO PAY HANDSOMELY FOR A BIT OF TROUBLE LIKE THAT. THE SCRATCJHING AND BITING ADD TANG TO THE SAUCE."

"This is pure witchcraft," insisted Abandonné.

She peered through a brass tube mounted atop her musket as she lay on a low grassy ridge southeast of the city. Chipay and d'Artagnan had chopped out a gap beneath a hedgerow to permit her to observe the farmhouse below without fear of detection. The marvelous instrument on her weapon contained clever lenses that did the impossible: it made far-away objects seem so near that she felt that she could touch them.

Beurre had assured them that they did not risk burning at the stake for using the thing. "No magic is involved. This is the newest advance in natural philosophy. It's a prototype developed by a clever optician named Janssen. We obtained it in trade by agreeing not to tell the Dutch authorities about his counterfeiting activities. He seemed to think it fair, this toy for his head."

"How does it work?" Treville asked, always interested in clever inventions, especially if they helped him do his job.

"Who knows? Something about bending light or some such thing. He says it's like when you put your hand in water and it appears bigger."

"Well, our friends down there appear bigger, whatever the reason," Abandonné muttered. "I swear I could shoot flies off their noses with this."

"Try to restrain your impulses in that direction," Treville advised. "You're only to fire if Krijger gets into difficulty."

D'Artagnan smiled. "Which is almost a dead certainty, with this scheme."

"Your confidence in my plan warms my soul."

"Just so long as our friends in the house are warmed, too."

The luckless Janssen's device was not primarily meant to make Abandonné's marksmanship sharper. Rather, she needed it to get a clearer view of who came out of the house and what they might be carrying. Maaike's role was to force them to do so with panic and alacrity. When that happened, those on the high ground would need to identify items of value and then work to take them from the Manqué. Secondarily, they would make things hot enough through musketry and other means to permit the Dutch spy to make her escape. She had reported to Guido as she often did, offering up bits of intelligence to them so that they would continue to trust her. Chiefly the information was either safely out of date or was carefully-designed by her masters in The Hague to seem legitimate while actually being worthless. Treville had spent many an hour crafting such things himself for Rosny.

Thanks to the lenses, they had gotten their first look at the man in charge of this end of the Manqué's business. Guido was a tall, dark, sturdy fellow, clearly a soldier, with the bearing of a man used to giving orders. His full beard and lush moustache, plus his long hair, were perfectly in the style of the time but somehow the way he maintained the growth gave the appearance of danger. Perhaps his zealot's eyes and resolute jaw were more to blame for that. At any rate, he did not look like someone to trifle with. In the few minutes that they had observed him with the telescope – that was what Beurre called the magnifying machine – he had already cuffed two of his men and kicked a third.

It was obvious that the house served as their headquarters, while the large barn and two smaller outbuildings were where they prepared their infernal devices. Small kegs were kept in a stone shed a pistol shot away from the house. Treville guessed that that was the powder magazine, set apart in case of an accident. He had enough experience with the stuff to know how unreliable and unstable it could be. Manufacturing it was as much art as science and not everyone who worked with it was a da Vinci. Plus, weather and other variables made it a dicey substance. His enemies may have been many detestable things, but they were not cowards.

Whatever the gunpowder was being used for was happening in the barn, a solid low structure of pale sandstone with a new slate roof. In the past ten minutes three kegs had been taken inside and nearly all the men on the property, at least a dozen, had gone in after them. A heavy wagon, of the type used to haul beer barrels, stood next to the barn. Krijger, Guido, and one other man remained in the house. So far things had proceeded as desired.

The first sign of trouble came from Fantôme, who was watching their rear to prevent ugly surprises. He appeared with no notice, like his namesake, and crouched beside Treville. "Horses coming. Four of them. Armed."

Treville made a sour face. "Anyone we know?"

"The leader has a shiny nose."

"That'll be La Haine. Can you delay them for a while? Without a major engagement?"

The doctor nodded and moved off as silently as he had arrived. Beurre replaced him at Treville's side. "My people will be in place in perhaps ten minutes."

"Good. Looks like we may need them. Lucky for us there's only one road in or out. I'm sure that's why our friends chose this house in the first place." Treville frowned as he stared down at the house, mumbling to himself. "Come on, Krijger, sooner would be better than later."

For another few minutes they all fidgeted, looking for some sign of success. D'Artagnan rotated a dagger between two fingers like the Dutch windmills on the horizon, while Abandonné kept fiddling with her new plaything. Beurre looked back at the road every three seconds, his head resembling a tavern sign swaying in the wind. For his part, Treville carved doodles in the dirt with one gloved finger.

Finally, it happened. "Smoke," Abandonné said, eye against her scope.

They all rushed to the tiny viewing gaps that they had made in the thick hedge. Black tendrils oozed out of a window at the rear of the house. Maaike had smuggled in enough oil to make for an alarming fire that would cause a swift reaction from the occupants. Her shrieks would gild the lily and ensure that Guido and company fled the place with whatever they valued most. Treville fervently prayed that the codebooks would be on that list.

To his vast relief, it worked to perfection...at first. Screams and shouts could be heard clearly even atop the hill. All three residents poured out the front, followed by ever-increasing inky smoke. They took a moment to cough and curse. Then Guido seized his man by the scruff of his neck and shoved him back inside with an unintelligible command. Maaike played the hysterical woman well, wailing with abandon to keep up the emotional pressure on the men. She had had the wit to set part of her skirt alight to deflect suspicion. Treville twisted his head around to check the road. No riders appeared. *Chipay must has done his work well, as usual.*

The reluctant fellow sent back into the supposed flames stumbled back out, hacking and complaining. He carried a small sturdy wooden chest with an impressive lock. As he fell to his knees to recover, his master gave him a boot and forced him up again. Guido pointed to the waiting wagon near the barn. His lackey grumbled but did as he was ordered. Krijger said something to Guido, who shook his head and waved her toward the wagon, too. Already the smoke was diminishing. Now the Manqué leader cocked his head, considered the situation, and stepped toward the house again, apparently to inspect the source. Suspicion hung on his body like a shroud.

Cavalry trumpets from the road made him stop. Shouted orders mingled with the brassy calls to advance. Martial noises grew louder. As the source was beyond the slight rise, Guido had no view yet of the horsemen. After a moment's hesitation he decided that he had sufficient evidence that soldiers were coming his way. He swore with enough ferocity to almost scorch the grass and ran toward the barn. Pounding on the door, he bellowed commands and caused a flood of men to stream out. Most sprinted for another outbuilding and began to lead horses from it. Weapons appeared in many hands, either swords or pistols. While they prepared for fight or flight, others carried kegs from the barn and the stone shed with a care that spoke of highly hazardous contents.

"Krijger told us no tall tale," observed d'Artagnan. "They wouldn't be handling those so gingerly if they were full of wine."

Abandonné pulled away from her scope. "That's a lot of gunpowder. Are they planning to blow a bridge, maybe?"

"Could be," Treville said with a shrug. "Though that seems a mundane use of all of this planning and coordination."

"Depends who's on the bridge at the time," Beurre pointed out.

The trumpets grew louder, as did the other noises of an imminent charge. That convinced most of the Manqué to mount and scatter into the surrounding woods, which turned out to be open enough for riding if one took care. In another minute the wagon, which could only use the road, was fully-loaded. Its burly black horses strained to get it going, possibly to plow through the enemy and be gone before the cavalry could turn on the narrow path. Only three riders remained as guard, the rest having fled their posts.

Gaining speed, the wagon rumbled past the house with a sound of distant thunder. Everyone on or around it lifted a blade or gun. But no attack came. They slowed, puzzlement on most faces. The exception was Guido, who realized at once that he had been fooled twice, by fire and horn.

"Good work," Treville told Beurre, who returned a little bow.

King Henri's man in Amsterdam had managed to assemble a band of musicians and actors to sell an imminent assault. They had been paid to make their deceptive cacophony twice and they go back to town, not being fighters. Already they would be heading home. If Guido crested the ridge he would see only an empty stretch of road. He had slowed the wagon, realizing the likelihood of that very thing. If he remained on the farm, Treville would have a much tougher time stealing that code box.

"Give him some encouragement," Treville advised Abandonné. "Try not to blow us all to the clouds."

She grinned and settled behind her musket, eager to see how the telescope would enhance or hinder her shooting. D'Artagnan and Treville backed away to mount their horses for this second phase of the scheme.

Treville asked Beurre, "Are your other boys ready?"

"They should be, so long as they haven't run into those riders in the woods. We hadn't counted on that."

"No shots from that way, so I'm thinking not."

There was a shot from their hedge, however. White smoke exploded from the musket's muzzle, befogging them all and giving away their position in a spectacular manner. As they were about to leave anyway, it mattered little. The bullet struck one of the outriders, only an arm's-length from Guido, tumbling him from his horse to be mashed by the wagon's wheels. That was the signal for the rest of the encouragement. Half a dozen more explosions came from the treeline behind the wagon, the smoke drifting across the field in the slight breeze. None of those in the wagon noticed that no musket balls flew past them. Beurre's men had simply lit fireworks in the brush.

Faced with fire on two sides and the clear realization that his base was no longer secure, Guido shouted to his driver to press on down the road. Hooves churned up turf as the four great horses responded to the whip. In another moment, the wagon crested the little hill and picked up impressive speed, hoping to escape the trap with its deadly load. Abandonné put another careful bullet just past the wagoneer's ear, to keep him motivated to dash off. Treville had made it clear not to hit the kegs or to kill Guido. They needed him to lead them to the rest of the gang and to the ultimate target of the plot.

But not until they lightened his load a bit.

As the wagon raced past them, Treville could make out Krijger in the back, atop a keg, playing her role of the terrified lady. Her terror might yet turn into the real thing if they could not rescue her. But he would have to manage it carefully so as not to alert Guido that she was a spy. The fellow already had his suspicions.

"Go, go, go!" he cried to his friends. D'Artagnan was already mounted, beside Beurre. Abandonné handed the Gascon her musket, accepted Treville's hands for her foot so that she could get up into her saddle, and took her weapon back. Beneath her split skirt she wore a man's leather pantaloons and riding boots, a fact that both scandalized and titillated her companions, as did the fact that she had eschewed a sidesaddle. She slammed the musket into a long scabbard alongside the horse's shoulder and caught up with the others, who had already begun galloping after the wagon. As they rode, each tugged a scarf up over the nose. Then they tugged pistols out of holsters and assumed their roles as highwaymen.

It took them longer than Treville expected to catch the fleeing wagon, but there was no doubt of the outcome of the race. Before it could clear the trees along the road and get out amongst houses and witnesses, they overtook it. D'Artagnan passed it on the right, crowding the horses and slowing them. When Guido lifted his pistol to fire, Maaike yelped and pretended to lose her balance, landing atop him. By the time he recovered, everyone on the wagon was staring down a gun barrel.

"Stand and deliver!" cried Treville in Dutch, feeling like an actor in some absurd play. "Portable valuables and jewelry, if you please, then you can be on your merry way. Oh, and toss the pistols onto the ground, too. Safety first, as my sainted granny always said. "

Guido sneered, "You dolts have fooled with the wrong people." His Dutch was flawless, but there was a lilt to it that said that it was not his first tongue.

"On the contrary, good sir, from where I sit you look to be precisely the right people. And well-supplied, too." He motioned to Abandonné. "Pop a shot into one of those kegs, sweetie, and let's see if his wine's any good."

When she swung her muzzle toward the wagon's load, everyone on the vehicle blanched and waved furiously. "No!" shouted the leader, carefully setting down his pistol. "You'll kill us all!" He pulled a leather purse from his doublet, jingling the coins. "Here. Just take the money and go."

Treville caught it with his free hand. "There's a good lad. Now the rest of you. Hurry up."

More purses were surrendered. He nodded at the box beneath Guido's feet. "That, too. Looks tasty, it does."

Guido's jaw stiffened, but he still managed to keep up his pretense. "Nothing in that but documents," he claimed with absolute sincerity.

"Well, that'll make it a lighter load than if it were full of gold, then. Hand it over. Mind that you do it with care. My companions get nervous when they smell heroism."

Grimacing, Guido did as he was told with little grace but even less violence. He had not survived the wars by taking mad risks. D'Artagnan collected the box and set it across the front of his saddle. As he moved his horse back Treville nudged his own closer, until the beast's nose nearly touched the driver's foot.

"One more trinket and we'll be off." He pointed to Maaike and curled his fingers. "That little morsel will do nicely."

To her credit, she acted the wronged woman magnificently. Squirming, whining, pleading, she nearly escaped before the fellow beside her wrapped her up tight in his arms. He looked to Guido for guidance. The Manqué boss frowned at Treville. "What the devil do you want her for? Does she look compliant to you?"

Treville had difficulty keeping a straight face at her antics and was grateful for his mask. "Oh, we have clients who pay handsomely for a bit of trouble like that. The scratching and biting add tang to the sauce, if you get my meaning."

To Treville's amazement, Guido displayed utter revulsion at the idea of selling her to a brothel. Apparently his Catholic views were sincerely held. For a moment it seemed as though he would refuse and take his chances in an uneven fight. But in the end, pragmatism won out and he motioned to his man to give the wriggling woman up. Treville slid from his horse, grabbed her before she could pretend to run away, and tossed her across his horse's neck. Once he had remounted, he patted her rump, feigning great delight in her outraged protestations.

"It's been a pleasure doing business with you all." He gave Guido an ironic little bow and guided his horse back from the wagon. "I still would like to sample whatever drink you're hauling." Again Abandonné made as if to shoot a keg. This time, though, Guido merely stiffened and glared, daring her to shoot.

The purported highwaymen laughed and rode off. Once out of sight around the first bend, they stopped so that Maaike could get off Treville's horse and give him a sound Dutch cursing as she clutched her sore middle.

"Charming language you Dutch have," said d'Artagnan with a grin. "Sounds like demons gargling."

"And French sounds like effeminate frogs arguing philosophy," she retorted.

Treville helped Krijger back onto the horse, this time in the more comfortable perch behind him. Once she was settled she leaned against his back, bit his ear hard, and breathed, "Tang to the sauce, eh?"

It took all his will not to rub the aching ear. "Sorry about the indignities. Had to sell the product, after all. If it's any consolation, you were magnificent."

"Well, when you put it like that, I may ease your inevitable punishment."

With that worry added to his list, Treville shed his mask and led his band toward home. One concern that he did not have was pursuit by Guido, for d'Artagnan had cut the wagon reins and some of the bridle straps. Replacing that worry was anxiety for Fantôme, for he had not turned up since going off to intercept La Haine's riders. Those horsemen had also not made an appearance, so his friend must have at least partially accomplished his mission to prevent them from interfering with the operation at the farm. But where had they all gone? The road, lined with trees for nearly a league, showed no sign of man nor beast. Had they chased Chipay in the other direction into open country and then town? Or had they all mixed it up in the woods? Treville alerted his companions to search the ground as they rode, for signs of a tussle.

D'Artagnan found it first, a spot not far from the end of the forested section of the road. The path was chewed up by hooves in a much wider swath than anywhere else, extending into the trees on one side. Nothing was immediately visible in the wooded darkness, so Treville had them all keep moving in case danger lurked there. Once they reached the end of the woods, he left Abandonné and Beurre on guard with the box and the horses, then circled around with d'Artagnan to come at the suspicious spot from the rear. It took longer than anticipated to make their way through the brambles and swampy patches. Eventually, they came upon a small clearing where horses had been recently. Their tracks led in and out on the same narrow animal path, leading back to the spot they had found on the road. Someone had bled in the clearing... more than one, to judge by the amount and how widespread the gore was. Bootprints told a story of a sharp fight against mounted and dismounted opponents. Tree trunks bore sword cuts. A slashed glove lay on the ground.

"Looks like he got their attention," said d'Artagnan.

Treville nodded. "So it would seem." He turned a full circle, frowning. "So where are they?"

"Maybe they overwhelmed him and took him off with them."

"Could be. Let's hope not. That'd put us in a poor bargaining position when we've just taken the one thing they didn't want to lose."

After another careful examination of the clearing, they headed toward the road in search of more clues. They didn't get more than thirty paces along the track, though, before d'Artagnan held up a hand to stop so suddenly that Treville ran into him.

"What?"

All but one of the fingers on the Gascon's raised hand curled. The remaining digit pointed straight up. "Holland has a peculiar type of rain in the spring." He turned so that Treville could see the drop of red on his hat brim.

Both tipped their heads back and peered up into the foliage. Twenty feet above, in the crook of an oak's branch, lay the bleeding Chipay, his face camouflaged with mud.

18

AMSTERDAM

"I'M FAIRLY CERTAIN THEY AREN'T LOOKING TO KILL A GREEK GOD."

D'ARTAGNAN LAUGHED. "OH, I DON'T KNOW.
THEY KEEP TRYING TO DO ME IN, AFTER ALL."

It took great creativity and effort to fetch Fantôme down and get him back to Amsterdam. Hours later, as the day was nearly ended, they had him installed in his room at Beurre's house. His blood stained nearly everyone, as the thigh wound had bled freely before they managed to get it wrapped. But after closer examination it proved to be not quite so debilitating as they had feared. 'Messy but not deep' had been the declaration. The victim himself talked them through the medicines and stitchery needed to treat it. All were amazed at his calm demeanor throughout the process.

"My people learned to suffer in silence," he explained when it was all done and he lay back in the bed smoking a long-stemmed clay pipe.

"One wonders," Treville said, "how you managed to do your suffering up that tree."

Fantôme then related all that had happened after being sent to delay La Haine and his men. Diverting them had been the easy part. The weighted hunting ropes had tangled the front legs of the leader's horse and sent both to the ground in a tangle. All the others piled up behind the fallen horse on the narrow path. Chipay pounced upon them before they could react, his swift empty-hand attacks forcing them to interrupt their journey to deal with the annoyance. After they had all received numerous kicks, punches, and elbows, they abandoned their journey to the farm in lieu of a single-minded pursuit of their tormentor. He led them into the trees, using all the devilish woodland combat skills that had earned him his nickname of Ghost. His description of the battle in the clearing sent chills up the spines of his audience.

All four enemies had proven to be more than capable fighters; they had cooperated in a tactical way to finally hem into a place where he had few options. A lucky rapier strike to his leg slowed him down, forcing the physician to reluctantly abandon his vow to avoid killing, as otherwise his friends would have found a cold corpse in the woods. So he had disarmed one of the foes, taking his parrying dagger and his life in one flash of movement. That weapon enabled him to keep the others at bay, inflicting wounds on every one of them even while his own was weakening him. Eventually the same happened to his enemies, who abandoned the fight with curses and threats of vengeance. No doubt they would have gone to the farmhouse for succor, but just then the trumpets and shooting had begun, convincing them to retire toward the city.

"But why did you climb the tree?" asked d'Artagnan. "More to the point…how?"

"As for the first, I felt my strength fading and felt that it was unlikely that I could survive if they returned with fresh men. It was also doubtful that I could get back to the road before failing completely. So I resolved to put myself where wild pigs and such would not eat my body when I passed away. We bury our dead on scaffolds above the ground, so it seemed fitting." He shrugged. "As for how? Perhaps Misimanito granted me the power of his Great Spirit as a final boon."

"Not so final, as it turned out."

"No, but it could have been, if not treated." He bowed his head to them all. "I have a debt."

Treville waved that away. "We swore an oath on that sword. Brothers care for one another. Debts don't enter into it."

With that they left him to sleep and met in the dining room again. While waiting for Beurre's weekly communication from Rosny, it was time to open the chest and see if all their risks had paid off. Though it had a sturdy iron lock, a hammer and chisel eventually conquered it. Inside lay half a dozen leather-bound volumes, all with innocuous titles in Dutch, French, Latin, even English. Casual examination of each revealed little of interest. None of them bore the title 'Secret Manqué Codebook.'

Treville frowned, then spread out the page of scrambled letters from the Louvre and the parchment with cut-outs taken from the dead assassin in Ostend. The former still made no sense, which was to be expected. That was the point of a code, after all. His eye naturally went to the **ZE1** on the corner of the grille. It had to be a key, telling the user which reference book to use. So again he looked at the spines of the books they had removed from the box. None of them had authors or titles beginning with a Z. He opened them all to their title pages where, in the traditional manner, the subtitles went on for the length of a Bible, illustrated with woodcuts advertising the subjects of the tomes.

'De secretis mulierum libellus, scholiis auctus, & à mendis repurgatus.' 'A true and excellent historie of my journie to the Antipodies.' 'De Geografie van Zeeland, eerste editie.' 'Le sang des saints martyrs de la France.'

He slapped his thigh and whooped "Zeeland, first edition! That's the one."

This time he gave it no cursory reading, but inspected every page. After five minutes he discovered the book's secret. The first and last hundred pages were the original book, so that if anyone idly looked at it he would likely not notice anything amiss. Between those points, however, the pages had been replaced with line after line of coded letters and what they stood for. All were in random clusters of three to make it nearly impossible to decipher without the key. ERK meant 'attack at dawn with all of your force,' while MGW stood for simply 'no.' Several hundred pages of tiny print went on like that, covering a stunning array of possibilities. One section was a list of every European ruler and all his or her subordinates. Another was of geographical sites: cities, rivers, bays, etc. Yet another gave activities: investigate, steal, invade, abduct, kill, even seduce. It was staggeringly thorough.

"Well, hasn't somebody been a busy little bee?" muttered Abandonné.

D'Artagnan squinted at the pages. "A whole hive, from the looks of it."

Treville placed the cut-out parchment atop the Louvre document, lining them up with tiny marks barely visible on each. The open slots cleanly made three-letter groups visible, either vertically, horizontally, or diagonally. He read them out and had Abandonné write them down. Then they worked their way through the codebook, translating each until they had the message in plain language, which turned out to be Dutch.

Extinguish Hercule as he kisses the Horn.

They stared at it in silence for a full minute. Finally d'Artagnan sighed and said, "Well, that's certainly clear as crystal."

"Isn't it though," groaned Treville, seemingly no better off than he had been before. *Damn these spies and their codes within codes. Just say what you bloody well mean, for once.*

"Suggestions?" he asked of the group.

"Looks like an assassination order," Maaike observed. "Extinguish is pretty straightforward. And with a bomb they'll extinguish everyone in the building."

"Is *Hercule* supposed to mean Hercules, like in mythology?" Abandonné asked.

"That would make sense," Treville said. "Though I'm fairly certain that they aren't looking to kill a Greek god."

D'Artagnan laughed. "Oh, I don't know. They keep trying to do me in, after all."

Abandonné rolled her eyes at that, but could not hide the warmth in them as she looked at him. "Remind me, which god are you supposed to be again? Coalemus?"

At the mention of the obscure god of stupidity, he laughed. "Ooh! Somebody's been to school." The Gascon blew her a kiss and winked.

She shook her head and addressed Treville. "What I mean is, there's no S at the end. In Dutch that's how you would spell Hercules."

Treville grunted. "Truly?"

Beurre, having spent decades in Amsterdam, agreed. "She's right."

"So...this would mean that they're talking about a Frenchman?"

"Looks like it."

"But a Frenchman in Holland. That ought to narrow it down. Though why he'd be kissing a horn is anybody's guess."

D'Artagnan pointed at the message. "That word is capitalized. Is it important?"

"I'm expecting every detail to be significant."

"What if it means a person, not a thing?"

"Which person?" Treville turned to Beurre. "Is anyone here who's worth the killing named Horn?"

Krijger slammed her fist into a palm. "Holy hell!"

"What?"

"Not his name, but it's on his coat of arms."

"Who? Don't be mysterious, I need some plain speaking, for once."

"A hunting horn is the symbol of the House of Orange," Beurre explained, grabbing a book from a shelf and opening it to the title page. It was a history of the current Dutch ruling family. The woodcut image on the page was of a shield with a typical cattle horn used for hunting calls. "Like this."

"Then the Horn would most likely mean...?"

"The head of the House would be Philip William, Prince of Orange, half-brother to the *Stadtholder*, Maurice."

"Why would he be kissing a French Hercules?"

"He might not be. He is on poor terms with Maurice. The Prince is a fervent Catholic. Lived in Spain until just a few years ago. Not enamored with the Protestant turn his country has taken during the revolt against the Hapsburgs. In fact, he's not happy with the revolt itself. Neither is his sister Maria, who's been fighting with Maurice over Philip's right to the title and to the city of Breda, in the south. Philip's there now."

"The Manqué hardly seem to be interested in killing an ally."

"I agree. But what if the Horn is really Maurice, the de facto holder of the House of Orange's power right now?"

"The general who's been giving the Spanish fits? Makes sense. The Manqué is predominantly Catholic and would no doubt love to remove that piece from the board while achieving its primary aim. I do wonder what their Dutch East India Company partners might get out of it, though. And that still leaves us with the mysterious Frenchman to identify."

Maaike interrupted with her own hard-won intelligence. "My sources tell me that although Maurice was in at the founding of the Company, and was instrumental in ensuring that it received the authority to wage war in the name of the United Provinces, he is not a popular figure with some factions of the Company. While public disputes are avoided, behind closed doors his desire for more control of the organization than they prefer to give makes him an obstacle to the more ambitious members of the Council, and even more so to the deep-pocketed investors behind the scenes. Nearly half of them are exiles from the Spanish-occupied southern provinces, but they would rather have a truce right now and pile up profits and power than continue to wage endless campaigns. Maurice disagrees, and desires to push the fight even harder, while Spain is short of money and men. So it's not beyond belief that some of his own people might not shed a tear at his permanent removal."

"But wouldn't a nice quiet poisoning, or a bedroom knifing, serve their turn better than bombs and bullets?"

"Not if the whole point is to make a statement, to get attention and demand that they be taken seriously. Or place the blame elsewhere."

Beurre excused himself to answer the complicated knock at the back door that meant that his dispatches from Paris had arrived. The others stretched and refilled their wine glasses.

D'Artagnan spoke up. "Let's say that Maurice is the Horn, and that they'll move on him and this Frenchman soon. Where would that be, most likely?"

"When he's here in Amsterdam," answered Maaike, "with the whole world watching. Dispatching him at the front would probably be dismissed as the fortunes of war. Poison or some private murder would be explained as an unfortunate act of God, covered up by the government. But a splashy public massacre couldn't be denied."

"Do you know his schedule? When would be their best chance to get at him that way?"

"In three days, when he meets with representatives of the States-General from The Hague. They will tour the new Stock Exchange, the East India Company headquarters, and hear his assessment of the military situation. After that there will be a public assembly in the New Church, to hear complaints from citizens and requests for civic action. Sanitation, law enforcement, canal maintenance, that sort of thing. A few foreign representatives will probably be there. They're always invited to see the glories of Dutch government."

"Any French ambassadors?"

"Possibly. The list hasn't been made public yet."

"Well, this sounds like a tempting target, French kissing or no," Treville said. "Do you think you can get back inside the Manqué without too much trouble? "

"Maybe. We did sell my abduction with great panache."

"You'll have to sell your miraculous escape with the same aplomb."

Beurre returned with the coded letters Béthune had just sent. He deciphered them quickly while the others debated the relative merits of Krijger going back into Manqué's embrace. Abandonné was dead set against it, d'Artagnan was always up for a risky venture, and Treville was of two minds. On the one hand, he could see how dangerous it was, since Guido had been suspicious of the fire. Would he simply torture her for the truth, on mere speculation of treachery? *I wouldn't put it past him. He seems like a nasty piece of work. La Haine, too.* On the other hand, though, Maaike was terrifyingly clever and an adept liar. She could probably convince the Pope to convert to Mohammedism.

Before a decision was reached, as if Krijger would feel herself bound to what French agents might say anyway, Beurre completed rendering his messages into readable text. When he saw the first one he fell back in his chair with an exclamation. "No!"

Treville looked at him with concern. "Trouble?"

"Yes, of the spectacular variety." Beurre held up the message. "This identifies the Frenchman Maurice will be kissing in that church. Things have just become much more dangerous."

"Why? Damn your suspense, who is it?"

"Henri de Bourbon, King of France."

The room grew quiet as the bottom of a well, and nearly as gloomy. Abandonné's mouth hung open in surprise, while Maaike's was twisted in a disgruntled half-frown. D'Artagnan's expression was a mix of apprehension and excitement. All Treville felt was irritation.

"Damn your joking! Who is it, really?"

Beurre held out the paper for him to examine. "My sense of humor atrophied long ago in this job. See for yourself."

Treville's annoyance only increased as he read Rosny's note. Sure enough, the king would soon be in Amsterdam to secretly consult with the Dutch *Stadtholder* about Spain and other issues affecting both nations. He was traveling incognito and would impersonate his own Foreign Minister for a brief appearance at the public gathering in the New Church.

Naturally, d'Artagnan knew the perfect thing to say. "Mothers of Amsterdam, lock up your daughters."

"Lock up the king!" snapped Treville, kicking the table leg. "What's he playing at?"

Beurre shrugged and handed him another message. "He's playing at being God's anoited, of course. We just get to watch."

"But we can't watch, not well enough to guarantee his safety. He'll have to cancel. Claim illness, or a broken carriage wheel, or a balky mistress...something."

Abandonné asked, "Send a message to Paris, tell them what's going on here."

"Too late. He's already en route. Besides, he's a seasoned warrior. He'd take our plea as an insult." Treville turned to Krijger. "You need to tell your people about this, get the event cancelled."

Maaike laughed. "You think they don't already know? I'm not the only spy in the United Provinces."

"They know of the Manqué's general danger, but not the specifics of this plot. Inform Maurice of an imminent assassination, get him to stop the gathering."

"He'd never do it, and for the same reason your king wouldn't. Generals don't want to be seen shying away from hazards, him especially. He's fought the best soldiers of Spain his whole life."

"Yes, but this time he's endangering hundreds of innocent citizens. Didn't you say that he's entertaining petitions?"

Her eyebrow went up and she nodded. "Hmm. That's a point more likely to sway him. I'll pass it on. But he's just as liable to feel that it would be an outrage to call his people cowards, and they'd rather share the risk."

D'Artagnan began sharpening his dagger on a whetstone he always carried. "Then we should assume the worst: that it's up to us to catch them before they blow that church all the way up to heaven."

Krijger fished some rope out of a cupboard. "I agree. To that end, I need to get back in with them, all suspicions swept aside." She held the cords out to Treville. "Sir, would you do me the honor?"

Catching on to what she wanted, though not happy at the prospect, he tied her wrists until the rope bit cruelly into her fair flesh. "Tight enough for you?"

She gave him a naughty smile. "Reminds me of a saucy evening in Antwerp where we... well, never mind." Gritting her teeth, she wrenched her wrists to and from until an alarming amount of blood seeped out from under the lashings. Abandonné begged her to stop. "I don't dare, missy. They have to believe that I was a true captive and not feigning. If you're too squeamish to watch this, then you should probably leave the room for the next part." Maaike fished a washcloth from the basin and tucked part of it into her mouth, between the cheek and her teeth. The rest hung out like a fuse. "Don't be too gentle," she mumbled to Treville.

Looking into her eyes to confirm that she was certain of her course and getting a curt nod, he punched her in the face. Twice.

Now everyone leaped to his or her feet in horror, trying to intervene. But Maaike waved them all off. She made a clawing motion with her fingers and offered Treville the other cheek. He raked his nails across it, creating a series of livid lines. The room was full of loud objections and exclamations. Treville understood their outrage, but he had been on the receiving end of such necessary abuse and knew that it was the only way to convince Guido that Maaike had stood up to her captors and managed to flee. When she dragged herself to Manqué with damage that could not be easily self-inflicted, it would make her story easier to swallow.

"Enough?" he asked her, hoping that it was. Just because it had to happen did not make it any easier to do.

"For now," she said as she pulled the cloth from her mouth. She snatched d'Artagnan's bottle from his hand and guzzled it. When she lowered it again she peered into the glass at her reflection. "Ooh, that eye may swell shut. You do good work."

Feeling slightly sick, Treville sat back down and went through the other decoded papers. "The Duc du Épernon has been seen on a ship for Holland. I doubt that it's a coincidence. And young Bethune was with him. Looks like all of the wolves are closing in for the kill."

"I'll set my people onto them," Beurre said. "Rosny's spawn, in particular, will probably make mistakes."

"I agree." Treville held up another message. "His father says here that they spent an entire day baiting the trap by giving out the same false intelligence, over and over again, to make certain that whoever was eavesdropping in the commode would overhear it."

Abandonné asked, "Did they catch anyone?"

"They did. Dr. Montalto."

Beurre was surprised. "Really?"

"So it says," Treville said. "But I'm skeptical. As a foreigner, and a Jew, he would be easy to blackmail into being the front man for someone else."

"You think his mistress is behind it?"

"The queen? Of course it's possible, since we already saw her out on a nighttime assignation, thinking she was making an ally of the Duc du Luynes. My money would be on Concini and his scheming wife. Her prescient fits seem a bit too on-the-nose for my liking. It's also possible that more than one person knows about that listening tube and Montalto was snared before they themselves blundered into the same trap."

"Anything else in there that we should know about?"

"Luynes is apparently innocent, as far as Rosny can tell. Marie tried again to suborn him and got nowhere. The same can't be said of the Marquise de Verneuil, who was seen rummaging through the king's bedroom cabinets. All she found was a paper that led her to believe that she and her son were going to be sent to exile in Geneva."

"Another false trail?"

"Of course, though utterly believable. When she confronted the king with it, he naturally inquired where she might have found it."

"That must have been an awkward conversation."

"Apparently it ended as it usually does, with her in tears and protesting that it was all done out of love for him. He smothered her with kisses and it continued from there."

"Are Concini and Madame Dori being watched, as well?"

"They are. Neither has been caught doing anything more disloyal than the typical lying and --damn!"

"What?"

"Dori. That babbling seizure she had in the library. I've been trying to puzzle it out ever since, as my Italian is hardly professorial. It just now struck me when I said 'lying'. That led to 'lion'. She said what sounded like 'Il leo...nay... intra...po..larey mol...lay in aut...unno', which didn't make much a sense. I've just puzzled it out. She really said *il Leone intrappolare molle in autunno.*"

"And that means...?" asked d'Artagnan.

"The lion trap springs in the fall." That garnered no reaction from his listeners, so he explained. "King Henri has been called the Lion of Bearn since birth."

Maaike frowned. "The fall. But this is spring."

"I know, but that's what she said. Maybe I'm getting it mixed up and it means 'the lion will fall in the spring.'"

"That's not how the Italian sounds, but, after all, she was having a seizure. We shouldn't put too much stock in specifics."

"So in her fits she speaks the truth, things she's heard or seen, plots she's a party to?" asked Abandonné.

"Looks like it. Even if not an active participant in this, she's at least heard of the Manqué's plans from somebody."

Abandonné rolled her eyes. "Is there anyone in the Louvre who isn't a spy, assassin, or traitor?"

"Not many. That's what it's for, to be a menagerie for the king's problem children, so he can view them up close and not have to search all of France for them."

"What do we with this precious knowledge?"

"First, Krijger goes back to Guido to confirm what we think will happen in three days."

Maaike shrugged. "Some folks drink, some folks dance. Me, I entertain myself with near-suicide."

D'Artagnan finished sharpening his dagger and stowed it. "And if she can't get out, if they keep her with them by force to make sure she can't talk to us?"

"He doesn't yet know that his mail has been read," Treville pointed out. "No time to change codes yet. Even if he holds onto her, it won't prevent us from interfering with his mass murder. And I suspect she has plenty of practice in getting messages out in such situations."

"That I do," said the Dutch spy with a pained grin. Her jaw and eye were swelling already. "I have a few enterprising local fellows who aid me in that."

"Good. So if you find out something we urgently need to know, such as a drastic change in plan or precisely where the gunpowder will be hidden, feel free to shout that from the rooftops."

"Oddly enough, that's almost precisely what I'll do."

"Do you know where to meet them, since they had to run away from that farm?"

"There's a refuge they use in case that sort of thing happens, yes. It's a disused stable not thirty minutes' walk from here. We have people watching it."

She explained her system for communicating, which was clever, complex, and might even work. Once that had been established to everyone's satisfaction, they worked on a plan for searching the New Church for the bomb, finding the Duc du Épernon and Rosny's son, while continuing to hope that they could convince King Henri to cancel his appearance altogether. But they had to assume the worst and expect to have to stop the explosion and sharpshooters from destabilizing Europe.

By the time that they had done all that they could, darkness had fallen. After checking on Chipay and finding him in good spirits, Treville took to his bed. His rest, though, had to wait, as someone was already in it. His dagger was at the interloper's throat before he realized the situation.

"Is that any way to treat a lady?" Maaike asked through puffy bruised lips.

"What the devil are you ---?"

"Not very perceptive for a spy, are you? What do you think I'm here for?"

"Since your clothes are hanging on that chair, I can pretty well guess. But this is a terrible idea and besides ---"

"I disagree. It's a wonderful idea. My face hurts. My wrists are aflame. I can't see out of the one eye. I believe you owe me some relief." She propped herself up on one elbow. "Quite apart from that, I've decided that I need some more ugly marks, beneath the clothes, to get the most sympathy from that dog Guido. If I claim that I was assaulted, that should do the trick." Lying back, she spread her arms wide. "Some scrapes and gouges on the belly and thighs will do nicely. They'll believe the worst." When Treville hesitated, still stunned, she winked her good eye. "Try to make it worth my while."

19

AMSTERDAM

"NO SMALL THING, HOLDING THE LIFE OF A KING IN ONE'S HAND."

When he awoke with a start at dawn, Treville was utterly relieved that Krijger was already gone. It had not been the first time that he had been in such a situation with a lady spy, but on the other occasions he had been playing the role of a rogue to seduce information out of her. Being put in the position of 'handy romantic abuser' had not only been off-putting, it had left him wondering just what had really taken place. It had not been love, certainly, or even attraction. He had the impression that Maaike had been making a point, playing a dominance game to make it clear that she was in charge of herself and her mission.

That's the first time I've ever been bedded by someone stronger than me, even if she did look like a victim of the Inquisition.

Putting the unsettling affair out of his mind, he dressed and then hobbled into the kitchen, keenly aware of injuries that he had not felt before bedtime. There he found a note from her thanking him for his diverse services and promising to communicate at dusk once she had insinuated herself back into the Manqué's favor. With a pained chuckle, he dropped the note into the fire that Beurre had already built up. After a hasty breakfast of bread, cheese, and honey, he struggled up the stairs to wake his people.

Abandonné was already awake, for she was not in her room. It was tidy, more organized than he expected for a girl who had been living on the streets. Perhaps having a space of her own made her fastidious. At any rate, she was elsewhere. *Probably polishing her musket.*

He rapped on d'Artagnan's door and went in with a sarcastic greeting. The words died on his lips when he saw Abandonné standing near the window, chemise in hand. D'Artagnan lay in bed, favoring her with a sly smile. Though he probably should not have been surprised, given the looks they had been exchanging since their first meeting, Treville's mouth gaped open nonetheless. But the mere fact of her naked presence was less startling than the scar on her arm. Against the pale perfect beauty of her skin, it reminded him of a fine painting slashed by a knife. Something else about it nagged at him; its shape made a bell ring in his mind, but he excused himself and backed from the room instead of puzzling it out. Shaking his head, he opened the last door.

His string of shocks continued. Chipay's bed was also empty, his clothes gone.

The physician's medical kit was missing, as well, so he was not merely visiting the commode. Somehow the wounded man had managed to recover sufficiently to get himself up, dressed, and out of the house on some errand of his own. Treville looked for a note of explanation but found none. Swearing under his breath, he hunted up Beurre, who was bringing in more wood from outside, and asked him where Chipay might have gone.

"Didn't know he was missing," was the answer. "But then, I never know what he's up to. The one man I can't read. His expression can be like a marble statue's."

"I have to agree with that, but he's not made of stone. He lost a lot of blood yesterday. I hope he hasn't fainted in the street."

"I'll go out to see if that's happened. I have a network of helpers for this sort of thing. If he's in trouble, they'll find him."

The little round agent donned a hat and cloak and immediately departed on his errand. That left Treville with only one ticklish problem, which he solved by ignoring it. When d'Artagnan and Abandonné came downstairs, separately, he made a point of fussing with documents while they ate breakfast and speaking of everything but their intimate situation. After all, he was hardly in a position to be judgmental. They obliged him, though the occasional suppressed snicker did escape.

"Krijger's already gone?" d'Artagnan frowned. "She's in that much of a hurry to lie down with those vipers again?"

"Well, that is her job. If she's survived all these months with them, she's clearly capable."

"Assuming that they don't cut her throat as soon as they see her, what then? Do you think that crazy messaging system she described will actually work?"

"It doesn't matter what I think, it's our only option. She says she'll send something out at dusk, so we'll have to be ready to receive it."

"And until then?" asked Abandonné.

"We keep to our plan from last night. You two play your roles as visiting merchants on your first trip to Amsterdam. That'll give you a reason to ask lots of silly and impertinent questions. Find out all you can about that church, your king's not-so-clandestine appearance, and any gossip pertinent to the event. Buy the local shopkeepers a few drinks. They'll soon tell you every bit of news that isn't an official state secret."

"And you?"

"I'm going to snoop around the church basement to see if I can find any likely places to set a bomb. Then I'll make a few friends among the soldiers and guards, see what their security procedures are. There may be gaps that Guido can exploit. No screen is foolproof."

Treville waited for an hour, but neither Chipay nor Beurre returned, so after preparing himself with some of Monsieur Le Coup's items, he dressed in a blue-and-gold doublet worthy of one of the Forty-Five and went out on his scouting errand to the New Church. Strictly speaking, the Nieuwe Kerk was hardly a shiny new coin, being nearly two hundred years old. But the building that it had replaced, the Oude Kerk, had been built two centuries before that. It looked a bit ramshackle to Treville's eyes, hardly the equal to what was considered a church in Paris or Chartres. Rather than soar to the heavens, it seemed to squat, with heavy bits protruding from it that made it look more like a well-dressed bank than a house of God. The Dutch had turned it into a Protestant shrine, which must have outraged the souls of its Catholic architects.

The interior was also a disappointment in comparison to the lofty and many-windowed masterpieces he was used to. Relatively dim, boasting the much simpler style of the new faith and of the new class of sturdy businessmen who had funded it, the church's ornamentation did not inspire. But a trained eye could tell that much money had been spent on quality materials, even if they were not gaudy. He took that all in at a single glance and focused his attention on the walls, which were thick enough to contain an explosion. There would be much carnage if the bomb were cleverly-placed. Little of its force would escape to the outside.

At the far end, where the king and Maurice would be on the day, an elevated rostrum and pulpit made for easy visibility...and an easy shot if muskets were employed. Treville saw countless sites for a sharpshooter to secrete himself. The place had many balconies, columns, odd corners, doorways, and other excellent hiding places. Escaping after the shot would be more problematic, but the Manqué likely would care little for that if its great aim were achieved. It would make martyrs of those who fell in its service as it crowed to all of Europe about how it was now a force to be reckoned with. He tucked himself into a niche near the main doors and sighted along his finger at the knot of four men on the rostrum. An easy shot, he concluded, especially with a gun like Abandonné had been given. As he peered along his arm, one of those in his sights turned, giving him a clear view of his face.

It was the Duc du Épernon, Admiral of France, governor of Provence and Normandy, occasional traitor to his king, standing there bold as brass.

Having seen the man many times, even protecting him when ordered to do so, Treville was in no doubt that it was Jean de la Vallette. The lean figure in sinfully-rich green fabric, gold-embroidered black cape, and tight white ruff was unmistakable. Also beyond doubt was the fact that the furious eyes and cruel mouth were directed right back at him.

Treville had been recognized.

After debating with himself for a moment, Treville decided to brazen it out. Better to be close to the enemy than be excluded. Hand on sword hilt, he marched up to the rostrum as if on parade, daring any man to challenge his right to be there. Ascending the wooden steps, he approached the quartet, stopped before them with a click of his heels, and bowed low, hat in hand.

"I am overjoyed to see that Your Grace is well," he said in his most oily manner.

Épernon cocked his head ever so slightly, making the single pheasant feather on his cap flutter. "I wonder..."

"No wonder, my lord. I am here as part of the king's protection force. That is my primary duty."

"So I understand, though so often you seem to be on detached service, performing other...functions."

Treville spread his arms. "Whatever France commands."

"And what has she commanded you to do this day?"

"Advance party, my lord, as a senior member of the Forty-Five. Investigating the site of the king's event, ensuring that nothing untoward can occur."

"Such as?"

"Fires, floods, collapsing roofs or floors, madmen wielding firearms, the odd explosion. That sort of thing."

The mention of explosions caused not the slightest change in Épernon's expression, though Treville looked hard for it. "This place seems safe enough from most of that. You worry about gunpowder in a church?"

"It is, admittedly, low on my list of concerns. But all unfortunate possibilities must be guarded against. I am tasked with preventing tragedy. Will Your Grace be in attendance?"

"I have the honor to have been invited by the king, yes."

Treville noted that the man had skillfully avoided the question. He wondered if the invitation had been sought, to deflect suspicion, or if Henri had insisted, feeling safer with his old enemy within arm's reach.

"Honor, indeed. I shall count it an honor on my part to guard your noble self on the day, also."

"I feel safer already," said Épernon with a barely-disguised smirk. "But there are so many of you here, I wonder who is protecting our sovereign back home?"

The well-dressed gentleman on the other side of Épernon, mostly hidden from Treville's view, stepped forward. "Oh, I think His Majesty is in good hands either way. Don't you?"

It was Antoine. For once, he was not with his Épuisant companions.

Treville made sure to give nothing away, though he came close. Would it have killed Rosny to have mentioned this in the dispatches he had sent? "Ah, yes. Saw you lurking there and wondered when you'd speak up. Sorry to horn in on you here, but the Marquis thought that a fresh pair of eyes couldn't hurt."

"Think nothing of it," the elegant Antoine laughed. "It doubles the chance of catching something dangerous before it threatens anyone important."

Épernon smiled, though it added no warmth to the room. "And spreads the blame."

Antoine introduced Treville to the other two men on the rostrum. One was the city's mayor, Barthold Cromhout, a soberly-dressed gentleman past fifty. His tall hat was as black as the rest of his garments, save for the enormous white ruff, offset by the gray of the long beard and the blue of his eyes. Next to him stood Marcus Raaf, sturdy of frame and severe of face, captain of Maurice's personal guard. They both gave polite nods to Treville, clearly regarding him an inconvenient lackey of the French king but apparently essential with so much at stake.

Raaf examined him with a soldier's grim eye, gloved hand on his businesslike rapier. His doublet was gray leather and the riding boots went all the way to the top of his thick thighs. "No small thing, holding the life of a king in one's hand." His voice sounded like cannonballs rolling about in an empty barrel.

"True," Treville agreed. "Sometimes it feels as heavy as a merchantman's anchor."

"And as slippery as an oiled eel."

"Let us hope, then, that our grip is firm and our arms strong."

"I prefer to rely on something more than mere hope." Raaf tapped his graying head. "Forethought. And putting myself into the mind of the enemy."

Treville smiled and nodded. "You and I are going to get on well together."

"I get on well with most men, provided they aren't Hapsburg infantry. But it's easier when they're competent professionals."

"Then, after my inspection of the church, I'd like to be professionally competent with you. Share security plans, prepare for contingencies." Treville looked over at Antoine to see if he wished to be a part of that and received a nod.

"As you wish," growled Raaf. "I'll be here as long as these gentlemen need me. If our paths don't cross again here, you may find me at the Mermaid across the street."

With that, Treville bowed to his betters again and toured the immense main area of the church. Part of him despaired of covering every potential assassin's site while the rest of him wondered about Épernon's presence. The man was implicated in yet more treachery in the Louvre, was hunted across France, yet here he was thick as thieves with those responsible for protecting two monarchs. He made a mental note to have Krijger put someone onto him and see what developed.

Krijger. Was she even alive? Guido might have already cut his losses and her throat. If he had decided after the affair at the farm that the authorities were aware of him, he might bolt. His sort of man would ensure that his trail would be hard to find by killing anyone who could be traced to him, whether they were proved to be treacherous or not. Granted, proof in Maaike's case would be a difficult matter. Even after being her intimate, in every sense of the word, Treville had not made up his mind if she was a fine double-agent or an even better triple one. Playing the role of a Dutch spy pretending to work for the enemy while actually being the enemy was something that Treville could well believe was within her talents.

He shook his head of those confusions and found the narrow door to the basement. That would be the natural spot to place a bomb, of course. The local authorities would have already been down there, but he preferred to trust his own eyes in these matters. The Manqué might have suborned the investigators with money, God, or threats of death. More checks would have to be made as the date of the king's appearance drew nearer. With nearly three days yet, the infernal device was almost certainly not in place yet. But detecting the most likely spot to put it would be time well-spent.

The steps were narrow and unlit. He took a candle from the altar with him and made sure to walk with care. If he tumbled down and broke a leg, he would probably starve before anyone found him. It smelled of the unlikely combination of dust and stale water, the latter being an Amsterdam staple, given its low altitude, canals, and proximity to the bay. Cobwebs were to be expected and this basement did not disappoint, but Treville had endured much worse and casually brushed them away as he scouted. At the bottom of the stairs he found a pair of oil lamps, well-maintained and recently used. As he had suspected, his was not the only visit down here lately. Lighting both with his candle, he left the tallow on a shelf near the exit and took the lamp as he continued into the further recesses of the place.

Now he could see the medieval roots of the 'new' church. Thick stone pillars branched up into masonry arches like great lilies, supporting the rest of the structure. White minerals coated the exterior walls, deposits left by the damp. The dank odor was more oppressive here, away from the only source of ventilation. It was also mostly empty the farther away he went from the door. Close to it the church elders had stored myriad items only used once a year for festivals, or odd old bits destined for the scrap heap. With every careful step he encountered fewer objects, unless one counted rats and their foul waste. Above him was the church floor, a solid mass as far as he could tell. But the space was vast and would take a long time to thoroughly inspect. Treville resigned himself to that drudgery and set to it, completely examining one section before moving to the next, leaving nothing to chance.

An hour later, covered in grime and seemingly half a league from where he started, he had found nothing. There were no other doors or stairs, no clever tunnels, no suspicious new constructions. He had spied a few boot prints, probably from earlier security-conscious guardians of public safety. Nothing to suggest that the Manqué had been planting infernal devices. With his lamps sputtering, he was about to turn back and go meet Raaf at the Mermaid for a drink when a ray of light stabbed him dead in the face.

Luckily, his hat brim caught most of it and gave him the split second to shut his eyes and not be utterly blinded. He set down the lamps and dove behind a pillar, dagger in hand. Near where he had just stood a clever contraption unfolded itself from the ceiling, a ladder that had been built into the trap door and extended to the basement floor when the hatch opened. Treville could just see through the narrow opening that it was located just behind the pulpit. An emergency exit if the flock became restive? The man coming down the steps gripped a rapier, waving it before him as if it were a magic wand. *Probably just clearing any cobwebs. Best to assume the worst, though.*

The newcomer crept forward, careful of where he placed his feet despite being the beneficiary of light from above and from the brass lamp in his hand. His cloak was wrapped around the lamp arm so it would not tangle in his heels. He reached the bottom without incident, shooing away a rat with the sword. After scanning the empty scene in a leisurely way, he spoke with his back to Treville.

"I wondered how long it would take you to get this far," Antoine said with a chuckle. "You've been down here a good while."

Treville waited for a reply. When none was forthcoming, he had to assume that his comrade was speaking to him. He moved out from behind the pillar, keeping the dagger in his hand but holding it casually along his thigh. "I thought I'd take my time, enjoy the atmosphere."

Antoine made a show of coughing up said atmosphere. "There's certainly plenty of it."

"Not your first trip down here, I take it?"

"Oh, no. We searched it straight off, of course. Nothing terrifying, at least in a political way. I would've told you that, but I knew you'd insist on seeing for yourself anyway. Satisfied?"

"No villains lurking, no sinister kegs of powder, only these two entrances that I can see."

"I know. Inexpressibly dull, eh?"

"I like dull. When the king needs protecting, dull is our friend."

"Agreed. Hercule must be guarded. Still, a soldier likes to have some excitement now and then."

And with that, Antoine launched his rapier point at Treville.

20

AMSTERDAM

"IF YOU KEEP US IN SUSPENSE, I SWEAR
I WILL CARVE YOU LIKE A CHICKEN."

Treville's dagger arm twitched, but he need not have been anxious. Antoine was merely skewering an aggressive rat that was chewing on his friend's boot. The creature shrieked and writhed for a moment, then expired. His executioner whipped the corpse from his blade.

"Nearly as many of these brutes down here as there are human vermin up top."

Treville returned his dagger to its scabbard. "You're unimpressed with the quality of the Dutch clergy?"

"And their civic equivalent." Antoine put his own weapon away. "They lack judgment, they lack discretion, they lack a proper religion. A pronounced dearth of most things we French would deem necessary for civilization."

"They seem to be a well-organized, educated, heroic, caring, people. Is that not civilization?"

"Oh, to be sure, they've created quite the clean, business-like nest here. But commerce has replaced God in most of their hearts." He shrugged. "But it's not my place to judge. Others will do that. I'm a mere hired sword, yes?"

"As am I. Shall we finish peeping into the rest of the corners down here?"

"By all means. Let nothing be overlooked."

They quickly checked every remaining inch of the basement and satisfied themselves that there were no ways for anyone to get into it other than from the interior of the church itself. It was possible, of course, that a tunnel from an adjoining building was being dug even as they stood there, but that would also be investigated soon. And the French and Dutch authorities would swarm the place with troops in two days, so that even if by some miracle the enemy managed to get in, they would have little chance of success before being overwhelmed.

After ascending to the pulpit area and shutting the trapdoor, they dusted themselves off and looked for Épernon and the others. But those worthies had moved on. So King Henri's men adjourned to the Mermaid Tavern across the street and met with a well-lubricated Raaf, who greeted them in a loud voice as if they had all been lifelong friends. Without sharing too many of the secrets he and his team had worked to hard to uncover in the past few days, Treville explained his concerns about the mysterious Guido and his gang. Antoine said that Rosny's sources had determined that such a political/religious group was set on causing trouble. That was why he had been sent on ahead of the others to try to flush them out. Raaf added that the Dutch spies had been quite busy trying to infiltrate operations like that, with varying success. He himself had broken one of them up, posing as a wealthy lord eager to fund their activities.

"A wealthy lord?" Treville asked with undisguised disbelief. The man looked terribly worn and coarse to have pulled that off.

Raaf sat up, shook the beer from his face, and said in an undeniably elegant tone, "Sir, you positively wound me!" His whole demeanor --posture, expression, vocal register -- had altered in an instant into that of a foppish courtier with more money than sense.

Treville was impressed. *Are all the Dutch spies this good? If so, we should be on our guard against them.*

"My apologies. You should start your own troupe of actors." It occurred to Treville that it would only take a larger nose and some gray paint in the hair and beard to turn the Dutchman into King Henri's twin. *That would be a performance worth seeing. I wonder if Henriette d'Entragues would notice?*

Raaf laughed. "Who says I haven't?"

They all traded more quips, downed just enough drink to feel able to conquer the world, and departed. Antoine said he was off to prepare for the arrival of Gaston, Louis, and the rest of the Forty-Five and would meet Treville the next morning for final planning of the king's appearance with Maurice. If anything important came up, Treville should immediately alert him at the Town Hall. Treville promised that he would do that very thing and bid him farewell at the door of the Mermaid. Feeling pleasantly relaxed, he left the tavern and strolled out into the square, intending to go back to the house and confer with d'Artagnan and Abandonné. But he had not gone five paces when he was brought up short by an unexpected sight.

Fantôme walked across his path, medical bag in hand, speaking to a prominently-ruffed Dutch burgher with a forked gray beard.

The physician either did not see him or was pretending not to, for though they passed within literal spitting distance, he made no sign of recognition. Intent on the other man's words, Chipay kept nodding his understanding as he walked. Treville fell in behind them at a safe distance, making certain not to lose sight of them. Only once did he pause, to ask a local citizen who the white man up ahead might be.

"Him, sir? Why, that's good old Johan van Oldenbarnevelt, the *Landsadvocaat*. Practically runs the country, he does."

Treville mentally kicked himself for not recognizing the Chief Minister of the United Provinces. While Maurice was the famed military commander and *Stadtholder*, Johan was the great politician who maneuvered with other rulers to keep Spain at bay. He had achieved the alliance with France and England in 1596 that had managed that very thing, though King James had just signed a peace with the Hapsburgs. And he had founded the very United East India Company that seemed to be at the heart of Treville's current difficulties.

Why's Chipay with him? And just how did he manage to get a private audience with the chief power in the land?

The second question was answered when the pair stopped near a cafe and van Oldenbarnevelt pointed to his own belly. Chipay frowned, asked a question, and prodded the spot with his fingers. That made the other man wince and reply.

Ah! A medical consultation. Chipay, you're a clever one. I just hope you aren't the one who ends up needing a physician most. You should be in bed taking medicine, not squeezing answers out of this old Dutchman.

Chipay took something from his bag and handed it to his patient, giving verbal instructions that the *Landsadvocaat* heeded with great seriousness. When the great man offered payment, Fantôme waved that off with great magnanimity, no doubt professing that it was a public service for the stability of the Dutch state. After offering it again, and again being politely refused, van Oldenbarnevelt surrendered the field and bowed. Treville smiled at how the fish had been played. Now the statesman owed Chipay a favor. That was like money in the bank to Treville.

After they parted, Treville caught up to the doctor. He noticed that the other man was limping, as well he should with such a wound. But that had not been evident the whole time he had been walking with his patient. Again, Treville was impressed by his iron will and ability to seemingly forget distress when a larger object was at hand.

"You should be resting," he said. "I know a physician who would tell you the same thing,"

"I know him, too," responded Fantôme, showing no surprise at Treville's approach. Catching an experienced warrior unawares would, of course, have been unlikely. "Pig-headed fellow. Can't get him to see any sort of sense."

"True enough. I'm considering having him dragged home by a team of wild horses and tied to his mattress."

"I doubt that it will be necessary. His reserves are nearly exhausted and he's more than willing to go without a struggle."

Now Treville saw how true the statement was. Even Chipay's dark skin could grow pale, it seemed. He looked gray and drawn, the struggle of the past few hours having taken too much out of him. The limp became a stagger, then a stumble. Treville caught him on a shoulder and aided him home, again too busy to notice the silver-nosed fly hovering nearby. They were met at the door by Beurre, who bustled Chipay back into the bed that he never should have left that morning. Despite his insistence that it was vital, Treville was allowed no opportunity to question the sick man about what he might have pried out of van Oldenbarnevelt. After several attempts, he gave up until his host was in a more forthcoming mood, heading down to the kitchen for a wash and a snack.

As he was finishing his cheese, d'Artagnan and Abandonné returned from their day at the market, wearing their wool merchant disguises. They looked utterly bored. Neither enjoyed inaction. The Gascon tossed a small sack of coins onto the table.

"Well, it wasn't a complete waste of time. We sold some of our wares. Didn't make much profit. Haggling with these Dutch is like negotiating with Spanish envoys. You know you're being cheated but their charm overwhelms your good sense. At the end of it you want to cut their throats just to feel that you've gotten something out of the deal."

"One hopes that you restrained that impulse," sighed Treville.

"We did," Abandonné answered, "and should get a medal from the king for it."

"Did anything at all come from your day?"

"Other than bargaining with the burghers? Does turning down eleven vile advances from various idiot men count as an accomplishment?" She gave d'Artagnan a sly smile, which told Treville all that he needed to know about the lad's bad temper.

"It's a testament to your self-discipline," Treville said, looking at her but aiming his words at d'Artagnan. "Any other interesting conversations?" He knew that their inexperience in espionage might lead them to overlook something of value.

He guided them through their day, getting them to relive it minute by minute to enable him to put himself with them, to see and hear as they had. Most of it was as mundane as they had claimed. Casual shoppers idly grazing the merchandise, sharp ones looking for an absurdly good deal. Even other cloth sellers, scouting the competition. Some friends and acquaintances had come by: Beurre, of course, keeping a quasi-parental eye on them. Chipay, at a distance, as he spoke to various important men in the square. *An amazing sight, a native from the forests of Canada treated as an equal by the masters of Amsterdam.* That kind and elegant guardian of the king who had helped save them in Pontoise, Monsieur Antoine. He had bought a bit of yellow silk to make into an extravagant handkerchief. *Typical of him.* Even the great lord the Duc du

153

Épernon had said hello, happy to speak French to fellow countrymen. In his graciousness he had purchased some lace for a certain lady who would have to remain unnamed. *I hope the queen likes it.*

"Did no one mention the New Church, or the assembly with King Henri's 'envoy' and the future Prince of Orange?"

D'Artagnan snorted while pouring wine. "Mention it? That's all anybody talked about, besides trying to cheat us of our profits. 'A great day for Amsterdam and the United Provinces', they'd crow. 'Now Spain has to take us seriously.' 'Catholics and Protestants in common cause against the world's bully!' That was a frequent one."

"Were any of them concerned about trouble at the event?"

"Several mentioned it on their own," Abandonné answered, "and most had an opinion if we brought up the subject. Patriotism runs high here. No one seemed to think that an enemy could get through their troops and constables, especially when bolstered by the French guards."

I wish I were that sanguine.

"Not quite true," d'Artagnan said, raising a finger. "Don't you remember that man of God who came out of the cheese shop?"

"The fat Protestant minister with the red nose from drinking too much of his own communion wine? The annoying swine groped me. Some man of God he was."

"He was the only one who worried about an attack. Hard to hear him sometimes. Kept coughing into his handkerchief like he had the White Plague. The cloth stayed in front of his face the whole time. So snotty that it was the color of one of those canary birds the Spanish sailors bring back from their travels. Don't think he'd ever washed it. Probably all for the best. Wouldn't want him spewing that all over me."

Alarm bells clanged in Treville's head. That fellow had been in the shop when he had inquired after Krijger. "What did he say? Be precise."

"I can quote him exactly," swore Abandonné, "because I was fending off one of his grubby hands at the time. "The pig said, 'True, a regiment of troops can repel a frontal assault, but they can only fight what they can see. Stealth can take a bag of gold if the watchdog thinks that the thief is its master. The dog wouldn't even notice the lack.'"

Treville slapped his hand onto the table so hard that the others jerked in surprise. "You'd swear that he said those words? No possibility of a mistake?"

D'Artagnan shook his head. "I remember it that way, too."

His mind whirling with scraps of conversation and bits of memory, Treville stood and paced about the kitchen. Images drifted before his eyes like puzzle pieces, sometimes interlocking and sometimes not quite matching. He kept them all dancing in the air, as would a talented juggler. Eventually they all settled into a single picture, with none left over.

"Bloody hell, that's it!" he cried, laughing in victory and relief that he had sorted the whole thing out. But part of him was miserable, too, for the triumph would be bittersweet this time.

"What?" asked all the others in unison, clearly perplexed.

"I know who the spy is who's been feeding Manqué our secrets. And I know what their plan is."

D'Artagnan drew his dagger. "If you keep us in suspense, I swear I will carve you like a chicken."

Treville snatched up the Gascon's wine glass and drained it. "They aren't going to blow up King Henri. They're going to kidnap him!"

21

AMSTERDAM

"OH, I COULD TELL YOU STORIES ABOUT MONKS.
THERE WAS THIS OLD ROUÉ IN THE NUNNERIES OF PROVENCE…"

Chaos ensued as the room erupted in competing questions and declarations. Treville let it run its course, then explained his thinking at great length. So thorough was he that there were few objections when he had finished. The most common reaction was shock. Beurre had the most important response.

"How do we test it?"

Treville replied, "By playing the fools. Let them think we are in the dark about their operation. We have two days to give them enough rope to make their own noose. Their cleverness will be their undoing. And while they think they are safe, we can quietly pry to confirm our suspicions. If I'm proven right, I also know how to ruin their scheme while letting them think they've succeeded."

Again he laid out his thoughts, and again they all heard him out with little opposition. It was not bold enough for d'Artagnan, of course, who preferred flashing swords to covert action. But he came to see that the king's safety was paramount and that the more violence the more risk to him. Abandonné advised canceling the event altogether, but again Treville explained that neither leader would countenance such an apparently-cowardly move. Each had a tenuous hold on his nation and dared not risk seeming weak.

"Besides, this is our best chance to sweep them all up and end the Manqué for good."

They worked on plans for a couple of hours, until Beurre announced that dusk was approaching. Treville thanked him and they both went to the garret atop the house, taking with them a detailed code sheet that Krijger had written out after explaining her communication system. Opening the window, they looked to the west and waited, heads cocked like curious dogs.

Three minutes later a lone church bell rang, in a very odd manner.

Its pattern was irregular. Not a steady single note, like the toll for the dead, or in precise groupings. Instead, the deep bongings made no sense to an experienced listener. Two would be followed by three, then one, then four. Pauses between were not all the same, either. People in the street below stopped, listened, shook their heads. Their confusion was not shared by the men atop the house, for by following Maaike's legend they could see that the bell spelled out words.

She had told them that she had developed a particular persona the entire time that she had been posing as a Manqué member. Her character, as it were, loved birds. For months she had fussed over larks, wrens, and anything else with wings, amusing her rough male cohorts with her silliness. Eventually she had begun keeping pigeons, giving them cute names and treating them almost like children. The others had never noticed that one bird seemed ever so much cleverer than the others.

Krijger had smuggled in a well-trained messenger pigeon.

With a bit of sly effort she had taught it to fly to the belfry of a particular church in the center of the city, a haunt of the Dutch intelligence service. From there coded messages could occasionally be sent out by way of the bells with no one the wiser. It was those bells that rang now, chiming out her first message. Treville listened well and wrote it down, with Beurre doing the same so that they could compare versions and make no errors.

"All...well...your...night's...work...fooled...them...let's...do...it...again... sometime..."

Beurre stared at Treville, one eyebrow raised. He received the most innocent of looks in return.

"Watch...New...Church...be...wary...of...old...women..."

Treville frowned. "Old women? What's that about?"

"Haven't the foggiest," Beurre said. "Are they recruiting grannies now?"

"Amsterdam has a lot of them, if we're expected to arrest them all."

The bell continued to speak." Trust...no...one...they've...got...their... hooks...in...all..."

"I think we puzzled that one out on our own," Beurre muttered.

"Will...talk...same...time...tomorrow...kisses...farewell."

Silence reigned as the bell finally petered out. "Well, someone certainly made an impression on her," Beurre snickered.

"Her idea of a joke, actually," Treville said, knowing that it sounded lame.

"We should all be the butt of such jokes."

"Frankly, I wish her on you. You'd be laughing less and limping more. Come on, let's share this with the others, little as it is."

They returned to the kitchen, where they found d'Artagnan and Abandonné playing at dice. As no coins were on the table, the stakes must have been of the alternative variety. To judge by the young woman's blushing face and somewhat swollen lips, there had been no losers. Treville ignored that and shared what he had heard from the belfry. It puzzled the younger partners, too.

"Old ladies? Well, perhaps she'll elaborate tomorrow," said d'Artagnan with a shrug.

Treville drummed his fingers on the table as he pondered the message. "Possibly. Until then, let's keep to our plan. That includes code names. Abandonné will be our eyes above, with her magical eye. Practice with it until it's second-nature to you. Temeraire will find that clergyman and stick to him like honey. Penseur will get with our friend Raaf for his role, and coordinate with the king and the Forty-Five when they arrive tomorrow morning. Beurre will send out his street folk to see what they can pick up. Otherwise, he'll remain here with Flan to ensure that Fantôme is lashed to his bed. I can't be bothered with any more of his heroics. There's too much at stake to risk having it all unravel because he takes on more than his punctured body will permit."

The next day saw no disasters, which warmed Treville's heart. Their damaged doctor remained obedient and supine, reading a Dutch medical tract on sleep aids. Abandonné polished her musket and lens, disassembling them both repeatedly until not a speck of troublesome grit remained to potentially clog the workings. Several ragged urchins and a few apprentices and shopkeepers came to the door to receive instructions from Beurre. Then they dispersed throughout the city to pass the orders along. After disguising himself as a dairyman, of all things, Temeraire took his cart loaded with milk, cheese, and butter around town, keeping a sharp eye out for the mysterious coughing minister.

That left Penseur to track down Marcus Raaf, who was conveniently warming a bench at the Mermaid again. When he explained the plan and what he wanted the old soldier to do, Raaf clapped his hands with glee and announced that he knew just the performative fellow to partner him in the enterprise, a man who often got into trouble for doing the very thing that Treville now demanded. After the requisite strong beer, they parted, Raaf to one of the Rederijker companies of performers and Treville to the City Hall to meet his fellows of the Forty-Five.

Counting himself, thirty of them were present, making for a raucous scene in the large banqueting room set aside for them. The other fifteen were on duty protecting King Henri, as always. Every eight hours a fresh group would take over, with allowances for leave and special assignments. At present the king was in the apartments set aside for him. As this was supposed to be a surprise appearance rather than an official state visit, his entourage was necessarily small. Treville passed through the cordon of his fellows to pay respects to His Majesty and request a brief audience. Henri saw the grave look on his man's face and immediately dismissed everyone for five minutes.

It took somewhat longer than that. The sovereign of France had no appetite for what Penseur suggested and said so with some heat. But the spy persisted, mixing cajolement with flattery and an appeal to the needs of the people. In the end, Henri not only accepted the recommendation, he adopted it as if he had thought of it himself, declaring it to be a brilliant stroke and no doubt the source of many rollicking tales in his dotage. His handlers were brought in, told the minimum that they needed to accomplish the task, sworn to secrecy, and dismissed. Treville bowed himself out, as well, and went in search of Gaston to arrange the rest. On the way, he spotted the Marquise de Verneuil, unusually quiet and unassuming, in what was for her a simple brown traveling dress, holding the hand of her, and the king's, young son.

"M'Lady," he said with a slight bow. "You look well." He bowed to little Gaston Henri, only four years old, wearing an adorable copy of the blue doublet the king wore that day.

"And you, m'lord, are getting to be a proper man already."

The lad grinned, drool oozing out of one corner of his mouth. Henriette's sole servant wiped his face with a cloth. When Treville turned to go, his mother let out a whimper and gripped his arm.

"Is it true? Is he in danger here? More than the usual, I mean?"

Penseur thought it remarkable that such a schemer could marshal concern for the man she so often upbraided for wronging her, whom she had even tried to overthrow with Spanish aid. Was she that good an actress, that empty inside? Or was this honest worry for the child's father and sole protector? "Somewhat. Steps have been taken. He is here with open eyes, have no fear of that."

"But I do fear it. We are in a vipers' nest here. The Dutch have no love of him, or of any of us, beyond what we can do to give them independence from the Hapsburgs. They are radical Protestants, after all."

"You think that they would endanger their own general just to embarrass France? Harm to our king would destabilize us and cost the Dutch their only support, since England has made peace with Spain. They are not madmen."

"Not the United Provinces as a whole, no. Eminently sane. But there are crazed factions, I hear…"

So her own spies had been at work. Or was she part of the Manqué, after all, and merely playing a double game? Treville wished that people would simply say what they honestly felt. Then again, he would be out of a job if that happened.

"Factions always exist. Men who believe that their petty desires should be granted, no matter the cost to everyone else. But in this case, they will fail."

"You are very certain."

"Self-doubt is the portal to defeat, m'lady. Good day."

He threaded his way through the press of courtiers and returned to the Forty-Five's hall, where he found Gaston holding court with a few of the lounging guards and even, to Treville's surprise, some of the Maréchaussée. Coupé and Colére both gave him ironic salutes.

"Is Paris so safe and dull that they could spare both of you for this?" he asked them.

"No," said Coupé, "but since disaster seems to follow in your wake, it was decided that the greater danger to the king is here."

Gaston slapped Treville on the back as if beating a carpet. "How have you been, you reprobate? I hear the most astonishing reports about you. They make me envious."

"All lies, I assure you. I live like a monk."

"Oh, I could tell you stories about monks. There was this one old roué in the nunneries of Provence ---"

Treville seized his arm and steered him into a corner with hasty apologies to the others. As he spoke in hushed tones, he kept a sharp eye on Coupé and Colére. "Say nothing, listen very carefully, and smile the whole time no matter what I tell you."

To Gaston's credit, he did precisely as ordered. He could be circumspect when duty required it. While Penseur filled him in on everything, he grinned like a fool, nodded, even guffawed a few times. No one watching would have guessed at the deadly seriousness of what he was hearing.

When Treville finished speaking, Gaston simply asked, "There can be no question?"

"I wish there were. It would make this easier."

"Agreed. But it has to be done, I suppose. Until tomorrow then."

With that unpleasant duty done, Treville returned to Beurre's house, where that gentleman reported that his minions had found nothing nefarious afoot in Amsterdam beyond what he had already discovered. There seemed to be no other operation in the offing. The Manqué's design on Henri and Maurice was not a diversion for a greater plot. That relieved Treville immensely. His greatest fear had not been the attack in the New Church, but having all those soldiers and guards tied down there so that something nearly as bad could succeed, like the assassination of the entire Dutch legislature. Now he could focus entirely on his single task.

"What about Maurice? Is he with us?"

"I gather that he was no happier about it than King Henri, but he is a pragmatist. I'm told that he also sees the potential for your idea to be of significant use in other situations."

"Such as touchy negotiations with Spanish envoys? Perhaps. One wonders what Raaf and his partner think of that prospect, though."

D'Artagnan dragged himself into the house, still dressed as a dairyman. He sagged into a chair and swilled wine straight from the bottle. "Milk...all day nothing but milk. How does anyone drink the stuff?"

"You did, as a baby," Beurre reminded him.

"Yes, but only because tits were involved. As soon as I was capable of rational judgment I abandoned it."

Treville laughed. "Speaking of rational judgment, did you employ any on our godly friend today?"

"I did, though I thought I'd have to employ a yard of good steel instead."

"Do tell."

"Well, if he's a man of the cloth then I'm the Pope. I followed him out of that cheese shop for a while and where do you think he went?"

"Not to church, I'm guessing."

"Far from it. He sat himself right outside our front door, pretending to read a book of psalms. But every half a minute he lifted his eyes to see if anything interesting was happening here."

"For how long?"

"Two hours. Oh, he was clever about it. Didn't stay in one spot for long. Every now and then he would shift, buy something in a shop, gossip with people. Twice he wandered around to look at the back of the house, too. But just to make sure, I arranged a little accidental 'beg your pardon, sir' collision. He's awfully solid for such a blubbery-looking old preacher. And no minister ever carried a brace of pistols and a dagger under his cassock."

"How did he take it?"

"Perfectly in character, I'll give him that. Coughed behind his yellow rag and told me not to worry myself about it. I got suspicious about the cloth and asked if he had seen a doctor for his condition. Tried to get him talking so that I could get in close. Sure enough, in the instant I managed it before he drew away, I spotted it."

"What?"

"He overplayed his hand. Rubbed his nose one time too many. I caught a glint of silver."

"La Haine! You didn't run him through, I hope."

"No, more's the pity. And I couldn't very well follow him after that, either, not without a change of costume. So I gave a coin to the street rat who seems to live on our stop and had him do it. Hasn't come back yet."

Beurre chuckled. "That street rat is Willem. Works for me. Very bright. He won't lose La Haine unless the man grows wings."

Treville counted that as a good day's work and went upstairs to check on Abandonné. She showed him how quickly she could sight in on a distant target by aiming at a steeple so distant it could barely be seen without the aid of her scope. Her glee resembled that of a child rejoicing over a birthday present. They went over her part of the next day's plan again and he left her to her toys. He looked in on Fantôme but the doctor was lightly snoring, which was just what Treville wanted him to be doing.

The rest of the afternoon was dedicated to planning, rehearsal, and weapons maintenance. At dusk Penseur and Beurre again trudged upstairs to listen for Krijger's bells. Just as before, they clanged out their hidden message. Only this one was markedly different from the previous day.

"We…have…your…little…cheesemonger…and…the…brat."

Treville kicked the wall and swore. It struck him that the Duc du Épernon's crest featured a bell at its center.

22

AMSTERDAM

THEN THE KING OF FRANCE VANISHED
IN FRONT OF A THOUSAND EYEWITNESSES.

His every instinct was to go charging to her rescue. It was everyone else's, too, when he told them what had happened. But eventually he let his passions cool and examined the matter logically.

"They want us to do that," he told his friends. "To rush blindly into an ambush and get butchered. Then their dance tomorrow goes off without interference."

"We can't just leave her there," Abandonné complained. "Or that poor boy either. They'll probably skin them alive for sheer sport."

"Not yet they won't. Guido's too canny for that. He may need something to bargain with. Dead hostages are poor leverage. We have some time. But it can't be any of us who go over there." When they complained again he held up a hand. "We know too much about them. They'd love to grab one of us and roast us over a spit until we talk. They'd change their plan for tomorrow and then where would the king be?" He turned to Beurre. "You have someone watching them, of course."

"Several someones. A report comes back every two hours."

"Good. Get every detail about the place: buildings, manpower, weapons, all of it. Then run the same ruse you ran at the farm. But not until the New Church meeting starts. We want to snare their boldest men."

"They'll never fall for it twice."

"Of course not. And just when they thinks it's all a show again and relax, real cavalry will storm the place."

Beurre laughed and made a show of looking around. "Whose cavalry?"

"Maurice's. It seems that our ailing doctor is owed a favor by Johan van Oldenbarnevelt."

"Yes? That's convenient."

"Isn't it? Chipay is a man of many layers."

Beurre dashed off to get intelligence from his runner and then take a note from Fantôme to the *Landsadvocaat*, stopping to have it countersigned by Maurice's office. The rest discussed precisely what they would do in the morning, when the King of France parleyed with the *Stadtholder*. Satisfied that they were as ready as they could be, Treville sent everyone to their beds -- their own beds this time, he cautioned -- with a watch schedule so that someone would always be up and alert, in case of a spoiling attack or an urgent message. None of the ringleaders would be with Maaike when the raid came, most likely. They would all be playing their parts at the New Church for God and glory…and probably East India Company gold, too. But a few would be left to guard the prisoners and secure the place until Guido and La Haine returned with the captives. Though how the Manqué thought they could gain anything other than a famous death was beyond him. Did they really think that they could bargain while thousands of troops surrounded them? What possible escape plan could they have?

Those questions kept Treville awake even when he was not on watch, but eventually he fell asleep. Predictably, the dream returned. As always, he tried to focus on the masked man, tried to glean some new detail that might help in recognizing him after so many years. But it was no good. All that came of it was sweat, panting, and anger. And worry over Maaike's fate did little to make him feel any better.

He was happy to rise, dress, breakfast, and strap on his weapons. The weight of metal reassured him. D'Artagnan seemed to be of the same mind, cavorting around the kitchen, whistling a cheery Gascon tune while his rapier banged against Beurre's cabinets. Soon Abandonné joined them, her hated dress left upstairs in exchange for male military trousers and boots beneath a long cloak that would hide her musket until she reached her assigned station. Only Beurre was missing, so Treville sighed and knocked on his door.

When repeated knocks received no answer, he barged in, fearing the worst. The man seemed dead, but closer inspection revealed that he only slept. Shaking would not wake him, however. His wine glass had an odd odor. Swearing at the top of his lungs, Treville burst into Chipay's room. Naturally, it was empty. A mortar and pestle there smelled just like Beurre's glass. This time, though, the physician had left a note.

'Apologies, my brother. You would not accept my help any other way. He will wake in an hour. I shall meet you when you are in most need.'

With nothing else to be done, Penseur swallowed his annoyance and informed the others of the development. They thought it charmingly hilarious, which hardly improved his mood. But duty called, so he jammed his hat onto his head and led them to the Neuwe Kerke, after first checking front and rear entrances to make certain that they were not being watched. He took an indirect route, just to be safe, and they arrived at the enormous house of God some thirty minutes before the king and *Stadtholder* were scheduled to appear. Cavalry and infantry surrounded it and lined the street approaches, keeping the packed and enthusiastic throng from pressing too close. An army band was getting ready to play the anthems of both nations. Old war widows in festive hats had set up a table and were selling yellow ribbons, souvenirs of the occasion. *Ah, the Dutch never miss an opportunity for commerce.* Schoolchildren sang patriotic songs near the steps.

A great black and gold carriage with the House of Orange crest crept up to the front door. The blue, white, and orange-striped national flag flew behind it. Soldiers struggled to contain the crowd as it surged forward to see its hero. Treville knew that they need not have bothered. That was all for show. Maurice and Henri were already inside the church, as were the few citizens permitted to take part in the spectacle.

The Épuisants were waiting at a rear door, preventing entrance except for those on the certified list. Gaston waved Penseur's team through with a curt nod. Treville informed him that Fantôme was at large and that he should be admitted if he appeared. A survey of the square showed no sign of him, nor of anything untoward, either. Looking up, he saw only happy citizens, plus Dutch musketmen atop the buildings.

Inside, all was courtly bustle. The guests of honor were sequestered in a back room until their time came, though their gilt chairs were already waiting. Other civic leaders would address the audience first. A music consort occupied the rostrum, playing patriotic tunes. Flags, bunting, and flowers decorated the space there and elsewhere. So many blossoms gave the room a more fragrant air than it might otherwise have had with hundreds of bodies filling it. Respectable merchants, bankers, aristocrats, and clergy milled about, filling the church with a low murmur. Abandonné moved to her assigned position while her two partners split up to scout the vast open space and hunt for anyone suspicious. Treville paced the exterior walls, holding his rapier close to the leg to avoid entanglement. No immediate concerns leaped out at him. He prayed that things remained thus.

The musicians played a fanfare and Mayor Cromhout ascended the rostrum to loud applause and a few cheers. Just like the other time Penseur had seen him, he wore the traditional dark and staid clothing of the Amsterdam city fathers and men of respect. He seemed nervous, almost trembling, which was only to be expected with the King of France and the *Stadtholder* waiting to be introduced. Others followed him on, members of the city council and church figures, nearly as anxious. As the room went silent, one of the latter spoke a prayer.

Penseur and Temeraire met near the main entrance after completing their inspection tours. Neither had come across anything to worry about. As the men on the rostrum took turns speaking to the assembly, mouthing the political platitudes one always heard in such circumstances, Treville began to think that the Manqué might have abandoned their rash scheme in the face of so much protection, not to mention the presumed assault on their headquarters.

Here's hoping that Maaike survived her own rescue. The guards may have orders to kill her if attacked. Even more likely, she might have joined the fight, even if tied up, and gone down swinging.

Colére joined them, two of his Maréchausée in tow. Raaf's lieutenant, a small terrier of a fellow, also appeared. He informed Treville that all was in readiness for the entry of Henri and Maurice, a sly smile on his bearded mouth as he spoke. Treville thanked him and asked if the basement had been searched again.

"Better than that," said Colére, "we have five men down there: two of mine, one of yours, and two of Raaf's."

"Good. No surprises from that quarter then."

The crowd erupted as Maurice of Nassau, renowned general and chastiser of the Hapsburgs, was introduced. Like the others on the stage he wore black, somber of shade but rich of fabric. His torso was covered in an etched bronze cuirass, a lace ruff perched atop it circling the thick neck. A narrow spade-shaped reddish beard hung from his round chin. Though a mighty warrior, he did not have the sort of face that inspired dread. It was pale, doughy, not very mobile, and more like a sad old hound than anything else, despite the man being only in his mid-thirties. He spoke so quietly that several hearers asked him to be louder. With a smile and a nod he did so, but not by much.

For a few minutes he talked about the nation, the revolt against Spain, the triumphs and tragedies and the long road ahead. None of it was particularly new or inspiring. In fact, Treville heard someone in the audience complain that it sounded like he was repeating an old speech given at a similar gathering two years before. Nonetheless, the people received it well and applauded mightily when he had finished and retreated toward his seat upstage. From there he announced a surprise, one of the far-sighted monarchs who appreciated their struggle and had allied with them to make it a success.

When King Henri IV's name was called silence reigned for a long moment, no one believing that they had heard correctly. But the sight of his homely, but regal, self strolling through the door cued them all to cheer lustily again. Like Maurice, he wore quasi-military attire as a symbol of the nature of their alliance against the Spanish. Like his fellow soldier on the rostrum, he seemed paler and stiffer than was his wont, but healthy enough. The two men of the hour embraced with proud smiles as the noise in the church reached a deafening level.

It subsided as they sat in their matching chairs. Cromhout gave a little speech, more haltingly than might be expected of an experienced politician, about the unbreakable bond between the two states, mentioning that the House of Orange had originally sprung from the south of France. Then those in attendance were invited to come up to the edge of the stage and ask that a boon be granted. Many did so, asking that a jailed relative be pardoned, the sewage removed from their street, or harbor fees reduced. Not all received the answer that they desired, but all took the replies with good grace and pride at being heard by the mighty.

Treville circulated through the crowd again, telling the others to do the same, looking for any last-minute signs of trouble. None appeared. Gaston came in and reported nothing outside was worrisome, either. Perhaps the military attack on the Manqué really had disrupted everything. Soon Treville could relax with wine and, with luck, Maaike.

Then the King of France vanished in front of a thousand eyewitnesses.

It was neatly managed. All of Amsterdam's city elders moved down to the edge of the rostrum for a final wave to their constituents, prompted by the mayor. Barely visible behind the tall black hats, Henri and Maurice stood to go. The *Stadtholder* walked to the upstage door he had originally come from, Henri following. But after three steps he simply disappeared as if taken by sorcery. Most in the applauding audience never noticed, their view blocked by Cromhout's cohort. Even Maurice remained unaware that his guest was gone.

Penseur and d'Artagnan spied it, though. In tandem, they shoved through the mass of people, ignoring the outraged cries. Vaulting onto the rostrum, their progress was blocked by the line of councilors. Cromhout remained rooted to the floorboards, unwilling to move out of the way.

"Stand aside!" Treville ordered. "What are you doing?" Then he noticed tears in the man's eyes.

"My wife," he sobbed in a whisper. "They said they'd kill her. I had no choice."

With understanding, Treville nodded and edged past him. *I should've prepared for extortion. A beginner's mistake.* He got to the spot his king had last occupied, already knowing what he would find. The secret trapdoor behind the pulpit, the one that Antoine had used, was just about to close. D'Artagnan saw it, too, and jammed a dagger blade into it before it sealed, a pistol in his other hand. As he tried to poke its barrel into the gap, a rapier blade shot up past his eye, forcing him to jerk aside. Treville stomped on it with his boot heel, pinning it against the edge of the opening. When it withdrew, he and his partner leaped upon the hatch together, overwhelming the mechanism and the man operating it. It gave way and opened fully. More agile and bolder, Temeraire slid down the ladder, gun spitting flame and smoke. By the time he landed at the bottom, his sword was out and Penseur was also through the passage.

The Gascon was too intent on pursuit and not on self-preservation. If Treville had not expected an ambush and shouldered him behind a sheltering pillar, the lad would have stopped a well-aimed pistol ball with his handsome face. Risking a look, Penseur saw two armed men towing the protesting king toward an empty section of wall. No door or window gave exit there, so it was a mystery what they thought they could achieve.

"Can't shoot back, that would endanger the king," he told d'Artagnan, who nodded and put away his second pistol. With swords and daggers they pursued, moving irregularly from pillar to pillar on separate tracks.

Soon they found all but one of the guards who had been placed in the basement to prevent just this thing. All lay dead from efficient stab wounds. Not one had drawn his weapon. They had all been killed by a supposed friend, of course, a fellow soldier whom they would had no reason to suspect. It proved that Treville's assessment of the traitor had been correct, but he had prayed to be wrong.

The treacherous one was at bay behind a pillar against the wall now, pistol to the king's head. His partner, a clean-shaven man dressed as one of the old widows outside, stood a few yards off at another stone support. Treville pointed his pistol at the man holding Henri.

"I don't suppose my heart-broken disappointment will entice you to surrender?"

"Alas, no," replied Antoine. "Though it does make me a bit sad that you feel that way. Besides, why should I surrender? I've won."

"I don't think that word means what you think it means."

"Um, 'achieving one's goal.' Did they change the definition?"

"You're pinned against a wall. Reinforcements are coming. All you've won is the right to be broken on the wheel."

"I think not. They won't risk their precious king's Protestant-loving skin. I'll be fine. We don't much care if we survive this, anyway. It's not about one man's life."

"To what end, though? Even if you escape with him, what have you gained?"

"Discord. Chaos. Upsetting the European apple-cart."

"Are you serious? Look around. There's no amity now. All you're doing is throwing a twig on a bonfire."

"Oil, not a twig. If we can snatch the Bourbon king, what can't we do? Every ass perched on a purple cushion will grow fearful, anxious that he'll be next. Especially all of the Protestant accommodators."

"This is all about whose church is in charge?"

"It's always about that, has been since we lived in caves. What is God, anyway? Power. The ultimate force on earth. And what flows from power?

Control. Control of gold, of property, of borders, of any damned thing you want. Can't make the world a better place without it."

"So now you're claiming the high road? You just want peace, justice, and amity?"

"Hell, no! I want the world to burn! Haven't you ever seen a forest after a fire? Lovely new green growth everywhere. Health follows disaster. It's nature's way."

"Then you should love the Protestants. They came along to cleanse your corrupt church."

"Your corrupt church too, Jean. But they want the baby into the ditch with the bathwater. They pretend to be so pure and holy, but what do they offer? Grim rituals, bland sermons, simpering platitudes. And what do they really want? Power and control, of course, just in a different name. Sixteen hundred years of glorious organization, government, and spectacle, all pissed away so they can pray in black clothes while looting the poor the same old way."

"You talk a good game about faith and tradition, but where does the so-very-un-Catholic East India Company come into this?"

"Well, sometimes you have to hold your nose and shake hands with your enemy so you can slay the dragon. Time enough to put them in their place later. For now, they have a lot of money...and the Spice Islands...and soon an invincible navy."

"Awfully flexible morals."

"Yours aren't? If the king declared himself a Mohammedan tomorrow, will you revolt? Or just shrug and follow the new orders?"

Before Treville could answer, voices and heavy booted footsteps came from the stairs. The promised reinforcements were coming, after all. D'Artagnan grinned and hefted his sword for the inevitable rush. Treville did the same. Antoine, however, remained cool despite impending doom.

"Ah, more for my little party. Perfect." He reached down to pick up a hammer from behind the pillar. "Let's bring on the entertainment, then."

He pounded the wall in a careful rhythm of two beats, three beats, two beats. Three times he did it, then tossed the tool away and knelt, putting the pillar between himself and the wall.

The exterior wall.

As the dozen troops raced up to them, Treville realized that he had had the Manqué's plan wrong. They had never wanted to blow up the church with all that powder they had accumulated. Just one bit of the wall...to make a new door.

He flung himself down behind his own bastion, bellowing for d'Artagnan to do the same. Then he tried to warn the others, to tell them to stop their charge, but the deafening boom overwhelmed all. Flame, smoke, dust, and noise filled the basement. His ears ceased to function, all sound replaced by a shrill ringing. Darkness from the debris made him blind, too. Crawling backward, he met an unmoving body, brought down by the explosion. Several others lay beside that one, some struggling. After a few moments, sight began to return as the dust was penetrated by light from the jagged hole in the upper wall where it met the floor. Antoine and the king were gone.

D'Artagnan recovered first. Sword in hand, he staggered to his feet and vanished up the ramp of rubble after them. Treville mastered himself and followed, still deaf but at least able to see where he was going. They passed through the wreck of a wagon, just so much kindling now, that had held the gunpowder and had been set against the wall. The widows had used it to hold their wares. Luckily, no passersby had been caught in the blast, though Antoine's luckless comrade in a dress lay nearby. Running on, Treville looked for Antoine's group. They were not in sight, though others were racing toward him in response to the loud catastrophe. Alarm in the eyes of one of them made him spin back around.

The man in the dress had risen with a pistol and was pulling the trigger.

Though he bunched his muscles to leap aside, Penseur knew that it was too late. He could never avoid the shot. But his own foresight saved him. A shot did come, but not from the treacherous Dutchman. A musket ball from the top of the church caught the fellow between the shoulder blades and knocked him down dead in the street. Treville let out the breath he had been holding and gazed up at a smiling Abandonné, peeking over her gunstock at him.

After giving her a salute, he turned in pursuit again to the square in front of the church, now hunting for crowd reactions that might indicate where Antoine had taken the king. Everywhere he looked he saw frenzy, people shouting, pointing, running. He was mildly thankful that he could not hear any of it, as it helped him to focus. His eyes scanned every segment of the scene. Where would Antoine take Henri that could remotely enable him to escape unpursued? Soldiers were everywhere, weapons ready, keenly alert. It was not possible to ---

Ah. Clever boy.

Antoine was calmly assisting the king into the royal carriage, the decoy that had provided the crowd with a show. He seemed to give orders to others to secure the building, for they saluted and moved away from the vehicle. Free of the aid that he dared not accept, Antoine climbed in after the king and waved to the driver to get moving.

That driver was La Haine, his face still made up like the clergyman but wearing a Dutch army uniform.

Screaming to no avail against all the other voices and horses, Treville looked around for d'Artagnan. The Gascon was moving in the wrong direction, not noticing the carriage. He was too far off for Treville to get to and still catch Antoine. In front of the church, Gaston and Louis barred entrance with drawn swords. In that direction the crowd and panic were slightly less, so Treville pushed over to them.

"What happened?" Gaston asked. Treville noticed that his hearing was finally returning, though the words sounded as if they came from the bottom of a well.

"He's getting away!" Treville shouted, so loud that his friends jumped back, startled. "Sorry. Bomb ruined my ears." He pointed to the moving carriage.

Louis shrugged. "So, go kill him, save the day...the usual thing we do."

"I need two horses."

Gaston nodded toward a cluster of mounts being held by a young and terrified recruit. "Take ours there. They need some real exercise."

"Fine. Your part of things is under control?"

The mountain of a man laughed as if nothing had gone awry that day. "Perfectly. Be sure to describe the look on Antoine's face when he finds out."

"I'll bring his head back and you can see it for yourself."

"Even better."

"Keep a sharp eye out. There may be more tricks and traps coming."

Half a minute later Treville was astride Gaston's horse and leading the other over to d'Artagnan, who instantly leaped into the saddle without comment and galloped after the coach. Side-by-side they raced, gaining with every second, shod hooves striking sparks on the cobbled street. Yelping pedestrians dove out of the way, other vehicles and horsemen swerved to safety, and once d'Artagnan even jumped his horse over a vegetable cart. Soon they were barely a strong stone's throw from the rear of the fleeing carriage and hopeful of stopping it.

Which was when the little hand bombs started bouncing their way.

A cart full of the false old ladies clattered into the street from a side lane, fuse smoke rising from it. The first grenade exploded harmlessly behind them, its fuse misjudged. But the second blew up uncomfortably close, making Treville's horse shy, and the third required spectacular effort to avoid. Deciding that getting closer than the fuse timing was safer, he urged his horse to top speed and closed next to the driver, ducking a pistol shot from one of the men in the rear. It was then that he realized that he had lost his pistol in the explosion.

Damn! Let's hope Le Coup's trinket does its job.

From the large pouch on the rear of his belt, he plucked a heavy brass dart nearly a foot long and flung it at the driver. Though it did not penetrate quite heavily enough to take the man out, it did cause him to swear in pain and alarm. He jerked the reins too hard and the carriage veered right. It rode up onto a cheese stand and rolled over, dumping out all its skirted occupants.

The royal carriage, though, was growing more distant.

"Isn't it time to play our ace?" yelled d'Artagnan.

"Not yet. Our trump card has strict orders. We want them to get to the leader first."

"Then maybe we should slow down and let them do that."

Treville nodded and brought his horse to a trot, then a walk, so that the carriage could move further off. When it turned west and headed out of the city, they were barely in sight of it. After an hour, the coach turned south and made for a series of windmills being used to drain the polder. Just beyond the dike lay the sea, where a ship lay ay anchor.

"Looks like they do have an escape plan, after all," d'Artagnan said.

"Let's make sure that ship waits a long time. They must have a longboat to get out to it. See if you can make it less than seaworthy."

With a laugh the younger man rode off on a roundabout route to do that. Treville walked his horse into hiding next to a mill two down from the one where Antoine had stopped his stolen carriage. From there he let the beast rest and graze while he waited for d'Artagnan's return. At the nonfunctioning windmill between him and the abducted king, a poor old worker hobbled about, fussing with one of the unmoving vanes. He nodded to Treville, unaware of the drama playing out beside him. *I'll have to make sure he not only doesn't get hurt, but that he doesn't see anything he shouldn't.*

Twenty minutes later, a smug d'Artagnan returned. There had, indeed, been a rowboat on the shore. Now it was so much driftwood. "What do we do now?" he asked.

"Nothing. Soon it'll be dark and then we can get closer."

"Until then?"

"Ride to the Manqué hideout and see what's happening there. Be careful, who knows what devilry is afoot. If Manqué could control the mayor, they might have been able to do the same to van Oldenbarnevelt's commander."

Temeraire cantered off to do as he was bid, while Penseur knocked on the door of his windmill. When no one answered, he let himself in with the picklocks he always carried. The great wooden-toothed mechanism, turned by the vanes outside, took up most of the ground floor. It was connected to pumps outside that helped to keep the polder drained and the sea at bay. He found fresh water and took a bucket out to his horse, then returned to explore. A cozy upstairs apartment suited him nicely. Its railed balcony gave him a perfect view of Antoine's mill. So he settled down in a chair to watch and wait.

D'Artagnan returned as dusk approached. Treville admitted him and handed him some water, for he had ridden hard. "Well?"

"There was no cavalry attack," his friend informed him, handing over a pair of fresh pistols. Treville quickly loaded and primed one.

"None? But we were promised ---"

"Oh, the troops went there, all right, but they made no charge. Didn't have to."

"Quit talking in circles. What did they find?"

"Half a dozen men trussed up tight, delivered to the soldiers as presents. No Guido, no Krijger."

"Surely neither of them did that?" Treville poured powder down the barrel of the second pistol.

"We questioned the prisoners. They claim that a ghost came just before dawn and subdued them all. Only Guido escaped. Left them to fend for themselves."

"And Maaike?" He dropped a lead ball down after the powder.

"The ghost took her away. That's all they knew."

Treville laughed as he rammed wadding down the barrel and tucked both guns into his belt. "A ghost. One with a limp, I'll wager. A fantôme, perhaps? They're probably both back at the house, teasing Beurre and wondering what happened at the church."

"That thought did occur to me."

"At least she's out of their hands and the gang is scattered. I do wish that we'd snared Guido, though."

"You may get another chance." D'Artagnan pointed at the far windmill.

Sure enough, the ringleader and two others were riding up to Antoine's hideaway. They threw themselves from their horses and dashed into the building. Treville rubbed his hands together.

"Lady Fortune must owe me a favor. Too bad you didn't bring some of those soldiers with you."

"They had to rush back to the city when they heard the explosion."

"Well...this way we won't have to share the glory."

"You have a cunning plan, of course."

"Naturally."

"And it is...?"

"Walk over there and knock on the door."

"Just like that?"

"Well, there are subsidiary details."

They spent a few minutes getting those items straight in their minds and gathering what supplies the mill offered, then went to pay their social call. As it was now fully dark, they had no need to approach with much caution. The mill in between showed no lights. Its old tenant must have already turned in, as such fellows generally did when the sun went down. Once past it, they stopped to make sure that Guido had posted no guards outside his mill. A circuit around the place discovered nothing except hobbled horses munching grass. So Treville sent d'Artagnan to his assigned post and knocked politely on the door.

Nothing happened, of course. He had not expected them to fling it open and greet him with open arms. But he knew that all their attention was now on him. That was the important thing.

Another knock, more insistent this time, was followed with feigned drunken bellowing in Dutch. "Abraham! Abraham van Gelder! I know you're in there, you thief!" More knocking, with kicking now. "Come out and face me! You stole my wife, you dog!"

Now movement could be heard from inside, and some arguing in multiple languages about what to do. Treville kept up his assault on the door to encourage them to decide. "Grietje! Come back to me, please!"

A gruff voice barked from just behind the door. "No Abraham here, sot! No Grietje, either. Go hammer on somebody else's door."

"Lies! I know this mill. I saw you take her in here. Grietje, babyface, it's Adriaan!"

Another voice ordered, "Oh, just thrash the fool and send him on his way. He's so drunk he probably won't even feel it."

The first man yelled to Treville, "All right, then, she's coming out!"

Noises of the lock being turned alerted Treville to set his feet. When the door opened to reveal one of the men that Guido had brought with him, fists clenched and lit by several lamps behind him, he wrapped his arms around the fellow with grateful sobs before the man could react. "Honeykins!"

Wrapped up with surprising effectiveness, the villain struggled to pry Treville's arms away. "Get off me, idiot. I'm not your wife."

"I know," Treville whispered in his ear. "Her voice is deeper."

His knee rammed up into the poor fellow's groin, followed by a vicious head butt that broke his nose. He yanked his victim's own dagger from his belt and shoved him into the figure standing behind him. As both tangled and fell into a corner, Treville threw the heavy knife at the shiny silver nose moving toward him from the left. La Haine nimbly dodged it and the blade smacked into the wall pommel-first, tumbling to the floor. *Never could throw a knife worth a damn. They need fins, like that dart.*

From the narrow stairs above Antoine snapped, "The three of you can't manage one drunken Dutch farmer?"

"Farmer, my arse," growled La Haine, "that's your damned Treville!"

"Really? Then three just might be enough. Welcome, Jean! Ears still ringing? Mine are."

Treville drew one of his pistols. "Let's make them ring some more."

His shot lit up the room like lightning for an instant, but the target had seen the muzzle rise and rushed back upstairs. The ball splashed harmlessly against plaster. La Haine snatched up a gun from a table and tried his own shot, just missing when Treville bent low and hurled his empty one at a recovering henchman. It caught him in the belly and doubled him over. His partner, the one with the freshly-broken nose, nudged him aside and stormed at Treville with an angry roar. With no time to draw his other pistol, Penseur simply tossed his hat into the attacker's face. The reflexive flinch that resulted gave Treville time to pivot out of the way and trip him with one spurred boot.

He collided with the door jamb and went down with a groan. Treville drew his remaining gun and turned to find La Haine.

But his foe had found him first, flicking a rapier tip at his arm. Treville managed to avoid the worst of it, but the blade smacked the weapon from his grip. Now empty-handed, he had no recourse but to retreat until he had time and room to unsheathe his own rapier. The Manqué swordsman pursued with a sneer, driving his enemy toward the man who had caught the useless pistol. Between two fires, Treville ducked beneath his own fallen gun, swung as a club, and then hopped up onto the frame of the rotating mill mechanism. He grit his teeth as he almost fell into the enormous grinding gears, but regained his balance and danced to the other side of the room, hopping into an open space near the stairs and drawing his sword.

La Haine came at him from the right, circling the apparatus, while the other advanced from the left. The third man had Treville's pistol and was maneuvering for a shot at its owner. Behind and above him, Treville could hear Antoine returning, perhaps with Guido and guns. All-in-all, things were not going well.

He drove La Haine's lackey back with a feint to the knee and a lunge at his face, but that only gave his master an opening that Treville barely managed to parry with a desperate sweep. *Lord, the man's quick! I won't last half a minute against him in a free duel.* Choosing the lesser of two devils, he charged at the other man, making sure to move irregularly so the one with the pistol would have to earn his murder. As the man with the sword moved away, Treville slid over to turn him into a bullet shield, desperately hoping that he did not discover the wit to simply duck down and give his friend a clear field of fire.

Luckily, the other bladesman was only of average ability and Treville managed him, so long as that was all that he had to do. But again the deadly La Haine moved in, like a clever machine made by some hostile watchmaker. None of his motions were hasty or wasted. All was as efficient as any practiced executioner. Once he made contact, Treville would be doomed. It was all that he could do to fend off the other man. To add to his troubles, it finally occurred to that one that all he had to do was run away and there would be nothing preventing the gunman from shooting Treville down.

Staring down the barrel of his own pistol, he almost laughed at the absurdity of it. *After all that I've survived, it ends this way? God's truly a comedian.*

And an ironist, as it turned out. When his killer pulled the trigger and the dog snapped onto the pan...nothing happened but a spark. Treville had forgotten to put priming powder into his own pan.

Now he did laugh out loud, from relief as much as mirth. But he only had a heartbeat to enjoy his salvation, for on came La Haine, in earnest this time. Treville beat away the first thrust and just survived the second by twisting his torso so that the tip slid past his ribs. His own riposte was parried with almost insulting indifference. Before he could withdraw it, La Haine neatly wrapped the arm and yanked the entire weapon out of Treville's grasp.

Almost the entire weapon, anyway.

As the silver-nosed villain placed his point at the hollow of Treville's throat, commanding surrender with a smirk of triumph, his victim raised his hands, making sure that his trump card was hidden up the sleeve of his doublet.

"It takes quite the set of stones to come in here alone," Antoine said from the stairs with a slow clapping of gloved hands. Behind him the half moon was visible through a large window. "Too bad La Haine will be keeping them as a trophy."

He nodded to his minion to dispatch the troublesome invader. Just as La Haine's arm tensed for the killing thrust, though, Treville slapped the point aside with one hand while slashing down at the foe's wrist with the other.

With Le Coup's clever and secret little stiletto, hidden in the pommel, which he had snatched free even while being disarmed.

As the rapier fell from the gouged hand, Treville flashed past La Haine, giving him a second strike to the eye. A viper-fast move saved him from blindness, but carved a bloody trench from cheekbone to jaw. No stranger to survival, the wounded man had the presence of mind to lash out at Treville with his own stolen weapon, even though it was a weak reversed strike as he held the weapon by the blade. It missed, but only by a whisker. Then he turned to face his enemy again, deftly flipping the sword into the air to catch it by the handle in his weak hand and come on guard. Treville swore, seeing that he had gained little, and raised his pitiful toy in defense.

"Hold!" commanded Antoine. "This is tiresome and pointless. Treville, you're beaten. Drop the cute little knife and submit."

Treville was about to spit out what might be his last saucy retort when he risked a glance at the stairs. Antoine held a dagger to King Henri's throat.

23

DUTCH COAST

"THE ODDS ARE ONLY FIVE-TO-ONE. AN EVEN FIGHT, FINALLY."

La Haine took a break from slaying Treville to admire the scene and laugh. "The vaunted King of the French, kisser of Protestant arse. Not so terrifying now, eh?"

"No," Antoine chuckled, "he's only fearsome when he has an army of Catholic conscripts at his back."

Glad of the dim light in the mill, Treville let him enjoy his moment of victory as he took note of the fellow with the pistol, now truly primed and deadly, slinking around behind him. The idiot seemed unaware that his reflection was visible in the window near the stairs. Something else was there, too, making a delightful double-image.

"Everything all right, Your Majesty?"

The King gulped and nodded, eyes wide with the fear that few men could honestly proclaim that they had ever seen in his eyes. Then one of those eyes did a funny thing. It winked.

"Stay strong, Sire. I'm here to rescue you."

That made La Haine almost wet himself. "Ha! You can't even save yourself."

Treville held up a finger. "Ah...watch and learn." He smiled up at the king and said odd words for the situation. Dutch words. "Long live the House of Orange!"

As soon as they rang out in the noisy mill, Henri slammed his elbow into Antoine's belly and bit the hand holding the dagger. The traitorous guardsman yelped and dropped his weapon, but retained his soldier's presence of mind. His other hand made a fist and backhanded his king across the nose.

Which instantly fell off.

Before anyone besides Treville could notice that, the disguised Marcus Raaf popped it back into place while shoving Antoine so hard so that he fell back onto the steps. Free of his captor, Raaf reached for the fallen knife. But Antoine kicked him in the shoulder from his supine position, tumbling him down the steps to sprawl at La Haine's feet. The maimed assassin crowed, "I've been hoping to kill a traitor to God. Looks like my lucky day."

But as he cocked his sword arm, the window just above him exploded, and d'Artagnan's silver-spurred boots landed on his head, driving him into the floor. The newcomer and La Haine ended up in a violent tangle. Treville had no time to see what ensued, for an instant before the window had shattered it had revealed the man behind him taking aim at his back. Ducking and spinning all at once, Penseur flung his little knife at the pistoleer. Once more Treville failed to get the point to stick, but it served its purpose by striking the man in the knee and making him squeeze the trigger prematurely. The spoiled shot flew harmlessly past him and over the two men still grappling on the floor. Before the shooter could recover, Treville dove and snatched up his fallen rapier, tossing it to the Dutch spy and yelling to Raaf to get upstairs and deal with Antoine.

Now unarmed, Treville turned back to the other fellow, who now moved against him with a heavy army sword. Without even his hat for defense, Treville had to use what was at hand: the enemy's own rage and the complicated room itself. To his right was an empty shelf, built into the wall. On his left, not four feet away, were the four great vanes turning the clattering apparatus outside. Not much room to maneuver. He taunted the swordsman by calling him a cowardly pig-lover in four different languages, inviting him to run his innocent foe through. The growling adversary obliged him, stomping forward to give a great but slow thrust. But Treville's helpless torso was not there to receive it. Leaping onto the shelf, he clung to it and kicked out with both feet, his boots solidly connecting with the other's head and shoulder. Stretched out in his failed lunge, the Manqué soldier had no means of resisting the kick.

A surprised *oof!* sound turned into terrified shrieking as he flew into the great churning gears of the pump mechanism. One arm was chewed up by the monster, which swallowed progressively more of him until his screams were cut short by the devouring of his head. Despite being lubricated by great splashes of blood, the cogs ground to a stop, jammed by all that meat.

Treville was not yet safe, however. Even as he mastered his nausea at the horrid sight, the remaining lackey took his dead friend's place, pistol in one hand and rapier in the other. His bloody swollen nose, plus the other cuts and bruises from being flung into the door jamb, declared an eagerness for cruel vengeance. Behind Penseur, the scuffling sounds had turned into a sharp steel-on-steel conversation. As much as he would have enjoyed watching that, he had to address his own problematic survival first. A quick scan all around him showed no available weapons. He even vainly patted his hip as if a sword might have magically grown there. No such luck. But his gloved hand did slap against the buckled pouch on his belt, where he kept money and spare bullets.

And some of the charming toys Le Coup had given him as he had left the Bastille, almost as an afterthought.

Left hand up in feigned supplication for mercy, to encourage his would-be executioner to pause and gloat, Treville slipped the other hand inside the pouch for the life-saving items. Palming them, he raised both arms in surrender, knelt, and play-acted a tearful terrified loser. "I beg you, monsieur…"

"Beg all you want," was the inevitable snarled reply. "My guess is that your God has abandoned you."

He leveled his gun to send Treville off to meet that deity. While the arm was moving and thus difficult to adjust, its target fell face-first onto the floor, one hand jerking. Intent on reacquiring his victim for the fatal shot, the Manqué killer never noticed the three little objects until they burst against his face and chest. A small cloud of white dust surrounded him. One heartbeat later he coughed, whimpered, and pawed at himself. In another moment he writhed on the floor, screaming and gagging. Le Coup's sinister devilries – tiny pudding-cloth bags of quicklime -- burned his lungs, eyes, and wounds like lava from hell.

With a certain feeling of pity for his victim, Treville kicked him unconscious and seized the pistol that had been meant for him. He turned with the idea of shooting down La Haine, but d'Artagnan was blocking the shot. As no one else was present to be engaged, all being upstairs, and the steps were blocked by the sword duel, he paused to admire the action until the way up was clear. There was plenty to admire. Treville knew that he himself was merely competent with a blade, good enough with hard-won experience to survive most normal encounters if he kept his wits about him. Before him, though, were two prodigies, the sort of duelists that people composed songs about.

La Haine was older, clearly a keen student who practiced for hours a day and challenged anyone foolish enough to so much as frown at him. Besides the missing nose and the new slice that Treville had just given him, he wore several other scars from his painful fencing education. No doubt there were many others beneath his garments. D'Artagnan, on the other hand, as Treville had seen in the Parisian cemetery melee, had been blessed in the womb by the god of war with the speed, reflexes, and cunning that few mere mortals ever received. And quite apart from his natural physical gifts, his keen observation of his opponent made him seem almost prescient, as if he could read his enemy's mind and know where the next strike was to be aimed.

Repeatedly La Haine's deadly point flashed out, only to be denied by an impossibly-quick parry or last-second avoidance. Then a terrifying riposte would flick out at the Manqué assassin, who would only be saved by his own experience and training.

Both men, though, had taken hits, grazes to sleeve and doublet mostly, and both were already tiring. Sweat ran down their faces, spoiling their vision, causing each at times to bound out of distance to wipe it off before the next attack came. Finally, Treville called out to d'Artagnan during one of those intervals to clear the stairway so that he could aid the outnumbered Raaf. The Gascon nodded and drove La Haine back with renewed fury until both surged out of the door and into the open air.

For the first time in many minutes Treville could relax for a moment, free of the need to dodge sword or bullet. He felt himself shake with the nervous tension. Fear was something one could master for a time, like a recalcitrant horse, but never shed completely. He found his hat and set it back on his damp head, then collected his pommel knife and a fallen dagger that its departed owner would never need again. Hefting the enemy pistol, he crept up the steps, alert for an ambush, since no sounds of fighting came from above. Unless others he had not yet seen lurked there, only Antoine and Guido should be left to defeat, so long as d'Artagnan contained La Haine. Mindful of the wicked hand bombs his former friend had already thrown, he made his way up with agonizing slowness. At last he poked his head into the loft room, pistol fanning left to right in search of danger.

There was none. The room was empty.

With even more concern for some sort of trick, Treville oozed up the final few steps. Standing in the low-ceilinged space, apparently meant to be the bedroom of the owner or operator, he set himself with his back in a corner and waited for a nasty surprise. When no one leaped from beneath the narrow bed or out of a cupboard, he made a quick search to satisfy himself that he was truly alone. All he found were burnt documents in a tin pail, drops of blood on the rug, and his own fallen rapier, which he seized. *Where the hell did they all go?* A look out of the seaward window showed a cluster of dark forms running toward the beach. The last remnants of the mostly-set sun cast their long shadows. One was slumped between two who seemed to be dragging him along, with a third in the lead. Surrounding them were half a dozen others, just arrived from the water, for the lone ship had crept much closer and launched a boat. It rested on the muddy beach, beside the one that d'Artagnan had ruined. Three more waited beside it.

Damnation, they're going to get away after all!

A more careful search revealed a cunningly-designed secret hatch in the western wall. There a polished wooden pole permitted a rapid descent to the ground behind the mill. After making certain that no one lay in wait for him below, Treville wrapped himself around it like a lover and dropped down.

When he landed he listened for sounds of bladeplay but heard none. A pistol boomed, however, from the other side of the building. Then a cursing figure sprinted past him. Treville nearly shot at him before recognizing d'Artagnan.

"Sneaking coward ran away!" the Gascon complained, tucking away his empty gun. "We were having a fine go of it, sparks flying from our swords, and then he just salutes and dashes off with a laugh like he had no worries in the world. But I noticed he made sure to jig back and forth to spoil my aim."

Treville frowned. "Wait a minute. You had a loaded pistol the whole time you were fighting him and didn't use it?"

"Where would the sport be in that? I've been looking forward to fencing that son-of-a-bitch ever since Abandonné told us about him."

"Stuff your sport! Next time, take every advantage you have. War isn't a game."

"Oh, relax. I already have a granny to fuss over me." D'Artagnan raised his sword. "So, shall we go get them? The odds are only five-to-one. An even fight, finally."

After d'Artagnan reloaded, they maneuvered with care, mindful of traps. But their enemies were only intent on escaping with Raaf. So Treville and d'Artagnan closed to within stone-throwing distance, their presence only revealed when they dropped two of the newly-arrived Manqué men with bullets.

"Pretty good shooting in the dark, if I do say so myself," the young Gascon cackled, dropping his pistol so that he could slap a parrying dagger into that fist.

Treville did the same, though without the self-congratulation. The sun was completely down now and the murk favored neither side. But their muzzle flashes had told the others where they were and an uncomfortably-large horde came straight at them. Both the king's men flung themselves into the tall grass when they saw arms raised at them. Pistol balls whizzed harmlessly past. Penseur feigned a cry of a man who had been shot. Two of his foes laughed and ran even faster at him. Rolling hard right several times, Treville crawled behind them. As they poked at the spot where they presumed him to be, he did the same to them. One gasped and fell, run through the body. His partner was more fortunate and only received a nasty gash in the back of the thigh before Treville continued his pursuit of Antoine's group. To the left, another man grunted in pain as d'Artagnan served him the same way. But the clash of steel said that someone else had managed to entangle his friend. Knowing that he was on his own for a while, Treville cleared the grass and felt the beach under his boots.

Sand and shells crunched. The going was slow, but those he chased were similarly handicapped. Their boat and safety lay perhaps half a minute's slog away. Now Treville could see that it was Antoine and La Haine who held the stunned Raaf, dragging him toward captivity and probable death. Guido was the one in front, making for the boat. He wished that he had Chipay's weighted throwing weapon to bring them down. Indeed, he longed for anything that might perform that trick. In desperation, he ran his hands all over himself, hoping that he had forgotten something and a miracle lay in a corner of a pocket.

If I let these scum escape, the king will lock me up and throw away the---

He laughed in relief at the unspoken word, like a man who had just received a reprieve from the headsman's axe. Panting from the effort of wading through ankle-deep sand, he fell to his knees, tucked away his dagger, and fished out the great key Le Coup had given him: the one with the tiny gun hidden inside.

With a shouted insult at Antoine he got his former ally to stop, turn, and spit out a savage retort in reply. With the trio thus frozen for an instant, twenty feet away, Treville thumbed back the little lock and pressed the sliver of a trigger. The key let out a surprisingly loud crack, accompanied by an equally-astonishing kick. At the same instant, the bullet struck home, forcing a curse from its victim.

Poor Raaf.

The prisoner, now fully awake from whatever beating had subdued him, yelped and sagged, struck in the arse. More insult to injury. *Good thing it's a tiny bullet. But I'll owe him a whole barrel of beer after this.* Though he bemoaned the result of his shot, Treville saw that it was fortuitous. Now Raaf was so much dead weight and too much for his captors to manhandle in the sand. They released him, drawing swords to deal with the oncoming Treville, who had resumed his rush as soon as the key had fired.

La Haine came on guard, his slashed face showing his eagerness for vengeance. But Antoine had a different priority. His arm drew back to slay Raaf, who lay on the beach clutching his wound, oblivious to all else. Still ten feet away, Treville hurled the heavy key. It smacked into Antoine's chest, forcing a gurgled complaint from him, and stopping his thrust. Before he could recover, his one-time friend crashed into him shoulder-first, bowling him over. As he lay helpless, Treville stabbed at him with all the rage of a betrayed man, only missing when Antoine rolled aside at the last moment. When he prepared for a second thrust, he felt movement behind him and began turning to meet La Haine's vicious attack, knowing that it would be too late. Feeling like a man underwater encountering a shark, he twisted with tragic slowness, already anticipating the cold point.

But he had not been the only one to do so. Just as he grit his teeth to die, the blade dove into the sand, kicking up a white cloud.

"Sorry I'm late," chuckled d'Artagnan. "That other fellow was a bit smoother than I'd anticipated."

Already La Haine was lifting his blade from where it had been spanked down by d'Artagnan's. The Gascon held it with his rapier and crunched the silver nose with the elbow of his dagger arm. La Haine stumbled back, choking on his own blood. To his credit, he recovered immediately, only now there was a great black hole where the shiny nose had been, like that on a death's head. His fierce grimace only increased the resemblance to a skull.

"You want to dance again, boy?" he spat. "Come on, then. I'll hold you close."

And they were off again, thrusting and parrying like deadly angels, just as they had done in the mill, though rather slower from the exhaustion of fighting and running. Treville knew how they felt. He could barely muster the strength to turn back to finish off Antoine. That opportunity had literally fled, though, as the traitor was already staggering toward the longboat again, where Guido waited. With the determination that came from treachery, Treville followed, every step heavier than the last. At least he retained the presence of mind to leave his pommel dagger with the downed Raaf.

"Stick the king-stealing dog once for me," Raaf requested with a grimace. He adjusted the false nose that he had had the presence of mind to replace. "Thanks for puncturing my poor bottom, by the way."

Treville made no reply, as he was already well past him, intent on catching Antoine and gutting him. He nearly managed it, too. But as he drew near to his mark, two of the four men at the boat advanced on him with swords, the third man staying at the small pintle gun, Guido leaning against the gunwale with a bored expression. Antoine squirmed between them and fell across the boat's bow, panting. Sighing, aware that now he had only his rapier left, Treville overacted his own distress, gasping and slowing, his guard dropping. As he had hoped, overconfidence welled up in his two new adversaries. They foolishly neglected to spread out, coming at him nearly single-file. The man in front barely bothered to make a proper thrust, so sure of victory was he. Penseur ruined the fellow's evening by hurling the handful of sand that he had scooped up when he had given Raaf the dagger. Blinded, his sword was easily slapped away, a stab to the hip dropping him in front of his comrade. Tangled, they went down together, out of Treville's path. Now no one could save Antoine.

Which was when the four men hidden in the bottom of the boat leaped out.

24

DUTCH COAST & AMSTERDAM

"THE GOOD PEOPLE OF AMSTERDAM BELIEVE
THAT STEAMING MOUNTAIN OF MANURE?"

"BELIEVE IT? THEY CLING TO IT LIKE HOLY SCRIPTURE."

All Treville's resolve evaporated.

He doubted that even a fresh and well-armed d'Artagnan could take on a quartet. These men certainly seemed to be that, carrying themselves with the air of seasoned men of war. *Plenty of those to be had around here nowadays. And Guido's probably paying them better than their own armies did. Ah, well, might as well sell my own self dearly, then.*

The fight lasted longer than he had had any hopes it might. His first enemy flinched when he feigned throwing more sand, despite the hand being empty. That gave Treville an opening to pink him in the forearm of the sword arm and disarm him. Another foe rushed him from the left. Treville hopped aside to put the first man between them while unbuckling his own sword belt. As the second fighter came around the wounded one, the heavy leather belt slapped him dead in the face. Treville's point skewered him between two doublet buttons. He coughed and sagged. Both the others, though, surged in from the other side, taking care not to get in one another's way. One got in a lucky blade slap to Treville's knuckles and the sword dropped from numbed fingers.

Treville tried swinging the belt again, but his intended victim merely stepped inside of the arc, wrapped his arm around it, and yanked it away. And when Penseur tried to pick up the fallen rapier, the same man kicked it away and slashed at him, forcing him back. His partner added a nasty thrust, just to add to Treville's troubles, which was barely evaded. Tripling the awful odds, Antoine chose that moment to strut back into the game, his wind and his courage returned. All three drove Treville, now armed only with the dagger from the mill, in retreat until he crashed into the little boat d'Artagnan had wasted his time wrecking. As if that were not bad enough, the wounded one arrived with his dropped sword and the two he had pushed through also hobbled into the picture. Alas, there was no aid forthcoming from d'Artagnan, as he and La Haine were still trading thrusts and insults a hundred feet away, and Raaf was still hors de combat.

Antoine held up a hand to interrupt the inevitable, as he could never pass up an opportunity to gloat. "Poor Treville, always a step behind. Impressive though your little interference was tonight, it's nonetheless inconsequential in our grand scheme."

"Which is?"

"A secret. It could hardly be much of a grand scheme if the entire world knows about it. Why, did you think I was going to unburden my soul to you as a last magnanimous gesture? You read too many romances."

Treville maintained his guard, futile gesture that it was. He let his eyes wander over to the man in the boat, the one with his hand on the swivel gun, a smoldering match in hand. While waiting for the sting of half a dozen lethal points, he squinted at the bearded face and fine clothes, not quite believing his own eyes. Then he chuckled and addressed Antoine again.

"Well, we know it all anyway," he lied. He raised his voice so the lone gunner could hear. "Quite the coup, kidnapping the king of France out from under us. Now all of Europe must take you seriously, wondering if any monarchs are safe. I wonder, though, why you didn't touch Maurice? Surely he would have been a greater achievement, snatching a vigorous young general out from under the cordon of his own men?"

To his gratification, the far-off fellow gasped in surprise and stared at Raaf, still some yards away from him. His expression shifted from triumph to outrage and he began a furious conversation with Guido. *He doesn't know Raaf's a fraud!* It relieved Treville to know that his final act had thrown a viper into their picnic.

"You'll just have to spend your days in hell wondering about that," said Antoine. "I will say, before we gut you, that killing a traitor to the Church means more to some of us than doing the same to a simple deluded Dutchman who at least sticks to his faith, though it be the wrong one." He stepped out of the way of his men's swords. "Besides, it's all been wonderful practice for the greater game to come. Gentlemen, if you'd do me the favor of ruining his hideous doublet, we'll be on our way."

Treville saw the rapier arms tense to dispatch him and he tried to sneak in a punch at the insufferable Antoine. But his late friend had foreseen that and made sure to remain just out of reach. As the others stabbed at him, the beach punched Treville in the face. Hard.

For the next few moments things were blurry and confused. His mouth filled with grit as something grabbed his ankles and dragged him beneath the upturned boat. Then he saw stars, literal ones, as that smashed hull rolled toward the swordsmen, pinning one to the sand as the rest scattered before it. By the time he spat out the sand and cleared his head, two more of Antoine's men were down and the rest were fending off some sort of dark demon with frantic swipes of their blades. Whatever was attacking them moved too quickly to be struck, though, and as it avoided the steel it also darted in to deliver bone-crunching blows. Soon Treville's head cleared and he could make out what assailed them all.

It was the old Dutch mill worker Treville had seen when he had first arrived.

At least, that was who he appeared to be, still clad in his rough garments and old cap. But it did not require much examination to recognize the feline moves of the New World forest, the relaxed grace of a warrior so wrongly termed a savage. Fantôme lived up to his name, seemingly insubstantial whenever a strike came his way. He proved to be all-too-solid, however, when he delivered a kick or punch. With the awareness of a woodland hunter, he seemed to detect an adversary behind him without even looking. Twice Treville saw him dodge a treacherous stab in the back. His fluid movements almost seemed to have been choreographed in advance rather than extemporized in the heat of battle.

It could not last, though. Still suffering from his wound, not having had time even for his own remarkable medicines to fully work, Chipay began to tire sooner than his wont. And his honorable resolution not to kill worked against him, as those he had felled recovered enough to rejoin the fray, even if they were much more cautious about engaging him again. Once they all realized that they only faced a mere mortal, however skilled, they cooperated to hem him in without getting in one another's way. Treville shook his head, grit his teeth, and struggled upright, intent on aiding his savior even if he had to do it empty-handed.

He only managed ten steps before crashing to the beach again. Something swift and solid collided with him. No sooner did he hit the ground than Antoine was coming at him, dagger in hand. Treville flung his hat at the man, but Antoine batted it aside and dove onto his prey, knife to the throat. Desperate reflexes allowed Treville to seize the murderous wrist, but that was only a stopgap, as the other man was atop him with superior leverage, his point pressing inexorably closer to the hollow above the collarbone. But Antoine, so confident of victory, did not notice that Treville had not flung all of his hat at him.

He had kept hold of Le Coup's secreted wire saw.

Antoine bellowed as the bits of diamond gouged a trough in his wrist. When he sat up, clutching it, Treville managed to get his knees up and shove him away. By the time he got to his feet and found his fallen sword, however, his enemy had done one better and retrieved a pistol.

"Where's that vaunted Treville luck now?" Antoine hissed through clenched teeth.

Which was precisely when his head exploded.

Treville flinched hard as gore rained down on him. The slack remains of his would-be killer slumped down to stain the white beach with blood. His own head pounding, Treville looked for the source of Antoine's fortuitous demise. All those surrounding Chipay did the same, fearing that they might be next. Even La Haine and d'Artagnan ceased their striving, the maimed Manqué man also taking the opportunity to disengage entirely and dash for the water. Had Abandonné arrived yet again to save him with her splendid musket?

He saw no sign of her. Who he did spot, though, was Jean de La Vallette, the Duc du Épernon, Admiral of France, standing in the bow of his longboat, a satisfied smile on his patrician lips as he waved away muzzle smoke from the tiny cannon he had just fired.

"He was growing tiresome," the great lord explained, seemingly as much to Guido as to Treville.

Penseur frowned in confusion. "Your grace?"

"The idiot kidnapped the wrong man, against my strict orders." He looked at Raaf. "I trust Your Majesty is quite well?"

Treville hoped the same, that Raaf would have the presence of mind to answer in character. He was not disappointed.

"Ah...yes," said the false king in that well-known Gascon accent, as cheerily as if on a promenade with his favorite mistress. No hint of the bullet wound could be heard in his voice. Instead, it was full of regal self-assurance. "Quite the adventure, wouldn't you say? Haven't had this much fun in years. Splendid shot with that toy of your, by the way. I'm sure Treville appreciates it."

"Indeed, sir," Treville said. "My humble thanks, m'lord."

Épernon shrugged. "He deserved it. I can't abide failure in my underlings, particularly one in a position of command."

"What was he commanded to do, I wonder?" asked Raaf.

Yes, we're all dying to hear you talk your way out of this.

As the duplicitous nobleman replied, all his men returned to the boat, leaving their dead comrades behind on the beach. Treville noticed that the ship offshore had drawn significantly closer and turned broadside, to point-blank cannon range, in fact. The threat was clear, if understated. Much more evident was Guido's reloading of the swivel gun.

"Is it not obvious, sire? The Dutch needed a warning. They are trying to climb too high, much above their station. A tiny pack of heretical shopkeepers pretending to great power. Building more ships than Spain and

France combined. Pouncing on the Spice Islands. Is that any way to behave? After all, they are the nether lands, yes? So we decided to take the opportunity of your visit to remind them of their place in the world. But that foolish guardsman decided to pluck you from the stage instead, for some imagined slight to the Catholic faith. He failed to understand that whatever your royal self does, it bears the imprimatur of God himself, correct?"

Treville observed Guido as the schemer listened to his master. The man's confusion was unmistakable. This was all news to him, though he dared do nothing else but agree to it.

Épernon's lying through his elegant teeth, saving his own skin with this pack of extemporaneous lies.

"But the Almighty does not speak through Maurice or his ilk, though they clearly believe that He does. All we did was disabuse him of the notion. There was no thought of actually harming him, I assure you, if for no other reason than that he is useful to France as a buffer against Phillip." Épernon raised his palms to the sky. "That's all that there is to this. If your men hadn't stormed the mill before I could be informed of Antoine's error, you would have been released instantly, as would have Maurice." He smiled. "Merely theatre, all of it."

"You acted out of the noblest of motives then?" inquired Raaf, barely able to maintain a straight face when presented with such an absurd tale.

"Would I slay my own man if it were otherwise?"

Raaf stood up as straight as any true monarch, mastering his wound. "Nonetheless, this has been a bloody affair. There must be a reckoning."

"And I will answer to you for it." Several men shoved the boat into the surf. "But not this day, Your Majesty. I have others to chastise. So I leave you in the care of your Forty-Five. I confess no little envy that you have them. Adieu."

As the longboat rowed out to the approaching armed sloop, Treville felt the sand tremble beneath his boots. He saw d'Artagnan and Fantôme wave at someone behind them and he turned to see Gaston, Louis, and several more of King Henri's guardians gallop up.

"Just like you to get here as everything winds down," Treville complained. "Where were you when I was facing off with a platoon of these rascals?"

"Protecting the real king, if that's all right with you," Gaston retorted. "And covering up this unholy mess with the mother of all tall tales."

"Regale me."

"Well, it seems that the whole thing was merely a realistic training exercise, and that King Henri and Maurice were just clever actors hired for the day."

"Really? And the good people of Amsterdam believe that steaming mountain of manure?"

"Believe it? They cling to it like holy scripture. They'd rather accept that explanation and sleep soundly tonight than live in fear. Now tell me your fairy story."

Treville gave his version of the day's events while they all pitched in to cleanse the beach and mill of bodies and weapons. A cart was fetched for Raaf and the failing Chipay, who was truly at the end of his powers. It took them straight back to the city to be tended by doctors. Another hauled off the mortal remains of those slain on the beach and in the mill. Those would be examined for anything of intelligence value: documents, coins, scars, tattoos. Already Treville had noted that nearly all bore the Dutch East India Company mark. The governors of that institution would have some questions to answer. He knew, however, that if they bore any guilt that they would already have a coherent explanation in hand.

"Here's the bothersome thing," mused Louis when they all sat outside the mill much later. "Where did all of that gunpowder go? They only used a tiny bit of it to breach the church wall."

Treville frowned. "It wasn't at the Manqué safe house?"

"Not a grain of it," said Gaston. "And the prisoners there all claim to a man that they don't know anything about it, even when strongly encouraged to do so."

"Well, that's not good. Can't leave that sort of thing to rattle around loose."

"Agreed. Though it's probably on that ship with Guido and Épernon."

"Perhaps we'll get lucky and the Dutch will catch it." Treville stretched, wincing as fire shot through nearly every sinew. "But I expect they bribed some naval officers to look the other way."

On the way to Amsterdam Gaston and Louis caught him up on what had transpired while he and d'Artagnan had pursued Antoine's crew. Maurice had ordered a house-to-house search for anyone potentially involved. At the same time he had ruthlessly questioned his own people and the city elders. After all, if the Manqué could force Mayor Cromhout to aid them, anyone else could been coerced. So far, no other conspirators had come to light. Dutch troops had secured the harbor and word had gone out to the navy to scour the sea for anyone suspicious. French and Dutch interrogators were hard at work on the farm captives, but they were proving resolute in their silence. Krijger had appeared in her bed at Beurre's house as if transported there by witches, her wounds, new and old, all stitched and wrapped. Abandonné was with her as both guard and companion.

"She's well?" asked d'Artagnan, who had barely spoken since the longboat had escaped. His concern sounded not entirely professional.

"Who? Your little sharpshooter?" asked Gaston, intentionally misunderstanding him. "Right as rain, apart from cursing us all for not letting her chase after you. But we thought it better to consolidate forces rather than scatter them in pursuit of shadows. She was certainly worth her weight in gold up in that rooftop perch."

"True enough," agreed Treville, recalling her lifesaving shot. He also recalled something else, a memory that had had been itching at his mind like a half-healed wound. *That'll have to be dealt with when we get back. I wonder if she already knows?*

"And no, Maaike didn't ask about you," Gaston added with a rumbling laugh. D'Artagnan forced a smile and urged his horse on ahead a bit.

Back in Amsterdam, the chaos had subsided. A curfew had cleared the streets, also advertised as part of the pretended drill, and there was no sign that anything exciting had occurred lately other than the hastily-patched church wall. Gaston explained that that had been passed off as a trainee having loaded a smoke bomb improperly. When Treville observed that the good burghers of the city were spectacularly gullible, he received no arguments. And though he was eager to rush to Beurre's house to see the valiant Maaike, his entire entourage was ordered into Maurice's suite instead. Even Raaf and Chipay were brought in, on litters.

The *Stadtholder* and general sat at an exquisite inlaid marquetry desk of ebony and cherry that probably cost more than Treville had earned in his entire life. Though it boasted innumerable drawers and pigeon-holes, the spy could tell that it doubtless also held several secret compartments. Its owner received them in only his shirt and breeches, looking more like a tired shopkeeper at the end of a long workday than a great lord. But he still possessed the energy and grace to see that the wounded men were looked after.

"I am told," the rusty-headed ruler said in good French, "that my new nation owes you gentlemen a debt. Not to mention my personal one."

"Your Excellency flatters us," Treville replied with a small bow. His head swam with pain and fatigue. "We merely did our duty."

"And not all are gentlemen," added d'Artagnan. "Two valiant women were involved."

"Indeed?" said Maurice. "I heard mention of one of my spies sacrificing herself for the cause. The other is yours?"

"She is, sir. Like your Krijger, she burrowed herself into the enemy's ranks in France and discovered their plans."

Treville smiled at the charitable description of Abandonné's former situation. "She is off tending Krijger's considerable wounds." *Half of them given to her by me. Let's hurry this up so I can make some amends.*

Maurice slapped a palm onto his desk. "I will send her my own surgeons. They will minister to these brave ones, too." He watched for a moment as those doctors set to their work on Chipay and Raaf. "Now, tell me everything, starting with introductions."

Gaston kindled his legendary charm and did the honors. His story did not disappoint, as he was known for his abilities as a tavern raconteur. The room fell silent as he spun his tale. In his hands it had all the attributes of a picaresque romance, full of rousing adventure and rollicking humor. Treville nearly forgot that it was his own story, too, so thrillingly was it recounted. At the end Maurice applauded. He fussed over Fantôme, whom he recalled having served him some years before. But his attention primarily went to his own spy, still made up as the king of France.

"Remarkable," he muttered, squinting at Raaf's face. "King Henri would feel as if he were gazing into a looking glass."

"I agree!" boomed a French voice from the main door, causing all but Maurice to bow low.

Henri IV swept in with the small retinue that he had brought on his half-secret journey. While Maurice seemed wrung-out like an old wash cloth from the day's drama, the French monarch was positively bubbly. He bounced about the room like one of his mistresses' yappy little dogs. Raaf's disguise was marveled at again, as were Treville's cleverness, Chipay's courage, and d'Artagnan's blade skills. Purses heavy with gold found their way into every man's hand. In addition, Treville received a silver ring with a black onyx stone.

"Keep it close," the king advised him in a whisper. "Only three others exist in all of France." He flipped the stone open to reveal a hidden compartment. Inside lay a tiny masterpiece of art: a golden crown with a fleur-de-lis above it. "Every servant of mine in the realm, from the Constable of France to the meanest tax collector, has been instructed to obey the orders of a ringbearer as if they came from my lips. Use it sparingly, but unhesitatingly if the need arises."

Nearly speechless at the honor, Treville could only nod and squeeze out a subdued thank-you.

But his spy's mind could not help wondering who the other three ring-holders were. *God help us if his mistress has one.*

There was some more royal gushing, then Henri left with Maurice and all their entourage, after giving orders that Treville, d'Artagnan, and Chipay should be taken to Beurre's house for a reunion with the ladies. Some thirty minutes later the team that had saved the leaders of two nations were embracing and opening wine bottles. Maaike had a head start on the latter.

"Behold the conquering heroes!" she crowed, flushed with drink. So swollen was her maligned face that the words were indistinct, though the Burgundy also played its part there.

"I don't know how much conquering we did," d'Artagnan grumbled, arms around Abandonné. "The ringleaders are on a ship to who-knows-where."

She waved her half-empty glass. "Actually, I might know where, thank you very much."

Treville sat on the bed beside Krijger, marveling at how good-humored she was after the beatings she had endured. Quite apart from what he had inflicted on her for show, the brutes of the Manqué had done much worse. One eye was completely shut, black as a thundercloud. The corner of her mouth was torn and one cheekbone looked to be broken. Much hair had been torn out, probably by seizing her there and yanking her violently to and fro. Her wrists were savaged from being manacled. His imagination conjured up dreadful horrors that might lay beneath the concealing garments.

He stroked her hair, not caring what anyone thought of the gesture. "Here I am, getting plaudits from the king, and you're the one who's given the most."

"It looks bad, I'll grant you," she laughed, "but at least you didn't shoot me in the arse. Hardly a scar poor Raaf will be eager to show in taverns to cadge drinks."

"Could this possibly have been worth the doing?"

She grew somber. "We stopped the plot, killed many of their men, took valuable prisoners, secured their documents. I would've suffered much worse for such an outcome."

Treville took her hand. Behind him, d'Artagnan did the same with Abandonné. "Documents, eh? Have we learned anything?"

"Well, the fools didn't write all of them in code. It seems this was mostly just a training exercise, though one with great benefits if it had succeeded. Their real objective is in England. They were cautious enough not to be too specific about when and where. And if that goes well, they hope to repeat the strike elsewhere. Germany, Sweden, other prominent Protestant centers. Some Hapsburg ones, too, to get both sides clawing at one another. I gather that some judicious looting in those wealthy places is part of the scheme. Then, when the Manqué is itself rich and strong, they plan to 'purify' Catholic states of regions and individuals too cozy with heretics, as they attempted today."

"That makes me wish I'd managed to snare Guido and the Duc du Épernon. Perhaps that might have ended this."

"I doubt it. They aren't the ones running things. Merely field operatives. Plenty more where they came from."

"Possibly. But Épernon is highly-placed and finding another Frenchman with his access wouldn't be easy."

"He's already mistrusted, though, thanks to past transgressions. One of the prisoners let slip that there are others, lily-white in your king's eyes, who are also involved."

"Well, let's see what comes of some insistent questioning of them, and of perusing those papers." Treville squeezed her hand and stood. "You do what the doctors tell you. No arguing."

He looked over at Chipay. "You, too. Though, in your case, perhaps they should do what you tell them."

Fantôme forced a smile. He held the beaded tally cord of his life-debt. "We shall see what sort of amicable accord can be reached. I am glad to see you well, brothers."

"As are we," d'Artagnan said, still clinging to Abandonné, who had been strangely quiet, almost meek, thus far. "Now cease all of the theatrical heroics and heal yourself. Plenty of other opportunities to charge after miscreants and threats to the crown."

"I believe I shall take your advice this time, young one." Penseur noticed that a couple more black beads had been removed from the cord and the same number of white ones added to the other side.

"And I believe that I shall take your amour," Treville said to d'Artagnan, grasping Abandonné by the arm and towing her away. "For a moment is all."

Down in the kitchen, Treville sat her in a chair and took another, sliding it in close to her. She gave him the look that a rabbit might give a hawk, but stayed put, wrapping her arms around herself. He wondered what had her so apprehensive. *Does she know what I'm about to say? How could she?*

Placing his left hand flat on the table before her, he invited her to inspect it. "It's been so long, you can hardly see the scar now, though I feel it in the depths of my soul. I have… nightmares. Well, one of them, at any rate, over and over. Reliving my worst childhood memory. When I was a lad, perhaps seven years of age, three masked men came to our little estate. One had a laugh like a banshee. Father had done a small favor for Henri III and the land and title were his reward. They demanded something of my parents. I don't know what it was, I was too small to understand. It didn't seem to be money, for they took none. My father proclaimed ignorance of this thing. There was an argument. They struck him down without warning or mercy. When my mother protested, they served her the same way, searched the house, then put it to the torch. As they left they abducted my infant sister, who squirmed free and ran blindly into the flames. I seized her arm and pulled her out before she could be severely burned. But her arm, where my little hand didn't protect it, did get singed. I imagine if she were somehow alive she would have an interesting mark there… an imprint of her brother's fingers on her forearm." He leaned back, laughed a little. "A strange tale, no?"

He waited, hoping that she would do the honors and not force him to pry it out of her. After a long moment, she took a deep breath and pulled up the sleeve of her dress. There, just as he had seen it that morning in d'Artagnan's room, was the white imprint of a tiny hand, seared into her flesh by the puckered burn that surrounded it.

"Not so strange, I think," she said in a tiny faint voice.

Good God, could it be true? Does fate have such a sense of humor?

"You knew?"

She waited a goodly while again. "No…not really. Just a feeling. After all, I don't remember anything at all that far back. I just know my various foster parents and the ugliness that came afterward."

Then what is she so nervous about? Something else is gnawing at her.

He took her hands in his. "That's all over now, my sister. My Mathilde."

"Is that my name? No one ever called me by it. After the orphanage I was passed from family to family."

I do wonder why those bastards took her in the first place. And why they parted with her. And how she ended up here with me. Coincidences make me itch.

"What name were you given, then?"

"Josephine. I hated it."

"Doesn't suit you."

"Does Mathilde?"

"Not really. Not now, though our mother chose it. I believe that you should name yourself. Surely something feels right to you."

She stood, almost trembling. "I have. And it does." With that she rushed away, hiding herself in her room. Treville did not pursue her. Enough had happened already that day without adding more anguish to it. She would tell him when she was ready.

He returned to Maaike's room. Chipay had already been moved to his own chamber, where a mild argument was taking place with Maurice's doctor about the efficacy of certain herbs versus a generous bleeding.

"I already told them to keep their damned knives away from me," Krijger said. "Lost enough blood at the hands of the enemy. Don't intend to sacrifice any more to medical ignorance."

"With any luck he'll utterly reform Dutch medicine by morning."

"I can only hope. Right now even my remaining teeth feel bruised."

"Can I do anything for you?"

She whimpered a bit. "You could, but alas, it'd probably be the death of me. A little death, at least. Not that I'd mind."

"But I would mind, so that will have to wait. Shall we speak of the Manqué to take your mind off that?"

"You certainly know how to ruin a girl's mood. No, I'm not interested in discussing that gang of murdering – oh, wait! I do have one item that you'll want to hear. It should help us track them. Guido, that charming bastard, has a real name."

"And that would be?"

"Fawkes. Guy Fawkes. An Englishman through and through."

"An absurd name. It's an obscene pun in English. You're certain it's not another alias."

"Well, it was in a document that we confirmed through army sources. He fought with the Spanish against us. Handy with gunpowder, it seems."

"Ah. That would explain why they're off to England. He can get into places no Frenchman could."

Maaike smirked saucily. "Most Frenchmen, anyway."

The front door slammed and Gaston's booming baritone filled the house. "Treville! D'Artagnan! You can kiss the ladies later! Get down here!"

Looking a bit sheepish, the gentlemen in question left the women's rooms and did as commanded. Once downstairs in the foyer, they met Gaston and Louis, who were dressed for traveling. Treville saw through the open door that dozens of men and horses waited out front, surrounding a drab carriage with its windows covered. The king was on his way home.

Gaston held up a rolled document that boasted the royal seal. "His Majesty neglected to give you this," he said to d'Artagnan. "Well, truth be told, it occurred to us to suggest it to him after you'd already gone."

"What is it?" the Gascon asked with as much suspicion as if it were a death warrant.

"Mother Mary, you're cautious!" said Louis. "It isn't poisonous. Hurry up and read the bloody thing, he's eager to get back to someone kissable."

D'Artagnan broke the seal and unrolled the paper. It was so fresh that some of the ink had smeared. His eyes narrowed as he read it all carefully, then looked up with a frown. "There's no such thing as a Cadet Apprentice Recruit to the Forty-Five Guards."

"Tell that to the king, then," snorted Gaston with a jerk of his head toward the door. "You know how much he likes being corrected."

"But what is this supposed to mean? Am I one of you now?"

Louis shrugged. "In a manner of speaking. We noted to the king that the Épuisants were now a man down and that you'd make a fine replacement. And we offered to teach you everything that you'll need to know if you truly rise to our exalted ranks."

Treville laughed. "Everything he needs to know? From you two? So that would be gambling, drinking, wenching, all of the noble virtues?"

"Could he have better tutors?" Gaston wanted to know. "After all, a good spy must be able to blend in with all sorts of people."

"A facile argument," Treville said, slapping him on the shoulder. He shook his head. "I don't like to lose him." He turned at the sound of footsteps on the landing to see a pale Chipay standing there, clutching the railing. "We have a sort of brotherly understanding."

"Truly?"

"We do," smiled Temeraire, nodding to the physician. "All for one..."

"...And one for all," answered Penseur and Fantôme.

Treville spied Abandonné, still looking grim, lurking behind Chipay. "I would be loath to part with the lad. I lost a sister once and only just recovered her."

Confusion clouding hiss features, Gaston said, "Nobody's abducting him, you know. Any time you need him, you know where he'll be. And he won't be going anywhere right off."

"What do you mean?"

"Our second errand. The king and Rosny have assigned you full-time to investigate this Manqué business, to the exclusion of all else. They're convinced the Louvre and the rest of France are rotten with their spies, if that devil Antoine's treachery is any indication. You're to start rooting it out, wherever it leads…and to whom."

"Starting immediately?"

Gaston gave him a saucy smile. "Well, he gave you five days leave for services rendered. If I were you, I'd use the time to do some, er, servicing. That poor Dutch lass needs tending to."

With that Gaston and Louis departed, vaulting into their saddles and leading out King Henri's train. As he watched them until they were out of sight, Treville was three-quarters certain that he spotted the young Béthune, lounging on his horse with several disreputable-looking characters. All were well-armed. The troublesome rake gave him a sour look and the group moved off to the south. Treville reminded himself to tell Raaf of that one's disturbing potential for mischief.

He headed up the stairs just as the flustered doctor was insisting that Chipay return to his bed. Snagging a wine bottle, he drank deeply on his way up to his sister and Krijger. Two encounters needed to happen up there. Somehow he knew that each would be painful in its own way.

ABOUT THE AUTHOR

Terry Kroenung has leapt out of perfectly functioning U.S. Army aircraft, taught Crips & Bloods on a wagon train, and been paid actual money to portray both William Shakespeare and Chuck E. Cheese. Oh, a side note: doctors cut his misbehaving heart out and threw it away. But at least he got a book out of it (*HeartSnark*).

Brimstone and Lily, the first novel in his Legacy Stone series, started as 'swords-and-sorcery Huck Finn' and went sideways from there. The books include shape-shifting swords, Civil War battles, magic cannonballs, combat pelicans, Captain Nemo's sub, kindly Arab terrorists, swimming trees, cyclopean ogres, 10,000 ancient Greek zombies, lady ninjas, and poop monsters. *Brimstone and Lily* won the Bronze Medal in Science-Fiction/Fantasy at the 2010 Independent Publishers Book Awards and was a Colorado Gold Rush Literary Award finalist. *Jasper's Foul Tongue* and *Jasper's Magick Corset* followed. *Jasper's Sloppy Smooch* will concluded the series.

An Advanced Actor/Combatant with the Society of American Fight Directors, he has choreographed or performed hundreds of swordfights, from *Hamlet* to *Peter Pan*. That's why his books have such an absurd number of fight scenes. He teaches Bartitsu (Sherlock Holmes' martial art, an actual Victorian discipline), because if you can't kill someone with an umbrella or a lady's hatpin, are you even civilized?

Paragon of the Eccentric, his Steampunk prequel to *War of the Worlds*, won the 2013 Colorado Gold writing contest and the Incite Denver contest for best first sentence ("When a Whitechapel whore waves her tentacles at you, attention must be paid").

He is retired from 30 years of teaching literature in Colorado, supported by his wife Janet and a completely whack-a-doodle basset hound named Moonbeam.

www.ingramcontent.com/pod-product-compliance
Lightning Source LLC
Chambersburg PA
CBHW020646260626
47157CB00008B/2928